# INDIGO RIDGE

# INDIGO RIDGE

*USA TODAY* BESTSELLING AUTHOR
# DEVNEY PERRY

Entangled Publishing, LLC
644 Shrewsbury Commons Ave., STE 181
Shrewsbury, PA 17361
rights@entangledpublishing.com

Amara is an imprint of Entangled Publishing, LLC.

Visit our website at www.entangledpublishing.com.

Edited by Elizabeth Nover
Cover art and design by Sarah Hansen at OkayCreations
Stock art by Nikola Spasenoski and Raul Pfammatter/Shutterstock
Interior design by Britt Marczak

ISBN 978-1-64937-666-4

Manufactured in the United States of America

First Edition February 2024

10 9 8 7 6 5 4 3 2

# ALSO BY DEVNEY PERRY

### THE EDENS SERIES

*Indigo Ridge*
*Juniper Hill*
*Garnet Flats*
*Jasper Vale*
*Crimson River*
*Sable Peak*
*Christmas in Quincy - Prequel*
*The Edens: A Legacy Short Story*

### TREASURE STATE WILDCATS SERIES

*Coach*
*Blitz*

### CLIFTON FORGE SERIES

*Steel King*
*Riven Knight*
*Stone Princess*
*Noble Prince*
*Fallen Jester*
*Tin Queen*

### CALAMITY MONTANA SERIES

*The Bribe*
*The Bluff*
*The Brazen*
*The Bully*
*The Brawl*
*The Brood*

### JAMISON VALLEY SERIES

*The Coppersmith Farmhouse*
*The Clover Chapel*
*The Lucky Heart*

*The Outpost*
*The Bitterroot Inn*
*The Candle Palace*

### MAYSEN JAR SERIES

*The Birthday List*
*Letters to Molly*
*The Dandelion Diary*

### LARK COVE SERIES

*Tattered*
*Timid*
*Tragic*
*Tinsel*
*Timeless*

### RUNAWAY SERIES

*Runaway Road*
*Wild Highway*
*Quarter Miles*
*Forsaken Trail*
*Dotted Lines*

### HOLIDAY BROTHERS SERIES

*The Naughty, The Nice and The Nanny*
*Three Bells, Two Bows and One*
*Brother's Best Friend*
*A Partridge and a Pregnancy*

### STANDALONES
*Ivy*
*Rifts and Refrains*
*A Little Too Wild*

# PROLOGUE

"Think you'll fly, little bird?"

A voice, a nightmare, whispered across the wind.

The rocks at the base of this sable cliff glowed silver as they caught the moonlight. A darkness so black and infinite began to pull, its tether on my ankle, as I took one step toward the edge.

Would it hurt, flying?

"Let's find out."

# CHAPTER 1

## WINSLOW

"Could I get another..."

The bartender didn't slow as he passed by.

"Drink," I muttered, slumping forward.

Pops had told me that this bar was where the locals hung out. Not only was it within walking distance of my new house in case I decided not to drive, but I was a local now. As of today, I lived in Quincy, Montana.

I'd told the bartender as much when I'd asked for his wine list. He'd raised one bushy white eyebrow above his narrowed gaze, and I'd abandoned my thirst for a glass of cabernet, ordering a vodka tonic instead. It had zapped every ounce of my willpower not to request a lemon twist.

The ice cubes in my glass clinked together as I swirled around my pink plastic straw. The bartender ignored that sound too.

Main Street had two bars—tourist traps this time of year, according to Pops. But I regretted not choosing one of those to celebrate my first night in Quincy. Given his attitude, the bartender, who must have thought I was a lost tourist, regretted my decision too.

Willie's was a dive bar and not exactly my scene.

The bartenders downtown probably acknowledged their customers, and the prices were listed on a menu, not delivered using three fingers on one wrinkled hand.

He looked about as old as this dark, dingy building. Like most small-town Montana bars, the walls were teeming with beer signs and neon lights. Shelves stacked with liquor bottles lined the mirrored wall across from my seat. The room was cluttered with tables, every chair empty.

Willie's was all but deserted this Sunday night at nine o'clock.

The locals must know of a better place to unwind.

The only other patron was a man sitting at the farthest end of the bar, in the last stool down the line. He'd come in ten minutes after I'd arrived and chosen the seat as far from me as possible. He and the bartender were nearly carbon copies of one another, with the same white hair and scraggly beards.

Twins? They looked old enough to have established this bar. Maybe one of them was Willie himself.

The bartender caught me staring.

I smiled and rattled the ice in my glass.

His mouth pursed in a thin line but he made me another drink. And like with the first, he delivered it without a word, holding up the same three fingers.

I twisted to reach into my purse, fishing out another five because clearly starting a tab was out of the question. But before I could pull the bill from my wallet, a deep, rugged voice caressed the room.

"Hey, Willie."

"Griffin." The bartender nodded.

So he was Willie. And he could speak.

"Usual?" Willie asked.

"Yep." The man with the incredible voice, Griffin, pulled out the stool two down from mine.

As his tall, broad body eased into the seat, a whiff of his scent carried my way. Leather and wind and spice filled my nose, chasing away the musty air from the bar. It was heady and alluring.

He was the type of man who turned a woman's head.

One glimpse at his profile and the cocktail in front of me was unnecessary. Instead, I drank this man in head to toe.

The sleeves of his black T-shirt stretched around his honed biceps and molded to the planes of his shoulders as he leaned his elbows on the bar. His brown hair was finger-combed and curled at the nape of his neck. His tan forearms were dusted with the same dark hair and a vein ran over the corded muscle beneath.

Even seated, I could tell his legs were long, his thighs thick like the evergreen tree trunks from the forests outside of town. Frayed hems of his faded jeans brushed against his black cowboy boots. And as he shifted in his seat, I caught the glimmer of a silver and gold belt buckle at his waist.

If his voice, his scent and that chiseled jaw hadn't been enough to make my mouth go dry, that buckle would have done it.

One of my mom's favorite movies had been *Legends of the Fall*. She'd let me watch it at sixteen and we'd cried together. Whenever I missed her, I'd put it on. The DVD was scratched and the clasp on the case was broken because I'd watched that movie countless times simply because it had been hers.

She'd always swooned over Brad Pitt as a sexy cowboy.

If she could see Griffin, she'd be drooling too. Though he was missing the hat and the horse, this guy was every cowboy fantasy come to life.

Lifting my glass to my mouth, I sipped the cold drink and tore my gaze from the handsome stranger. The vodka burned my throat and the alcohol rushed to my head. Ol' Willie mixed his cocktails strong.

I was unabashedly staring. It was rude and obvious. Yet when I set the glass down, my gaze immediately returned to Griffin.

His piercing blue eyes were waiting.

My breath hitched.

Willie set down a tumbler full of ice and caramel liquid in front of Griffin, then, without giving him the fingers to pay, walked away.

Griffin took a single swallow of his drink, his Adam's apple bobbing. Then his attention was on me once more.

The intensity of his gaze was as intoxicating as my cocktail.

He stared without hesitation. He stared with bold desire. His gaze raked down my black tank top to the ripped jeans I'd put on this morning before checking out of my hotel in Bozeman.

I'd spent four and a half hours driving to Quincy with a U-Haul trailer hitched to my Dodge Durango. When I'd arrived, I'd immediately jumped into unloading, only breaking to meet Pops for dinner.

I was a mess after a day of hauling boxes. My hair was in

a ponytail and whatever makeup I'd put on this morning had likely worn off. Yet the appreciation in Griffin's gaze sent a wave of desire rushing to my core.

"Hi," I blurted. *Smooth, Winn.*

His eyes twinkled like two perfect sapphires set behind long, sooty lashes. "Hi."

"I'm Winn." I held out a hand over the space between us.

"Griffin." The moment his warm, calloused palm grazed mine, tingles cascaded across my skin like fireworks. A shiver rolled down my spine.

Holy hell. There was enough electricity between us to power the jukebox in the corner.

I focused on my drink, gulping more than sipping. The ice did nothing to cool me down. When was the last time I'd been this attracted to a man? Years. It had been years. Even then, it paled in comparison to five minutes beside Griffin.

"Where are you from?" he asked. Like Willie, he must have assumed I was a tourist too.

"Bozeman."

He nodded. "I went to college at Montana State."

"Go Bobcats." I lifted my drink in a salute.

Griffin returned the gesture, then put the rim of his glass to his full lower lip.

I was staring again, unashamed. Maybe it was the angular cheekbones that set his face apart. Maybe it was the straight nose with a slight bump at the bridge. Or his dark, bold browbone. He was no ordinary, handsome man. Griffin was drop-dead gorgeous.

And if he was at Willie's... a local.

Local meant off-limits. *Damn.*

I swallowed my disappointment with another gulp of vodka.

The scrape of stool legs rang through the room as he moved to take the seat beside mine. His arms returned to the bar, his drink between them as he leaned forward. He sat so close, his body so large, that the heat from his skin seeped into mine.

"Winn. I like that name."

"Thanks." My full name was Winslow but very few people ever called me anything other than Winn or Winnie.

Willie walked by and narrowed his eyes at the sliver of space between Griffin and me. Then he joined his doppelganger.

"Are they related?" I asked, dropping my voice.

"Willie Senior is on our side of the bar. His son is mixing drinks."

"Father and son. Huh. I thought twins. Does Willie Senior have the same glowing personality as Willie Junior?"

"It's worse." Griffin chuckled. "Every time I come through town, he gets crankier."

Wait. Did that mean…"You don't live in town?"

"No." He shook his head, picking up his drink.

I did the same, hiding my smile in the glass. So he wasn't a local. Which meant flirting was harmless. *Bless you, Quincy.*

A hundred personal questions raced through my mind, but I dismissed them all. Skyler used to criticize me for going into interrogation mode within ten minutes of meeting someone new. One of many critiques. He'd used his profession as a life coach as an excuse to tell me anything and everything I'd been doing wrong in our relationship. In life.

Meanwhile, he'd betrayed me, so I wasn't listening to Skyler's voice anymore.

But I still wasn't going to bombard this man with questions. He didn't live here, and I'd save my questions for the people who did: my constituents.

Griffin looked to the far end of the room and the empty shuffleboard table. "Want to play a game?"

"Um...sure? I've never played before."

"It's easy." He slid off his stool, moving with a grace that men his size didn't normally possess.

I followed, eyes glued to the best ass I had ever seen. And he didn't live here. An imaginary choir perched in the bar's dusty rafters gave a collective *yeehaw*.

Griffin went to one end of the table while I walked to the other. "Okay, Winn. Loser buys the next round of drinks."

Good thing I had cash. "Okay."

Griffin spent the next ten minutes explaining the rules and demonstrating how to slide the pucks down the sand-dusted surface toward the point lines. Then we played, game after game. After one more round, we both stopped drinking, but neither of us made a move to leave.

I won some games. I lost most. And when Willie finally announced that he was closing at one, the two of us walked outside to the darkened parking lot.

A dusty black truck was parked beside my Durango.

"That was fun."

"It was." I smiled up at Griffin, my cheeks pinching. I hadn't had this much fun openly flirting with a man in, well...ever. I slowed my steps because the last place I wanted to go was home alone.

He must have had the same idea because his boots stopped on the pavement. He inched closer.

Winslow Covington didn't have one-night stands. I'd been too busy wasting years on the wrong man. Griffin wasn't the right man either, but I'd learned in my time as a cop that sometimes it wasn't about choosing right from wrong. It was choosing the *right* wrongs.

Griffin. Tonight, I chose Griffin.

So I closed the distance between us and stood on my toes, letting my hands snake up his hard, flat stomach.

He was tall, standing two or three inches over six feet. At five nine, it was refreshing to be around a man who towered over me. I lifted a hand to his neck, pulling him down until his mouth hovered over mine.

"Is that your truck?"

...

"**S**hit." I cursed at the clock, then flew into action, flinging the covers off my naked body and racing for the bathroom.

Late was not how I wanted to start the first day of my new job.

I flipped on the shower, my head pounding as I stepped under the cold spray and let out a yelp. There was no time to wait for hot water, so I shampooed my hair and put in some conditioner while I scrubbed Griffin's scent off my skin. I'd mourn the loss of it later.

There was an ache between my legs that I'd think about later too. Last night had been...

Mind blowing. Toe curling. The best night I'd ever had with a man. Griffin knew exactly how to use that powerful body of his and I'd been the lucky recipient of three—or had it been four?—orgasms.

I shuddered and realized the water was hot. "Damn it."

Shoving thoughts of Griffin out of my head, I hurried out of the shower, frantically swiping on makeup and willing the blow dryer to work faster. Without time to curl or straighten my hair, I twisted it into a tight bun at the nape of my neck, then dashed to the bedroom to get dressed.

The mattress rested on the floor, the sheets and blankets rumpled and strewn everywhere. Thankfully, before I'd headed to the bar last night, I'd searched for bedding in the boxes and laid it out. When I'd finally gotten home after hours spent in the back of Griffin's truck, I'd practically face-planted into my pillows and forgotten to set my alarm.

I refused to regret Griffin. Kicking off my new life in Quincy with a hot and wild night seemed a little bit like fate.

Serendipity.

Maybe on his next trip through town, we'd bump into each other. But if not, well... I didn't have time for the distraction of a man.

Especially not today.

"Oh, God. Please don't let me be late." I rifled through a suitcase, finding a pair of dark-wash jeans.

Pops had told me specifically not to show up at the station looking fancy.

The jeans were slightly wrinkled but there was no time to find whatever box had stolen my iron. Besides, an iron meant fancy. The simple white tee I found next was also wrinkled, so I dug for my favorite black blazer to hide the worst offenders. Then I hopped into my favorite black boots with the chunky heels before jogging for the door, swiping up my purse from where I'd dumped it on the living room floor.

The sun was shining. The air was clean. The sky was blue. And I had no time to appreciate a minute of my first Quincy, Montana, morning as I ran to the Durango parked in my driveway.

I slid behind the wheel, started the engine and cursed again at the clock on the dash. *Eight-oh-two.* "I'm late."

Thankfully, Quincy wasn't Bozeman and the drive from one side of town to the police station on the other took exactly six minutes. I pulled into the lot and parked next to a familiar blue Bronco and let myself take a single deep breath.

*I can do this job.*

Then I got out of my car and walked to the station's front door, hoping with every step I looked okay.

One disdaining look from the officer stationed behind a glass partition at the front desk and I knew I'd gotten it wrong. *Shit.*

His gray hair was cut short, high and tight in a military style. He looked me up and down, the wrinkles on his face deepening with a scowl. That glare likely had nothing to do with my outfit.

And everything to do with my last name.

"Good morning." I plastered on a bright smile, crossing the small lobby to his workspace. "I'm Winslow Covington."

"The new chief. I know," he muttered.

My smile didn't falter.

I'd win them over. Eventually. That's what I'd told Pops last night when he'd had me over for dinner after I'd returned the U-Haul. I'd win them all over, one by one.

Most people were bound to think that the only reason I'd gotten the job as the Quincy chief of police was because my grandfather was the mayor. Yes, he would be my boss. But there wasn't a nepotism clause for city employees. Probably because in a town this size, everyone was likely related in some manner. If you added too many restrictions, no one would be able to get a job.

Besides, Pops hadn't hired me. He could have, but instead, he'd put together a search committee so that there'd be more than one voice in the decision. Walter Covington was the fairest, most honorable man I'd ever known.

And granddaughter or not, what mattered was my performance. He'd take the cues from the community, and though my grandfather loved me completely, he wouldn't hesitate to fire me if I screwed this up.

He'd told me as much the day he'd hired me. He'd reminded me again last night.

"The mayor is waiting in your office," the officer said, pushing the button to buzz me into the door beside his cubicle.

"It was nice to meet you"—I glanced at the silver nameplate on his black uniform—"Officer Smith."

His response was to ignore me completely, turning his attention to his computer screen. I'd have to win him over another day. Or maybe he'd be open to an early retirement.

I pushed through the door that led into the heart of the station. I'd been here twice, both times during the interview process. But it was different now as I walked through the bullpen no longer a guest. This was my bullpen. The officers looking up from their desks were under my charge.

My stomach clenched.

Staying up all night having sex with a stranger probably hadn't been the smartest way to prepare for my first day.

"Winnie." Pops came out of what would be my office, his hand extended. He seemed taller today, probably because he was dressed in nice jeans and a starched shirt instead of the ratty T-shirt, baggy jeans and suspenders I'd seen him in yesterday.

Pops was fit for his seventy-one years and though his hair

was a thick silver, his six-three frame was as strong as an ox. He was in better shape than most men my age, let alone his.

I shook his hand, glad that he hadn't tried to hug me. "Morning. Sorry I'm late."

"I just got here myself." He leaned in closer and dropped his voice. "You doing okay?"

"Nervous," I whispered.

He gave me a small smile. "You'll do great."

I could do this job.

I was thirty years old. Two decades below the median age of a person in this position. Four decades younger than my predecessor had been when he'd retired.

The former chief of police had worked in Quincy for his entire career, moving up the ranks and acting as chief for as long as I'd been alive. But that was why Pops had wanted me in this position. He said Quincy needed fresh eyes and younger blood. The town was growing, and with it, their problems. The old ways weren't cutting it.

The department needed to embrace technology and new processes. When the former chief had announced his retirement, Pops had encouraged me to toss my name into the hat. By some miracle, the hiring committee had chosen me.

Yes, I was young, but I met the minimum qualifications. I'd worked for ten years with the Bozeman Police Department. During that time, I'd earned my bachelor's degree and a position as detective within their department. My record was impeccable, and I'd never left a case unclosed.

Maybe my welcome would have been warmer if I were a man, but that had never scared me and it certainly wasn't going to today.

*I can do this job.*

I would do this job.

"Let me introduce you to Janice." He nodded for me to follow him into my office, where we spent the morning with Janice, my new assistant.

She'd worked for the former chief for fifteen years, and the longer she spoke, the more I fell in love with her. Janice had spiky gray hair and the cutest pair of red-framed glasses I'd ever seen. She knew the ins and outs of the station, the schedules and the shortcomings.

As we ended our initial meeting, I made a mental note to bring her flowers because without Janice, I'd likely fall flat on my face. We toured the station, meeting the officers not out on patrol.

Officer Smith, who was rarely sent into the field because he preferred the desk, had been one of the candidates for chief, and Janice told me that he'd been a grumpy asshole since the day he'd been rejected.

Every officer besides him had been polite and professional, though reserved. No doubt they weren't sure what to make of me, but today I'd won Janice over—or maybe she'd won me. I was calling it a victory.

"You'll meet most of the department this afternoon at shift change," she told me when we retreated back to the safety of my office.

"I was planning on staying late one evening this week to meet the night shift too."

This wasn't a large station, because Quincy wasn't a large town, but in total, I had fifteen officers, four dispatchers, two administrators and a Janice.

"Tomorrow, the county sheriff is coming in to meet you," Janice said, reading from the notebook she'd had with her all morning. "Ten o'clock. His staff is twice the size of ours but he has more ground to cover. For the most part, their team stays out of our way, but he's always willing to step in if you need help."

"Good to know." I wouldn't mind having a resource to bounce ideas off of either.

"How's your head?" Pops asked.

I put my hands by my ears and made the sound of an exploding bomb.

He laughed. "You'll catch on."

"Yes, you will," Janice said.

"Thank you for everything," I told her. "I'm really looking forward to working with you."

She sat a little straighter. "Likewise."

"Okay, Winnie." Pops slapped his hands on his knees. "Let's go grab some lunch. Then I've got to get to my own office, and I'll let you come back here and settle in."

"I'll be here when you get back." Janice squeezed my arm as we shuffled out of my office.

Pops simply nodded, maintaining his distance. Tonight, when I wasn't Chief Covington and he wasn't Mayor Covington, I'd head to his house and get one of his bear hugs.

"How about we eat at The Eloise?" he suggested as we made our way outside.

"The hotel?"

He nodded. "It would be good for you to spend some time there. Get to know the Edens."

The Edens. Quincy's founding family.

Pops had promised that the fastest way to earn favor with the community was to win over the Edens. One of their relatives from generations past had founded the town and the family had been the community's cornerstone ever since.

"They own the hotel, remember?" he asked.

"I remember. I just didn't realize there was a restaurant in the hotel these days." Probably because I hadn't spent much time in Quincy lately.

The six trips I'd taken here to participate in the interview process had been my first trips to Quincy in years. Five, to be exact.

But when Skyler and I had fallen to pieces and Pops had pitched the job as chief, I'd decided it was time for a change. And Quincy, well... Quincy had always held a special place in my heart.

"The Edens started the hotel's restaurant about four years ago," Pops said. "It's the best place in town, in my opinion."

"Then let's eat." I unlocked my car. "Meet you there."

I followed his Bronco from the station to Main Street, taking in the plethora of out-of-state cars parked downtown. Tourist season was in full swing and nearly every space was full.

Pops parked two blocks away from Main on a side street, and side by side, we strolled to The Eloise Inn.

The town's iconic hotel was the tallest building in Quincy, standing proudly against the mountain backdrop in the distance. I'd always wanted to spend a night at The Eloise. Maybe one day I'd book myself a room, just for fun.

The lobby smelled of lemons and rosemary. The front desk was an island in the grand, open space, and a young woman with a sweet face stood behind the counter, checking in a guest. When she spotted Pops, she tossed him a wink.

"Who's that?" I asked.

"Eloise Eden. She took over as manager this past winter."

Pops waved at her, then walked past the front desk

toward an open doorway. The clatter of forks on plates and the dull murmur of conversation greeted me as we entered the hotel's restaurant.

The dining room was spacious and the ceilings as tall as those in the lobby. It was the perfect place for entertaining. Almost a ballroom but filled with tables of varying sizes, it also worked well as a restaurant.

"They just put in those windows." Pops pointed at the far wall where black-paned windows cut into a red-brick wall. "Last time I talked to Harrison, he said this fall they'll be remodeling this whole space."

Harrison Eden. The family's patriarch. He'd been on the hiring committee, and I liked to believe I'd made a good impression. According to Pops, if I hadn't, there was no way I'd have gotten my job.

A hostess greeted us with a wide smile and led us to a square table in the center of the room.

"Which of the Edens runs the restaurant?" I asked as we browsed the menu card.

"Knox. He's Harrison and Anne's second oldest son. Eloise is their youngest daughter."

Harrison and Anne, the parents. Knox, a son. Eloise, a daughter. There were likely many more Edens to meet.

Down Main, the Eden name was splashed on numerous storefronts, including the coffee shop I wished I'd had time to stop by this morning. Last night's antics were catching up to me, and I hid a yawn with my menu.

"They're good people," Pops said. "You've met Harrison. Anne's a sweetheart. Their opinion carries a lot of weight around here. So does Griffin's."

Griffin. *Did he say Griffin?*

My stomach dropped.

No. This couldn't be happening. It had to be a mistake. There had to be another Griffin, one who didn't live in Quincy. I'd specifically asked him last night if he lived in town and he'd said no. Hadn't he?

"Hey, Covie."

So busy having my mental freak-out that I'd slept with not only a local man, but one I needed to see me as a professional and not a backseat hookup, I didn't notice the two men standing beside our table until it was too late.

Harrison Eden smiled.

Griffin, who was just as handsome as he had been last night, did not.

Had he known who I was last night? Had that been some sort of test or trick? Doubtful. He looked as surprised to see me as I was to see him.

"Hey, Harrison." Pops stood to shake his hand, then waved at me. "You remember my granddaughter, Winslow."

"Of course." Harrison took my hand as I stood, shaking it with a firm grip. "Welcome. We're glad to have you as our new chief of police."

"Thank you." My voice was surprisingly steady considering my heart was attempting to dive out of my chest and hide under the table. "I'm glad to be here."

"Would you like to join us?" Pops offered, nodding to the empty chairs at our table.

"No," Griffin said at the same time his father said, "We'd love to."

Neither Pops nor Harrison seemed to notice the tension rolling off Griffin's body as they took their chairs, leaving Griffin and me to introduce ourselves.

I swallowed hard, then extended a hand. "Hello."

That sharp jaw I'd traced with my tongue last night

clenched so tight that I heard the crack of his molars. He glared at my hand before capturing it in his large palm. "Griffin."

Griffin Eden.

My one-night stand.

So much for serendipity.

# CHAPTER 2

## GRIFFIN

*Winn*. She'd told me her name was Winn.

Winn, the sexy woman with silky dark hair, deep blue eyes and legs for days. Winn, the lady with Bozeman license plates. Winn, the tourist with freckles across her nose.

It happened sometimes, that a tourist would stumble upon Willie's for a drink. It annoyed the fuck out of Willie—Junior and Senior—because neither liked outsiders in their bar. I'd considered myself one lucky bastard that I'd made the last-minute decision to swing in for a drink and pull up a stool beside Winn.

Except she wasn't *Winn*.

She was Winslow Covington, a name I sure as hell would have recognized. Dad had been talking about her for weeks since the hiring committee had selected her as the new chief of police.

Not a tourist. Definitely not a tourist.

She was supposed to be a goddamn tourist.

"Fuck," I muttered as the truck bumped and rolled down the gravel road toward Mom and Dad's place.

"You okay, Griff?" Conor asked from the passenger seat in my truck.

I grunted.

"Okay," he drawled, turning his attention to the green pasture out his window.

What a fucking mess. It had been two days since lunch at The Eloise and I was still pissed at myself.

Winslow Covington.

Not someone I should have fucked in the backseat.

Maybe I should have put it together. Maybe I should have tied Winn to Winslow. But Dad had spoken so highly of her and her experience that I'd pictured an entirely different woman in my mind. Someone older. Someone harder. Someone rougher.

Winn was nothing but smooth edges and unrivaled desire.

Two days and I was still struggling to fit Winn to Winslow.

Those preconceived notions were a bitch to erase.

Dad had taken his role on the search committee as seriously as he had any job I'd seen him tackle, including managing the Eden ranch. He was the kind of man who took every responsibility to heart, no matter how big or small. It was a trait he'd passed to me.

Though the way he'd jumped into the search committee had been borderline zealous. Mom blamed boredom for his enthusiasm for a nonpaying position. Since Dad had retired and handed me the reins for the ranch three years ago, he'd been spinning his wheels.

There were other family businesses that still required his attention, like the hotel. But those mostly ran on autopilot these days. The time commitment was nothing like it was for the ranch. This land had been his priority for decades, second only to his family. Us kids were grown. The ranch was mine.

He'd needed that search committee almost as much as they had needed him.

I had to give my father credit. A lot of farmers and ranchers struggled to pass the baton to the next generation. I had friends from college who'd abandoned their family's operations to work a desk job simply because their parents refused to step away.

Not my dad. After his retirement, he hadn't given me a single piece of unsolicited advice. If a hired hand asked him for input, Dad would send the man to me. He'd pitch in whenever I asked, but besides a few slips that first year, he'd stopped giving orders to everyone, including me. There were no critiques when I introduced a new idea. No muttered censures when I made a mistake. No guilt trips when I stopped doing something his way.

I loved my father. I respected him above any other man on earth. But for fuck's sake, couldn't he have mentioned, just once, that Winslow Covington was a beautiful, vivacious woman who was going to turn a hell of a lot more heads than just mine?

Instead, he'd praised her energy. He'd said twice that she'd *outshined* the other candidates. She was *sharp*. She had the *tenacity* to take the police department into the future.

In my mind, I'd pictured a brawny woman with a masculine haircut and narrow nose like her grandfather's. Certainly not the bombshell who'd been sitting at Willie's.

I'd been blinded by Winn's looks, that smile and her wit. I'd come in for one drink and thought, what the hell? When was the last time I'd seen such a stunning woman?

I preferred to hook up with tourists because their time in Quincy was temporary. If she had brushed me off or not shown any interest, I would have walked away. But the desire in her gaze had matched my own, and I'd just...had to have her.

That was the most erotic night I'd had in years. Maybe ever.

I clenched my jaw and tightened my grip on the steering wheel to keep myself from glancing at the backseat. Winn's scent was gone but it had taken all of yesterday for her sweet citrus to vanish.

Now it reeked like Conor.

Bless that kid and his sweat glands.

He'd started working for us in high school, stacking hay bales and doing odd jobs around the ranch. He'd tried college in Missoula for a year, but after flunking out, he'd come home to Quincy. Conor was the youngest full-time employee at the ranch and this kid moved nonstop.

There weren't many men who could keep up with my stamina. At thirty-one, I felt just as fit as I had a decade ago. But the ten-year age gap between Conor and me, combined with his work ethic, meant he could run me into the ground.

He'd spent the morning cleaning out the barn by my place, and what normally took me three hours, he did in half that time. Sweat ringed his plaid shirt and the brim of his baseball cap. The hat was as sun-bleached as my own, the black fabric having faded to brown. The Eden ranch brand—an *E* with a curve in the shape of a rocking chair's runner beneath—had once been white stitching and was now a dirty gray.

Conor was a good kid. But damn, did he stink.

I hated that I missed Winn's perfume.

"Nice day," he said.

"It is." I nodded.

Rays of pure sunlight streamed through the cloudless blue sky. The heat had already melted away the morning dew, and as we drove, I could practically see the grass growing. It was summer days like this when, as a teenager, I used to find an open field, lie down and take a power nap.

I could use one of those naps today after waking up at four, hard and aching for the woman who'd invaded my dreams. Sleep was risky, so I'd settled for a cold shower and my fist before retreating to my home office. Paperwork had been a decent distraction. So had work in the barn. But it was moments like this, when the world was quieter, that she crept up on me again.

Try as I might, there was no shoving Winn out of my mind.

Her tight body. Her sweet lips. Her long, dark hair that had brushed over my bare chest as she'd straddled my lap and sunk down on my cock.

*Hell.* Now I was getting hard again.

A relationship with her or any woman was out of the question, hence my streak of one-night stands over the past year. My focus was my family and the ranch. By the time most days ended, I barely had time for a shower before my head hit the pillow. The bachelor lifestyle suited me just fine. I answered to no one but the land. If I needed company, I had five siblings to call. A woman would require energy I just didn't have to spare.

Tourists didn't ask for commitment.

Except she wasn't a tourist.

Had she known who I was at Willie's? *No way.* She'd looked as shocked to meet me at lunch the other day as I'd been to see her. Whatever. None of it mattered. I had no intention of repeating Sunday night.

Winslow was an outsider, and though tempting, I'd keep my distance.

There was work to be done.

"I'm going to drop you off at the shop," I told Conor. "You can take the fencing truck and head out to the meadow that runs along the road to Indigo Ridge. We'll be turning out cattle into that pasture in the next few weeks and I noticed some spots that need fixing when I was driving out there the other day."

"Sure thing." Conor nodded, his elbow sticking out the open window. "How far should I go?"

"As far as you can. By Friday, I'd like to have that whole area finished."

Ranch headquarters remained by Mom and Dad's log house. Though my place saw more and more activity every year, the main shop and the stables would probably always be here, where Dad had built them.

"Call me if you need anything," I said, parking beside Mom's Cadillac.

"Will do." Conor hopped out, then jogged across the wide, open lot that separated my childhood home from the ranch buildings.

Mom walked out of her front door as my boots hit the gravel. "Hi, Conor."

He slowed, spinning to tip his hat. "Ma'am."

"That boy is a dear. Has been since he was in diapers." She smiled at me as I climbed the steps to the wraparound porch.

"Hi, Mom."

"Hello, son. Got time for coffee or are you already off to the next thing?"

"I need to keep moving, but I wouldn't say no to a travel mug."

"I just brewed a fresh pot." She waved me inside and headed straight for the kitchen.

Dad sat at the island with the newspaper spread across the granite countertop.

The *Quincy Gazette* came once a week, every Wednesday. When I'd been a kid, those weekly papers would have gone mostly unread because neither Mom nor Dad had had time to read them. Mostly, we'd used them to start fires in the wood stove. But now that Dad was retired, he spent hours poring over every printed word.

"Hi, Dad."

"Hi there." He straightened, taking his glasses off. "What's going on today?"

There was an eagerness to his voice like he was waiting for me to extend an invitation for a project. As much as I enjoyed time with my father, today, I needed some time alone. Time to get my head straight and off a certain woman.

But maybe he could save me a trip to town. Going anywhere near city limits seemed risky today.

"I was hoping you might have time to run into town and pick up a bundle of steel fence posts at the Farm and Feed," I said.

"Sure." He nodded. "I'll do it when I'm done with the paper."

"He's only read it twice already." Mom rolled her eyes from the coffeepot.

"Just the one article about Winslow," he argued. "The Nelsens did a piss-poor job on this one."

I stepped closer to the island, leaning in to read over his shoulder. My gaze landed on her pretty face. The photo took up half the front page. Winn was dressed in a black uniform shirt, the top button choking her slim neck. Her hair was pulled back into a slick knot. Her expression was the definition of neutral.

The photo had to be ten years old. Maybe one taken at the academy.

"They might as well have called her a child." Dad huffed and pushed the paper my way.

If the picture weren't bad enough, the article certainly didn't help. Below the headline—*QUINCY CHIEF OF POLICE*—was a column that read more like an exposé on small-town politics and favoritism.

No surprise, given the reporter listed was Emily Nelsen.

She loved to stir up drama. And when it came to the women in town who'd made it their mission to chase me, Emily was the leader of the pack. Good thing she didn't know I'd hooked up with Winn. The article was bad enough already.

Emily's parents owned the paper and the disdain for Walter Covington was as clear as the black-and-white ink on each page.

"Are you really surprised?" I asked Dad. "You know the Nelsens have always hated Covie. Ever since that squabble at the basketball game over the air horns."

"That was seven years ago."

"Does it matter? It could have been seventy and they'd

still hold a grudge."

The Nelsens had brought two air horns to a high school basketball game. My younger brother Mateo had been playing as a sophomore on the junior varsity team along with the Nelsens' son. They'd run those goddamn air horns in the gymnasium for an hour straight. Finally, Walter had asked them to pipe down.

Our mayor had taken the hit for everyone in the bleachers that day. The articles printed since hadn't been kind to Covie. I guess the Nelsens had no plans to be kind to Winn either.

The article left out most of her experience, though her age had been mentioned three times. Along with the word *preferential*.

Thirty was young for a chief of police. Had Dad not been on the hiring committee, I would have called it favoritism too.

What kind of experience could Winn have this far into her career? If something disastrous happened, I didn't want the chief dropping the oars in the water when we'd need a steady captain at the helm. Maybe, despite a shitty delivery, Emily Nelsen had a point.

But since I wasn't in the mood to argue with my father, I took my coffee mug from Mom and kissed her cheek. "Thanks for the refill."

"Of course." She squeezed my hand. "Dinner tonight? Knox isn't working at the restaurant and Mateo doesn't have a shift at the hotel. Lyla and Talia both said they could come over around six."

"What about Eloise?"

"She's coming over after the night clerk arrives at the hotel, probably around seven."

It was harder and harder to get us all under her roof and at the same table these days. Mom lived for the rare occasion when she could feed all six of her children.

"I'll do my best." This was a busy time on the ranch and the idea of a family dinner already made me tired. But I didn't want to disappoint Mom. "See you later. Thanks again for picking up those posts, Dad."

He raised his own coffee mug, his attention rapt on the paper and a scowl fixed on his face.

A calico cat darted across the porch when I stepped outside. It ducked beneath the bottom stair, and when I reached the ground, I bent to see her tucked into a corner, nurturing a chorus of tiny meows.

Kittens. I'd have to take a few of them to my barn when they were weaned. Mom had at least ten cats already. But since they kept the mice away, none of us had ever minded grabbing the occasional bag of dry cat food.

I set out across the gravel, heading for the shop. The mammoth steel building was the largest on the ranch. With the barn and stables at one corner of the lot, Mom and Dad's home at the other, the shop was the third corner of the triangle.

Our hired hands came here to clock in and out of their shifts. My office manager and bookkeeper each had a desk here, though they both preferred to work at the office space we kept in town.

My boots echoed on the concrete floor as I walked into the cavernous space. One of the swathers was parked just inside the sliding doors.

"Hiya, Griff." My cousin, who worked for us as a mechanic, poked his head out from beneath the machine.

"Hey. How's it coming?"

"Oh, I'll get it fixed."

"Good news." I'd already bought two new tractors this spring. I'd prefer to bump another major equipment expense to the winter.

I kept walking as he went back to work on the machine. There was a mountain of office work for me to do today, either here or at home. We were short a man for the summer season and I was a week late on getting an ad into the classifieds with the paper. Avoiding Emily was the reason, but I couldn't keep putting it off. Except one glance at my darkened office and I turned around for the door.

In total, the ranch consisted of ninety thousand acres. Most days, I was more of a business manager than an actual rancher. I still wore my boots and the belt buckle I'd won from a bareback ride at a high school rodeo. But the business degree I'd earned was put to use more often than my fencing pliers.

Not today.

June was a beautiful month in Montana and the blue sky beckoned. There was a cool breeze coming off the mountains, carrying the scent of pine trees and melting snow into the valley.

Sunshine and sweat would do my head a lot of good. I needed a day of hard, manual labor. Maybe if I exhausted myself, I'd sleep without dreaming of Winn.

I'd just reached the tool bench, ready to load up on a fresh roll of barbed wire and galvanized post clips, when my phone rang in my jeans pocket.

"Hey, Conor," I answered.

"Griffin."

My heart stopped at the panic in his voice, but my feet were already moving, jogging toward the shop door. "What's wrong? Are you hurt?"

"It's…"

"It's what? Talk to me."

"I started at Indigo Ridge. That corner post."

"Yeah." When I hit the gravel past the door, I was running. He might be young, but Conor didn't get spooked. "Conor, tell me what happened?"

A sob escaped his mouth.

"I'm on my way," I said but didn't end the call. Instead, I got into my truck, let my phone connect to the Bluetooth and kept Conor on the line with me as I drove.

"Breathe, Conor."

A whooshed breath escaped his lungs. My foot dug into the gas pedal as I raced to the turnoff.

"I'm just pulling off the gravel road," I told him, taking the two-track path that ran along the fence line.

He didn't respond other than to continue those heartbreaking, muffled sobs.

The truck rattled so hard my bones felt like they were shaking loose. These roads weren't paved or smooth, just worn from the times we drove through the fields. The tracks were spotted with holes and rocks and dips. They weren't meant for anything more than five miles per hour. I was going twenty.

My stomach twisted with every passing minute. God, don't let him be hurt. If he'd cut his hand or arm or leg and was bleeding, it would take us time to get to the hospital. Too much time. And I'd sent Conor to one of the farthest ends of the ranch.

Finally, twenty minutes later, I spotted the fencing truck in the distance. The mountains loomed on the horizon.

"I'm here," I said, then ended the call. My tires skidded

to a stop. A cloud of dust billowed from the road as I shot out of the truck and jogged toward Conor.

He was seated against a tire, his knees pulled up and his head hanging between them. One arm hung loose beside him. The other had the phone pressed to his ear.

"Conor." I put my hand on his shoulder, doing a quick scan. No blood. No apparent broken bones. All ten fingers. Two ears and two booted feet.

He looked up, his phone dropping to the grass. Tear tracks stained his tanned face. "It's Lily."

"Lily..."

"G-green," he choked out. "Lily Green."

Green. One of the nurses at the nursing home where my grandmother had lived before she passed was a Green. "What about Lily Green?"

Another tear dripped down Conor's face. "Over there."

"Over..." I trailed off and my stomach found a new bottom.

*No.* Not again.

I swallowed hard and stood, knowing without asking what I was going to find.

On leaden feet, I walked through the tall grass to the corner post and climbed the fence. My boots followed the same roughly trodden path that Conor must have taken.

Above me, the tower of Indigo Ridge rose into the blue sky. Its bold rock face caught the sun. This place was as intimidating as it was beautiful. A solid wall of rock that cut through the fields in such a harsh line that it was like the mountain had been cleaved from top to toe. The rocks at its base were as black and harsh as the cliff's face.

I climbed toward the rocks I'd avoided for ages. I hadn't been on this side of the fence in years. Not since I'd found the body.

The last body.

My gaze landed on a streak of blond hair. On a white dress. On mangled limbs. On a river of blood.

On Lily Green.

# CHAPTER 3

## WINSLOW

"I'm going to run home and grab a new shirt," I told Janice, frowning at the mess I'd made of my white blouse.

My sleeve, stained with black coffee, was as much of a disaster as my desk. Folders, reports and sticky notes cluttered the brown wooden surface. Or was it gray? I hadn't seen it in two days.

I was officially buried.

When Janice had come in to tell me that it was time for the weekly staff meeting with the administration crew—an unofficial standing meeting that hadn't been on my calendar—I'd been in such a rush to join them that when I'd gone to grab my coffee mug, a blob had leapt out of the cup and splattered my shirt.

"Will you call me if anything comes up?" I asked.

"Of course." She smiled and walked for the door, pausing

at the threshold. "You're doing great, Winslow."

"Am I? Because I feel like I'm drowning." Something I'd only admit to Janice. She was my one and only ally at the station. Winning people over was going slower than I'd expected. Much slower.

It was my age. No one had outwardly admitted that they thought I was too young—not to my face. But the sideways looks had held unspoken words. Doubts.

*I can do this job.*

Maybe the others doubted me but I wasn't about to doubt myself. Much.

"You're drinking from a fire hose right now, but it will get easier," Janice promised. "And the folks here will come around. Give it time."

I sighed. "Thank you."

She gave me a sure nod, then slipped away for her spotless desk.

Taking my purse from the bottom drawer, I scanned the piles of reports to review and officer résumés to read. Tonight, I'd take another stack home and read over them like I had last night. I was in learning mode, trying to familiarize myself with the staff. I'd also had Janice pull every case file from the past three months so I could glean what type of crimes happened in Quincy.

So far, it had been nothing more than four drunken drivers, a busted high school kegger, one bar fight and a domestic disturbance. Janice had warned me that there was a meth arrest hidden in the mix but I hadn't reached that file yet.

Overall, the officer files were thin, too thin. The reports were short, too short. And everything was handwritten on paper templates.

Pops hadn't been kidding when he'd told me that the Quincy Police Department needed a shove into the future. Though shove seemed too gentle a word. What we needed was a bulldozer.

I was that bulldozer.

Walking through the bullpen, I waved at Allen, one of the day-shift officers.

He nodded, his eyes darting to my sleeve. The corner of his mouth turned up.

I shrugged. "Coffee attacked me."

"That's why I'm partial to our black shirts and pants. Hides the spills."

"My uniform order is supposed to get in today. Then I'll be sticking to black shirts too." I smiled and headed for the door.

Okay, that was nice. Allen hadn't avoided eye contact. Progress, right?

I waved at Officer Smith when I passed him for the lobby, hoping for a nod. "I'm going to run home quickly. Would you please call me if anything comes up?"

He ignored me, like he had for the past two days. Even when we'd bumped into each other in the break room yesterday, he'd acted like I hadn't even been there. The heat from his glare burned down my spine as I walked out the door.

Early retirement. We were definitely going to discuss an early retirement if he didn't change his attitude.

I plucked my sunglasses from my purse, using them to shield my eyes from the glare and cover up the dark circles under my eyes—sleep hadn't been easy this week. My Durango was parked beside Allen's cruiser. The leather seats were warm and the air stuffy. I cracked my window, drawing in the scent of summer sunshine.

Located in the heart of western Montana, Quincy was about an hour from Glacier National Park. The town was situated in a valley surrounded by snowcapped mountains, their slopes covered by a dense evergreen forest. The Clark Fork River cut a path through the trees and provided a natural border on one side for the city limits.

Pops would take us camping along the river when I was a kid. My family would spend a few precious summer weekends at his favorite sites, where we'd fish and hike and roast s'mores.

At every turn, Quincy held a memory.

Visiting Pops had always felt like an adventure. My father had grown up here, and for him, Quincy was home. Mom and Dad would have loved to see me living here. They probably would have followed me from Bozeman.

Though if they hadn't died, I doubted I would have moved to Quincy.

If they hadn't died, a lot would be different.

At every turn, Quincy held a memory.

I had yet to decide if that was good or bad.

Pushing the past aside, I took in the tourists meandering down the sidewalks on Main. Because of our proximity to Glacier, Quincy would be bustling until fall with out-of-town visitors.

As the mayor, Pops loved the influx of cash to his small town. As a resident, the tourists tended to grate on his nerves. The abundance of visitors was the reason he loved whisking us away to the mountains for summer campouts.

It had been during the fall and winter visits that we'd actually stayed in Quincy to explore. Not much had changed since my childhood. There was comfort in the familiar.

As in most small Montana towns, Main Street was a segment of the highway that led in and out of town. Everything branched away from Quincy's downtown, like arteries from a thriving heart. But the bulk of the commerce was right here, all clustered together in the town's core.

Restaurants, bars and retail shops were the primary appeal for our seasonal visitors. Offices and banks filled the gaps in between. Mom's favorite stop had always been the antique shop. Dad's, the hardware store. The grocery store and two gas stations acted as the bookend to one side of Main. Quincy Farm and Feed was the other.

The community took pride in this street. The window displays were artful and charming. Flower baskets hung from lampposts in summer, holiday garlands and twinkle lights in winter.

I loved this town.

*My* town.

It hadn't quite sunk in yet that Quincy was mine.

Maybe because I felt more akin to the tourists than the locals.

I slowed at a crosswalk, waiting for a couple to navigate the intersection. Between them was a little girl wearing a yellow jumper and an adorable smile. Her parents swung her between them after every count of *one-two-three-yippee*.

Once upon a time, I'd been that little girl.

"What is wrong with me today?" I shook my head, snapping myself out of the past, then I took the next side street on my route to home.

Mom and Dad had been a constant on my mind these past two days. Probably because I was in Quincy. Probably because so much had changed in just a week.

A new house. A new job.

Moving was the right decision, but that hadn't made it easy. I missed my friends in Bozeman. I missed my old department and my coworkers.

Sure, I had Pops, and it was wonderful to see him every day. In time, I'd fit in here. But at the moment, being new felt a lot like being alone.

Was that why I'd slept with Griffin on Sunday?

I cringed for the hundredth time just thinking about his face at the restaurant.

Pops and Harrison Eden had chatted through the entire meal, carrying the conversation. Griffin had barely uttered a word. He'd simply sat there, glowering at his plate, while I'd forced a smile and done my best to make small talk with his father.

The tension radiating off of Griffin's shoulders had grown exponentially over the meal. Regret had been so plainly written on his handsome face that I'd nearly faked a stomachache to escape.

Thankfully, he'd bolted first. The moment he'd finished his club sandwich, he'd excused himself from the table.

I was still mad at myself for checking out his ass as he'd walked away.

With any luck, a few months would pass before we bumped into each other again. Maybe by then I'd stop thinking about his naked body in the backseat of his truck.

Griffin Eden was a one-time mistake, and with any luck, not a soul in Quincy would find out I'd screwed him my first night in town.

My house was a single-story Craftsman painted dove gray with white shutters. I parked in the driveway and made my way up the brick porch steps to the red front door.

The door was the reason I'd bought this house—that and

because there had only been three places on the market.

This two-bedroom, one-bathroom house was the perfect size for my simple life. I didn't need a large yard. The extra bedroom would become my office because I didn't need a guest bedroom—I rarely had guests.

I hurried inside and ignored the disaster that was the living room. Boxes crowded the couch in the center of the room. They'd gone untouched since Sunday because I'd spent every evening since reviewing case files.

My bedroom was in the same state—maybe worse.

On one side of the room, three suitcases were open, their contents spilling onto the hardwood floors. Somewhere under this roof there were hangers, I just had yet to find them. I dug through the closest pile of clothes, finding a new shirt, then stripped off my stained blouse, tossing it into the growing pile of laundry.

My new washer and dryer were arriving on Friday. The rest of the furniture I'd ordered had been delayed, so for now, my mattress was on the floor with my wardrobe.

Maybe tonight I'd search for the hangers. Maybe not.

Dressed and no longer smelling like stale coffee, I hurried outside and into the Durango, reversing onto the street. Then I retreated the way I'd come toward Main.

I was slowing at the intersection when a flash of red and blue streaked by, the wail of a siren splitting the air.

That was Allen's cruiser.

I pulled my phone from the console, seeing nothing on the screen. He'd been doing paperwork today, not out on patrol, so where was he going? Something had happened. Why hadn't anyone called me?

Instead of taking the left that would lead me to the station, I turned right, following Allen down Main. When he hit the edge of town, he punched the gas and shot down the road.

My heart hammered as I hurried to keep pace, driving with one hand while dialing into the station with the other.

"Quincy Police Department," Officer Smith answered.

"Hi, it's Winslow."

He grunted.

"I'm following Allen out of town. Can you tell me where he's going?"

"There was a call from out of town. Emergency in the mountains."

"Okay." I waited for more of an explanation. He didn't give me one. "What emergency?"

"Someone found a body at the base of Indigo Ridge."

I gasped. "W-what? Why didn't you call me?"

"Slipped my mind."

*Asshole.* "Officer Smith, you and I will be having a conversation when I return to the station."

With that, I ended the call, tossing my phone aside so I could concentrate on catching Allen.

His brake lights glowed as he slowed for a turnoff. There was no road sign or marker, but I followed his trail of dust down the gravel road, the mountains growing closer with every minute. One cliff stood out from the rest, its vertical face daunting as it towered above the trees and meadows below.

Three trucks were clustered together in the grass ahead, parked on the other side of the fence. Allen slowed when he approached, easing the cruiser toward the ditch.

I parked behind him, snagging my phone and shoving it in a pocket. Then I rifled through my purse for a small notepad and pen before climbing out.

"Chief." Allen stood on the side of the road, waiting for me to join him.

"What's going on?" Officer Smith's short explanation had been lacking at best.

"One of the ranch hands for the Edens stumbled across a body this morning."

"This is the Eden ranch?"

It was a stupid question. When I followed Allen's gaze to the men standing beside the trucks, I spotted Griffin instantly.

His legs were planted wide as he stood beside that familiar black truck. His hands were fisted at his hips. The words *go away* might as well have been etched on the brim of his faded black hat.

I steeled my spine. "Lead the way, Allen."

"Yes, ma'am." He set off through the tall grass, walking to the four-row barbed-wire fence past the ditch. With one hand pulling up the second wire and a booted foot pressing down the third, he opened a gap for me to duck and slide through.

I took his place, holding the wires for him, then it was my turn to lead, walking toward Griffin.

"Winslow." His voice was flat. Unreadable.

"Griffin." My voice sounded much the same. I had a job to do. "Can you show us the body?"

He nodded for us to follow him past the line of trucks.

A younger man was sitting against the tire of the last pickup in the row. Beside him crouched another man, older, with a handlebar mustache and a tan cowboy hat.

The kid on the ground looked pale. Tear tracks stained his cheeks. He must have been the one to find the body. I'd seen enough faces like his to know who was the first on the scene.

"Conor found the girl," Griffin said, keeping his voice low as we walked toward the corner of the fence. Beyond it, rocks clustered at the base of the cliff.

"I'll have to question him later."

"Sure." He nodded. "He works for us. I sent him out here to fix fence."

"What time was that?"

"Around ten. We worked in the barn first thing this morning for a couple of hours."

"Did he touch the body?"

"Probably." He sighed, then led the way over the fence.

The posts were wooden here, the wires too tight to stretch, so I planted a boot on the bottom brace and swung my legs over. Then I set off toward the cliff, walking slowly to take it all in.

A trail of broken grass had been made, probably from Conor and Griffin. Otherwise, the area seemed untouched.

Griffin and Allen stayed close behind as I set the pace to the rocks, moving as methodically up their steep face as I had through the flat meadow. We climbed until I reached a landing spot.

And a broken body.

I flipped off the switch in my mind that panicked at the blood. I shut down the emotions that came with a gruesome death. I swallowed hard—I did my job—and surveyed the scene.

The body was of a young woman, facedown. A few errant strands of blond hair blew in the breeze. Death blackened the area beneath her smashed skin and bones.

Most of the blood had dried and hardened in sticky pools and trickles from where it had flowed. She wore a white dress, the skirt mostly unharmed where it brushed her ankles. The bodice would never be clean again.

Her arms were splayed to the sides. One leg was bent at an unnatural angle. Only a few patches of smooth, graying skin remained on her calves. Otherwise, bone protruded from the surface of her limbs.

"Another one," Allen whispered.

I looked over my shoulder. "Another what?"

He pointed to the ridge above us.

There was a trail cut into the rock about halfway between us and the cliff's pinnacle. I hadn't noticed it on the drive. The path disappeared around a bend, probably where it descended down the hillside, but the end was directly above us.

Had this girl been pushed? Had she jumped?

"What am I looking at, Allen?"

"Suicide," he explained.

*Damn.* "Why do you say that?"

Allen and Griffin shared a look.

"What? What am I missing?"

"You're new here." Griffin spoke the word *new* with such scorn it was like he'd taken those three letters and thrown them in my face. "This isn't the first body found at the base of Indigo Ridge."

"How many others have there been before?"

"Two."

Two. This made three. *Holy. Shit.* What the hell was going on? What had I just walked into?

"We've had a string of suicides in the past ten years."

I blinked. "A string of suicides."

"Seven total."

"Seven?" My jaw nearly dropped. "That's almost one a year."

Allen's shoulders slumped. "It's been like this domino effect. One kid does it. Another decides to do it too."

I pointed to the ridge. "And this is where they come?"

"Not always," Griffin said.

I took in the girl's bare feet. The smocked sundress. Had she been in shorts or jeans, I might have thought this had been a hiking accident.

"Do we know who this is?" I asked.

"Lily Green," Griffin answered. "Conor thought so, at least. They are about the same age. I think they were friends."

There was nothing left of the girl's face. So how had Conor recognized her? Maybe from the blue butterfly tattoo on her wrist.

"Allen, are you good to take photos of the scene?"

"Yes. I was, um… I was here for the last one."

The last one. My stomach rolled. "All right. I'll call the station and get the medical examiner out here so we can get the body moved. The sooner we can identify her, the sooner we can notify next of kin."

"You got it, Chief."

"I'll need to talk to your employee now," I told Griffin.

He answered by retreating down the rocks.

My head was spinning as I followed.

Seven suicides in ten years. That was crazy. That was too many. Suicide rates were higher in rural areas than cities, but seven suicides in ten years…that was too many.

I knew it happened with young kids. And Allen was right, sometimes it could become this domino effect. We'd had the same thing happen at the high school in Bozeman for a few years. Three kids had attempted suicide, two had died.

The principal and teachers had jumped all over it after the second death, making sure they were watching the kids more closely and providing outlets for other students to report friends who might be at risk.

Seven suicides.

In this tiny community.

How had I not known about this? Why hadn't Pops told me? Why hadn't this been brought up during my interviews? I'd asked plenty of questions about past criminal cases. Though maybe they hadn't considered these crimes. Had these at least been documented?

The questions rolled through my mind as I followed Griffin to the fence and climbed over. Then I put them all away when we joined the other two men at the trucks.

"Conor, this is Winslow Covington." Griffin crouched beside the young man. "She's the new chief of police and she's going to ask you some questions."

The kid looked up from his spot on the ground, his face etched in sheer heartache and terror.

I bent so he wouldn't have to stand. "Hi, Conor."

"Ma'am." He sniffled and dragged a forearm across his nose.

"Mind if I ask you some questions?"

He shook his head.

The man with the mustache clapped Conor on the shoulder, then stood and walked to the truck's tailgate, giving us some space.

Griffin stood, but his feet didn't move. He towered over us as I asked my questions and took my notes.

It was fairly straightforward. Conor had come out to fix the fence per Griffin's orders. He'd caught sight of Lily's dress on the rocks and rushed to the body. He hadn't tried to move her but he'd picked up her hand to check for a pulse. The tattoo, as I'd suspected, had given her identity away. From there, he'd climbed down and called Griffin.

"Thank you, Conor." I gave him a sad smile. "I'll probably have a few follow-up questions for you."

"Okay." A tear streaked down his cheek. "We went to high school together. Lily and me. We dated our junior year. Broke up but she was always…"

The tears came faster.

Finding a dead body was never easy. Finding someone you loved…this would haunt him. "I'm so sorry."

"Me too." His chin quivered. "Wish she had talked to me. Wish I had talked to her."

"This isn't your fault." Griffin's tall body dropped beside mine. "You head on out with Jim, okay?"

"What about the fencing truck?"

"I'll take care of it."

Conor shoved to his feet, his balance unsteady.

Griffin stood and clamped a hand around Conor's arm, escorting him to where Jim was waiting.

I followed at a distance, watching as Griffin hugged the kid and helped him into the passenger seat of a white truck. The door was marked with an *E* and underscored with a U-shaped bar beneath—the Eden ranch emblem.

Griffin spoke to Jim for a moment before the older man nodded, then went to the driver's side.

"Will he stay with Conor?" I asked Griffin as Jim and Conor pulled away, rolling down a two-tire track.

"He will."

"I need to keep this quiet for a little bit so I can ensure we have the right identity, then notify next of kin."

"Lily's mom is a nurse at the nursing home. Allen can

get you her information."

"What if it's not Lily?"

"It's her, Winslow. We know our own people."

As in, I wasn't one of them. *Ouch.*

A new trail of dust followed a vehicle down the main gravel road. Hopefully it was the medical examiner.

"This is your property, correct?" I asked.

"Yes."

"Is this road ever closed? With a gate at night or something?"

"No." He shook his head. "The property on the other side of the road used to belong to another ranch, but I bought it two years ago. This is all Eden property now. There's no reason to gate it off other than to segment pastures for cattle."

"Do you ever have people drive out here?"

"Not really. It's private property." He fisted his hands on his hips. "Why?"

"Have you seen any strange vehicles coming and going this week?"

"This is a huge ranch. It's impossible to keep track of traffic." His jaw clenched. "Why are you asking?"

I looked up and down the gravel road. There wasn't a vehicle in sight that might have belonged to the girl. She'd been barefoot. Where were her shoes?

"I'm simply asking questions." That's why I was here.

"That girl jumped to her death. Her mother is probably worried sick about her. How about you stop asking questions and start providing answers?"

"How about I leave the ranching to you? And you leave investigations to me? I'm just doing my job."

He scoffed. "You want to do your job, go tell Lily's

mother. Anything else is a waste of fucking time."

Without another word, he stormed away, marching to his truck. He left me standing in a field, watching his taillights disappear.

"That went well," I muttered. "Shit."

I tipped my head to the sky.

Maybe this wasn't how the previous chief would have handled it. Maybe he would have taken one look at that poor girl and known it was suicide. But...

"I'm the chief now." And we'd do things my way.

Whether Griffin Eden liked it or not.

# CHAPTER 4

## GRIFFIN

The ice-cold beer bottle had barely skimmed my lips when the doorbell rang.

"Christ," I grumbled. "Now what?"

It had been a hell of a long day and I wasn't in the mood for visitors. But it was probably an employee—the members of my family didn't know how to ring doorbells—so ignoring my guest wasn't an option.

With my beer bottle in hand, I padded down the hallway to the door in my bare feet. If I was lucky, a rare occurrence, I wouldn't have to put my boots back on for whatever this visit entailed.

There were times when it would be nice to put some space between home and work. To live off the ranch where I wasn't as easily accessible—to the staff or my family. But there wasn't a place on earth I'd rather be than on this ranch.

Even when people showed up at my doorstep unannounced.

I pulled the door open, expecting, well...anyone else besides Winslow.

Her eyes, the color of ripe blueberries, seemed bluer in the fading evening light. One look at her beautiful face, and for a moment, I forgot to breathe.

"Hi," she said.

I tipped the bottle to my lips. Then I chugged.

Drinking seemed necessary around this woman.

Probably not a brilliant decision considering alcohol was the reason I'd gotten into this mess with her in the first place, but one look at those eyes and that silky hair and my cock twitched beneath my jeans.

Why the fuck couldn't I control myself around her?

Her pretty gaze narrowed as I gulped half my beer. "Thirsty?"

I forced the bottle away from my lips. "Something like that."

There was no need to ask her how she knew where I lived. Not only could she look it up in her database at the station, but anyone in Quincy could give her directions. Hell, three minutes on Main and she'd likely bump into a relative. Finding an Eden in this town was about as easy as looking for leaves on a tree in June.

"What are you doing here?" I asked.

"You never answered my questions on Wednesday."

Wednesday. A day I would like to forget. I'd been in a shit mood for the past two days. I'd barked at everyone the way I'd barked at her at the scene. In my defense, that had been the second time I'd found a dead woman on my property.

"So you came to my house?"

"Would you have come down to the station if I'd asked?"

"No."

"That's what I figured." She raised her chin, her feet planted firm. Winn wasn't going to leave until I talked to her, and this time, I couldn't exactly walk away.

I sighed and stood aside, jerking my chin for her to come inside.

She stepped past me and her sweet citrus scent wrapped around me like a vine.

My body reacted instantly, tightening in all the wrong places. I took another pull from my beer. The only rational explanation for this infuriating desire had to be lust. I'd gone too long without sex, and now I was acting like a randy teenager.

Lust. Definitely lust.

And those freckles on her nose. Goddamn it, they did it for me.

I was too busy to be studying her freckles.

"Did you know who I was?" I blurted.

"Pardon?"

"At Willie's. Did you know who I was?"

"No. You said you came through town. I assumed you didn't live here."

"You said Bozeman. I thought you were a tourist."

"You really didn't know who I was?"

"I wouldn't have fucked you in my truck had I known. As a general rule, I don't do hookups with locals. Gets messy when women realize I'm not interested in a relationship. I'm too busy."

"Ah. Then you're in luck because I have no desire for a relationship. And as far as I'm concerned, it never happened."

Like fuck it had never happened. That night was burned into my brain. But if she wanted to pretend it hadn't happened, that was fine by me. No one in Quincy needed to know I'd given the chief of police three orgasms.

"Back to the reason for my visit. I'd like to know more about that road to Indigo Ridge." She was all business tonight, her shoulders square and her expression stoic. Just like it had been Wednesday. Not a ghost of her mesmerizing smile graced her soft lips.

Probably safest that way. "Want a beer?"

"No, thanks."

"On duty?"

"That's why I'm here."

I finished my bottle, making her stand there and watch, then I retreated to the kitchen for beer number two. Maybe two Bud Lights would dull my senses enough so I wouldn't have a raging erection while she was in my house. At the moment, my dick was ready to say *fuck it* and carry her to my bedroom.

We hadn't had a lot of room to maneuver in the backseat of my truck. On a king-sized mattress, Winn and I could have some fun.

*Jesus.* I scrubbed a hand over my face as I opened the refrigerator. What was wrong with me?

Winn was here to talk about a dead girl, and I was thinking of sex. The mental image of Lily Green's smashed body was sobering, and I closed the fridge, forgoing the beer.

"Did you talk to Lily's mother?"

"I did." A wave of sadness broke her neutral composure. "It didn't take long to confirm Lily's identity through fingerprints. I spoke to her mother on Wednesday evening."

"Have you ever done that before? Notified a parent that

their child was dead?"

She gave me a single nod. "It's the worst part of this job."

"Sorry."

"My mentor at the Bozeman PD used to tell me that it was our duty and our responsibility to ease the burden any way we could. That we never know how we'll change the lives we touch with this job. He once had to tell a woman that her husband had been killed in a liquor store robbery. Years later, he bumped into her. They started dating and they're married now. He'd always remind me that even the dark days pass. That we heal from our losses. I don't know if that's true when you lose a child. But I hope, for Lily's mother's sake, that in time, she finds comfort. And I hope that I was able to soften the blow, as much as that was possible."

I studied her as she spoke, gentle honesty and vulnerability in her words. If she'd spoken to Lily's mother like this, with such truth and compassion, then yes, she'd softened that blow. As much as that was possible.

The news of Lily's suicide had traveled quickly through Quincy, as expected. I'd gone into town this morning to place a classified at the paper and the Nelsens had been buzzing with the news. No doubt it would be next week's headline. Emily had fished for more information and, when I'd stayed quiet, had made a not-so-subtle offer to trade sex for secrets.

I'd decided to post my help-wanted ad online instead of in the paper.

Emily had been a one-night mistake last year. A mistake I was still paying for.

I hoped Winslow wouldn't turn out to be the same.

"Was there a note?" I asked. "From Lily?"

She ignored my questions and asked one of her own.

"Can you tell me more about the road to Indigo Ridge?"

"It's a gravel road. There's not much else to tell."

"There's a trail going up the ridge. I walked it yesterday. How often do you or staff members of your ranch use it?"

"Why does it matter?"

"Because this is an ongoing investigation."

"Into a suicide."

"Into a young woman's death." She spoke like Lily could have been murdered.

"Don't drag this out looking for something that's not there. You'll only make it worse."

Her fists clenched. "I'm asking questions because I owe it to that girl and to her mother to do my job."

"Your answers would have come with a suicide note."

Winn didn't even blink.

"So there was no note."

She crossed her arms over her chest. "I stopped by your parents' place before coming here. Your dad said you've taken over management of the ranch. I'd prefer to talk with you because he said you were the one who'd know most of the day-to-day routines. But if I should head back there and ask them these questions—"

"No." Damn it. This was not a topic I'd put on Dad.

The first suicide off Indigo Ridge had been years ago. He'd found the body and taken it really hard. To this day, he avoided that road at all costs. I wouldn't make him relive that, even if it meant reliving it myself. "Let's talk in the living room."

My house wasn't nearly as big as my parents' six-thousand-square-foot home, but half that size suited me just fine. The open concept and vaulted ceilings gave my rancher character and an open feel. With three bedrooms and an office, it was plenty for me. I didn't have six kids to wrangle, unlike Mom and Dad, who'd needed to add on twice to fit us all.

I walked to the couch and took a seat as Winslow went to the opposite side of the coffee table, sinking into a leather chair.

She glanced at the framed photo on the end table. "Your siblings?"

"All six of us. I'm the oldest. Then Knox. Lyla and Talia, the twins. Then there's Eloise, who manages the inn."

"Pops introduced me to her after lunch on Monday."

That awful, tense lunch. "Mateo is the youngest. He's working here on the ranch and at the inn until he decides what he wants to do."

He'd probably take over a family business or start one of his own. That's what the rest of us had done. My parents had instilled their entrepreneurial spirit in us all. And their love for Quincy.

Each of us had moved away for college. Knox and Talia had stayed away the longest, but eventually, the pull of Quincy and family had brought them home too.

Winslow studied the photo, memorizing our faces. Plenty of people had a hard time telling me and my siblings apart, especially when we'd been young. Our ages were close. Knox and I had the same build, though his tattoos set him apart. The girls were undeniably sisters.

But I suspected Winslow wouldn't have any trouble recognizing my siblings. She was smart. Focused.

Good qualities in a cop.

"Okay, Chief." I leaned my elbows onto my knees. "What do you want to know?"

She shifted, retrieving a small notepad and pen from

the back pocket of her jeans. It was the same one she'd had on Wednesday. She flipped it open and the ballpoint pen hovered above the paper. "The trail up Indigo Ridge. What's it used for?"

"Nothing these days. Before we bought the neighboring place, we used that trail to move cattle up the mountain. Even then it was rare. We'd only take it if we were having a drought and were short on grass. There's a cutoff that winds to the back side of the ridge where we've got about two hundred acres."

Her pen flew over the paper. "I think I saw that cutoff when I was up there."

"It's pretty overgrown now. After I bought the neighboring place, it gave us a direct road to the mountain. We haven't moved cattle on that trail since." Part of the reason that I'd pushed so hard to buy the neighboring property was because I hated moving cattle up that trail. It was steep and required we go single file, following the cattle by horse.

"I believe I saw that road too. Though road is probably a generous term. It was more like two tracks through the trees."

"That's the one."

"Does anyone go up there? Or is it strictly for cattle?"

"My uncle. He lives there now. After I bought the neighbor's place, he built a cabin in the mountains. It's right on the border with the forest service. He's been there for about a year."

Her pen scratched on the paper as she made a note. "And would he have recalled seeing anyone coming up or down the trail?"

"No. His place isn't anywhere near that trail." And

Briggs was struggling when it came to recollection these days.

"Do people come out there to go hiking?"

"Not without permission. And even then, I wouldn't give it." Not to Indigo Ridge.

"So no one ever goes out there."

"Kids sometimes," I admitted. "Curious kids who know that's where two girls committed suicide. I caught a group of them last fall. Haven't seen anyone up there since."

"Was Lily with that group of kids?"

"No, they were younger. In high school."

Her pen scratched another note. "The medical examiner determined that the time of death was likely late Sunday night, into early Monday morning. Would any of your employees have been in the area at that time? Or perhaps your uncle?"

"You want alibis."

"Call it alibis if you'd like. I'm trying to determine if anyone would have seen her go up there and if she was really alone. We found her car parked off the highway. From where it was parked to the place where she would have jumped, it's seven miles. I walked it yesterday, and it took me almost three hours. I'm wondering if someone might have seen her during that time."

"No one who works for me."

"If it was at night, she would have had to have a flashlight. We didn't find one on the trail or by her body. We also didn't find shoes."

"What are you getting at?"

"Where are her shoes? If she walked it without them, her feet would have looked like ground meat. Her feet had some scratches but not seven miles' worth. How did she get up there in the dark? By eleven it's pitch black."

"You said the medical examiner suspected it could have been Monday morning."

"At the very latest. But again, that's time of death."

"Maybe she went up during the day. Stayed there for a while. I don't know."

Winn flipped to a new sheet on the notepad. "Would anyone have been around early Monday morning to see someone leave the ridge?"

"You think someone went up there with her."

"Possibly."

"And what? Killed her?" I shook my head and sighed. "It's a suicide, Chief. Just like the other girls who jumped off that ridge. I don't know why they did it. My heart aches for their families. But it's exactly the same as the other two times. I know because I was there for all three."

She blinked.

"Didn't know that, did you?" I muttered. "Dad found the first body. I found the second."

"And now Lily Green."

I nodded. "It's awful. Truly awful. What we need are more resources in town for these girls, not to go looking for a killer when there isn't one. Which you'd understand if you were from here. But you're not."

She opened her mouth, then closed it before speaking. Her nostrils flared.

"What?"

"Nothing." She sat a little straighter. "Is there anything else you can tell me about the other girls?"

"It'll all be in a report, I'm sure."

"Yes, I'm sure. But I'm asking anyway."

"The girl I found was two years ago. She was one of

Eloise's friends. It shook us all up. Eloise knew she was having a hard time but didn't think it would go this far." So now my sister carried that guilt. We all did. "The girl Dad found was five years ago. She'd been friends with Lyla."

"I'm sorry. That had to be hard on your family."

"It was."

Winslow closed her notebook, then stood. "Thank you for your time."

"That's it?"

"For now. I'll show myself out." Without another word, she strode out of the living room.

The smart thing to do would be to let her go. Keep some distance. Let her walk out the door while I stayed right here on this couch. But I stood, the manners my mother had ingrained in us from an early age nagging. We escorted guests out and thanked them for stopping by.

I caught up to Winn just as she was about to reach for the handle. I stretched past her, crowding way too close, and opened the door. Another manner. Men held doors for women.

She glanced up at me, her breath catching. Once again, that sweet scent of hers filled my nose. Her mouth parted but otherwise she didn't move.

An inch, maybe two, separated our bodies. That tiny gap crackled, the electricity between us just as strong as it had been at Willie's. She was more beautiful than I'd realized sitting in that dark, musty bar.

Winn's blue eyes broke from mine, and the moment her gaze dropped to my mouth, I was done for.

I leaned closer.

"What are you doing?" she whispered.

"I have no fucking clue." Then my lips were on hers.

One sweep of my tongue against her lower lip and we weren't standing by my door. We were at Willie's, locked in my truck. Our clothes were stripped and strewn on the floor. Our mouths were fused as she straddled my lap.

Days later and I could still feel the way she'd moved over me, rocking her hips up and down and up and down. The fingernail marks she'd left on my shoulders had faded, and damn it, I wanted them back.

I let go of the door to wrap Winn in my arms, pulling her flush against my chest.

She came willingly, her tongue tangling with mine as I savored her sweetness. Her lips were soft, yet frantic. Her hands gripped my T-shirt, balling it in her fists as I slanted my mouth over hers for a deeper dive.

My pulse throbbed in my veins. My arousal was like steel, as hard as the gun holstered on her hip. I was a second away from kicking the door closed and carrying her to my bedroom when the sound of a horse's whinny broke us apart.

Winslow tore her lips from mine, our breaths mingling. Her eyes widened as she stepped out of my arms.

My chest heaved as I worked to regain my breath, and before the haze of desire had cleared, she was gone. She walked away without a backward glance.

I stood in the threshold, arms crossed over my chest, and watched her climb into her SUV and tear down the gravel road, disappearing into the grove of trees that surrounded my property.

"Shit." I rubbed her kiss from my lips, then went inside for that second beer.

Anything to get her intoxicating taste off my tongue.

The second bottle didn't work. Neither did the third.

# CHAPTER 5

## WINSLOW

**W**hy had I kissed him? Over the past three days, that question had bounded through my mind like a sugared-up kid on a trampoline.

I'd lived in Quincy for eight days and I'd kissed Griffin at two of our four encounters. Questioning my decision to move—questioning my sanity—had become a regular part of my daily routine. And nightly, since sleeping had been difficult. This morning while brushing my teeth, I'd considered for a split second going home to Bozeman.

Except there was no home.

And quitting wasn't in my nature.

Time. What I needed was time. I'd survive the second week like I'd survived the first. If I could make it through the next eight days without kissing Griffin Eden, maybe I'd be able to get that man out of my head.

Work demanded my full attention. My focus was on building any kind of positive rapport with the officers. So far, things at the station were...strained. Eventually the staff would warm up to me, right?

"Good morning." I walked into the break room and conversation stopped.

The three officers standing around the coffeepot scattered, each nodding as they passed me on their way to the bullpen.

I swallowed a groan and refilled my mug before retreating to my office, closing the door behind me. Then I sagged against its face. "I'm not quitting."

The attitude in the station had grown colder. Even Janice had given me a few sideways looks when I'd started asking questions about Lily Green, Indigo Ridge and the abundance of suicides in the last decade.

Apparently it was a no-touch topic. Everyone looked at me like this was a no-touch subject. Maybe Griffin was right. Maybe I needed to let it go and accept it at face value. I didn't want to drudge up painful memories and make it worse for families and friends.

But it just felt...off.

The best cop I knew had once told me to always follow my instincts.

Files were scattered over the surface of my desk again, despite the hour I'd spent organizing last night. I still hadn't made it through the past three months' worth of cases, but I'd asked Janice to pull another three anyway, expanding my window to six months.

Janice had delivered this morning. On top of them were the files of each suicide in Quincy.

Seven deaths.

I'd read through each report three times already, hoping that it would squash this uneasy feeling. It hadn't. What was I missing? Something, right?

I shoved off the door and walked to my chair, setting my coffee aside. Then I picked up the phone and dialed the number I'd been meaning to call for a week.

"Cole Goodman," he answered.

I smiled at his warm voice. "Hey."

"Who is this?"

"Funny," I deadpanned. "You better not have forgotten about me already."

He chuckled. "Never. Is this your new work number?"

"Yep. I think my personal phone was swallowed up by the unpacked boxes at home. I haven't seen it for days."

"Sounds about right," he teased.

Cole had spent many hours listening to me complain that I'd lost my personal phone. In my defense, I had yet to misplace my station cell or a radio.

Organization wasn't necessarily a weakness. I could be organized. But I didn't mind a little chaos either. When my focus was on one lane, everything else became a little blurry. Unpacking and finding my phone just didn't seem as important as wrapping my head around Lily Green's death.

"I was just thinking about you," he said. "How'd the first week go?"

"It was, um…interesting."

"Uh-oh. What's going on?"

I sighed and the truth came rushing out. "No one likes me here. I keep getting looks like I'm too young for this job and only got it because of Pops."

"You knew this wouldn't be easy."

"I know," I muttered. "I just…hoped."

"Hang in there. It's only been a week. You're a great cop. Give them time to see that."

All things I'd told myself, but somehow hearing them from Cole gave me a boost of confidence.

Cole had been my mentor in Bozeman. When I'd been promoted to detective, he'd been there to help me every step along the way. Whenever I had a difficult case, Cole was my go-to person to talk it through.

In our years working together, he'd become more than a colleague. He was also a cherished friend. His wife, Poppy, owned my favorite restaurant in Bozeman. Their kids were the sweetest souls on earth. When I'd lost my own family, his had been there to see me through the darkest days.

"I miss you guys. I'm homesick for the Goodmans."

"We miss you too. Poppy was talking about taking a weekend trip to visit."

"I'd love it." For them, I'd actually unpack my house.

"Tell me about the station."

"Actually, if you have a few minutes, can I run something by you?"

"Always."

I spent the next fifteen minutes telling him about Lily Green and the other suicides. I'd told him how Lily's mother had collapsed into my arms when I'd gone to her home and told her the horrific news. Her scream had been so full of agony that I'd never forget that noise.

Heartbreak was an ugly, black sound.

I'd stayed with Melina Green for hours that night. I'd held her hand as she'd called her ex-husband and told him about Lily. Then I'd waited with her as he'd driven the two hours from Missoula. When he'd arrived, his eyes red rimmed and his soul broken over his daughter's death, I'd given him my condolences, then left them to grieve.

Yesterday, I'd stopped by Melina's house to check on her. She'd answered the door wearing a bathrobe and tear-stained cheeks. And once again, she'd fallen into my arms, and I'd held her as she'd cried.

But Melina was a strong woman. She'd collected herself and begun to talk about Lily. For an hour, she'd told me about the bright, beautiful light her daughter had been.

Lily had been twenty-one and living with her mom to save money. When I'd asked Melina if she'd found a suicide note in Lily's room, she'd confessed that she hadn't had the emotional strength to check. But her ex had gone into Lily's bedroom while he'd been in Quincy and hadn't found anything.

"I'm trying to be sensitive and not push too hard with the mother," I told Cole. "But my impression was that she and Lily were very close. She's shocked. Truly shocked that Lily would kill herself."

"I can't imagine her pain," Cole said. "She might not want to think about the signs that she missed. Or that her daughter was hiding anything from her. You need to talk to other people who knew Lily."

"That's my plan. I started with the officers and staff here."

"And what did they say?"

"No one knew her well. One of the officers said that her son graduated with Lily, but they'd lost touch when her son moved away for college. Most of the others just knew her from the bank where she worked as a teller. Everyone says that Lily was always smiling. That she was a happy young woman."

That didn't necessarily mean anything. I knew how it

felt to feel entirely lost and alone but force a smile for the outside world.

"What about the other suicides?"

"The reports are thin."

The former chief hadn't been a stickler for details. That was something the staff here was going to have to change because I wasn't going to let short, hurried reports be the standard.

"Last year, a seventeen-year-old boy hung himself in his basement. Before that, it's all been women. Three, including Lily, jumped to their deaths off a cliff. Another slit her wrists in the bathtub. Another downed a bottle of prescription pills. And the first, ten years ago, shot herself with her father's pistol. I guess he was a cop."

No one in the station had wanted to talk about that case.

"Damn." Cole blew out a long breath. "That's a lot for such a small town. Especially because it's mostly women."

"Exactly." Suicide rates were over three times higher in men. Yet in Quincy, it was like the statistics had flip-flopped.

"It's not unheard of but it gives me pause."

"Me too. It's not necessarily out of the normal range, but the girls were all in their twenties. Typically, I would have expected them to be younger. Dealing with high school stuff, you know? These girls were all working and transitioning to their adult lives. The high school problems should have largely been behind them."

"Were they all from Quincy?"

"Yes."

"Even though they were older, they were probably still connected to it. Their old acquaintances, good and bad. The town."

"True."

"What does your gut say?" he asked.

"It's unsettled," I admitted. "Maybe if we had found a note or a journal or anything that showed this girl was struggling, I wouldn't feel so uneasy."

"Keep looking. Keep talking to people."

"I'm ruffling feathers."

He laughed. "You're quite good at losing your phone and keys. But you're fantastic at ruffling feathers."

"Ha ha," I muttered, a smile on my lips. I'd missed Cole's teasing.

"Rile 'em up, Winnie. If that's what it takes until your gut stops screaming, ruffle all the feathers you need."

"Thanks." A knot of anxiety loosened in my stomach. Cole often told me what I already knew. That didn't make his words any less powerful.

"Call me if you need to talk it through again."

"Okay. Give Poppy a hug for me. Brady and MacKenna too."

"Will do. I'll shoot you a text with some weekends that work for us."

"Can't wait." We said our goodbyes and then I sat back in my chair, staring at the mess of files to review.

Maybe I was reading too much into Lily Green. Quincy was a small town and I had to think that my officers had a good pulse for what was happening. If there was any reason to suspect foul play, they would have seen it, right? And Pops too. He hadn't mentioned a thing about the suicides.

Except what if the reason no one had questioned these suicides was *because* they were from Quincy? I was the only person who hadn't spent years working in this department. Not only that, but every staff member had been born and raised in this county.

Maybe to them, this was normal.

The saddest truth would be if they were right.

A knock came at the door.

"Come in," I called.

Janice poked her head inside. "Emily from the newspaper is on line one for you."

"Would you please tell her I'm in a meeting and take a message?"

"Sure thing." She eased the door closed, leaving me to my own thoughts.

I swiveled in my chair, right then left, right then left. My eyes never wandered from the stack of files.

Why? Why was Lily's death bothering me?

"No note." That was the biggest missing piece.

"Her car." Why had it been miles away from Indigo Ridge? Who'd taken her up there?

"Her shoes." If she'd walked, where were her shoes?

On Saturday, after a fitful night's rest on Friday thanks to the man who'd kissed me dizzy, I'd returned to Indigo Ridge. I'd canvased the area, hiking the ridge not once more, but twice. Then I'd walked the path to where we'd found Lily's car again.

No clues in sight, certainly no missing pair of shoes.

What I really felt like doing with my day was heading out to the trail again, but the stack of files wasn't getting smaller, so I took a sip from my now-cold coffee and got to work.

Eight hours and too-many-files-to-count later, there wasn't anything particularly noteworthy, though I had added three more items to my list of new paperwork requirements. Janice had scheduled one-on-one meetings with every officer in the department, and starting tomorrow, I'd sit down with each to talk on an individual basis.

I had positive praise for each person—except Officer Smith—but there were critiques too. I doubted I'd win many friends by the time these meetings were complete, but whatever. This was my department now, damn it, and we were going to start creating reports worth reading.

By the time Janice came in to say good night, I was exhausted and starving. I was in the middle of packing up a few files to take home for the night when my phone rang. "Hey, Pops."

"I'm grilling burgers for dinner."

"I'm on my way. Need me to pick up anything?"

"Cold beer."

"On it." I smiled and hustled out the door. After a quick stop by the convenience store for his favorite, Coors Original, I headed across town.

Pops lived on the outskirts of Quincy, in a neighborhood nestled against the river. The house had been his and my grandmother's before she'd died fifteen years ago. In all my life, the house hadn't changed. The outside was still the same pea green. The interior was a symphony of beige.

My grandmother had loved chickens, and her collection of rooster and hen statues sat proudly above the kitchen cabinets. Walking through the front door was like walking into my childhood. His love for her clung to the outdated floral curtains, crocheted afghans and cross-stitched toss pillows she'd left behind.

"Pops?" I called from the entryway.

He didn't answer, so I headed toward the back deck. The smoky scent of his barbeque greeted me as I stepped outside, along with another familiar face.

"Well, there she is." Frank, my grandpa's neighbor and

friend, popped out of a deck chair. He clapped once, then opened his arms. "I've been waiting for you to come over here and visit."

I laughed and walked into his embrace. "Hey, Frank."

"Missed seeing your face, cutie. Welcome. Glad you're one of us now."

Was I one of them? Because I felt like an outsider, and the niggling in my stomach warned me that it might always be that way.

Frank let me go, putting his hands on my shoulders to look me up and down. "You're all grown up. Still can't believe you're our chief of police. I look at you and see that little girl in pigtails who'd come over and make mud pies in Rain's garden."

"How is Rain?"

"Come on over. See for yourself. She'd love to visit."

"I'll do that," I promised, feeling bad for not stopping by already.

Rain and Frank had moved in next door when I was little. We'd come to visit Pops and Nana that weekend and I remembered thinking how cool it was that their U-Haul had been from Mississippi.

They were older than my parents and younger than my grandparents, but after Nana had died of a sudden heart attack when I was fifteen, Frank and Rain had adopted Pops. They'd been here for him through his wife's death.

And when he'd lost his son and daughter-in-law.

Frank and Rain had been here for Pops when I couldn't. They were part of the family. Frank was my grandfather's best friend. Now I was here and we could all be a family.

"Are you staying for dinner?" I asked.

"Can't. I've been fixing up this old Jeep for Rain. The

new fender just got here, so I need to do some tinkering." He smacked his flat stomach. "And she promised me paella for dinner."

Frank, like Pops, was a silver fox with a broad physique and muscled frame. The two of them went hiking together nearly every weekend in the summers, and during the week, they'd carpool to the local gym.

"I'd better get on," he said.

"So good to see you, Frank."

"You too, Winnie." He gave me a kind smile, then turned and shook hands with Pops. "Feel like fishing tomorrow after work?"

"Absolutely."

"Good deal." Frank waved, then walked down the deck's stairs, crossing the lawn to disappear into his garage.

"How's my girl?" Pops came over and wrapped me in a bear hug.

"I'm okay." I sagged into his broad chest. His heartbeat was strong beneath my ear, a comforting rhythm that had been a steady beat my entire life. "How are you?"

"Hungry."

I laughed and let him go. "What can I do?"

"Fetch me that cold beer."

While he grilled burgers, I readied the buns, toppings and napkins. Then the two of us ate on the deck, the river beyond the yard providing the evening music.

"Thanks for cooking dinner," I said when the dishes were done, and we set off for an after-dinner stroll down his block.

"Of course. Glad I could track you down. I tried calling your other number. It said your voicemail box was full."

The messages were probably all from Skyler. Our

breakup had been four months ago, and the constant calls were wearing thin. "I can't find that phone. I don't even know when I lost it."

"I figured as much." He laughed. "How are you holding up?"

"I'm...okay." Not great. Not bad. Just okay. "It's been a week."

"I still can't believe sweet Lily Green. Breaks my heart."

"Mine too." Melina's distraught face popped into my mind. "You never said anything about the suicides."

He tucked his hands into his khaki pockets. "Didn't want to put that on you while you were dealing with so much in Bozeman. And awful as it is, that's part of life. Here and anywhere else."

"Seven in ten years. Don't you think that's a lot?"

"Of course I do. Each time, we put more resources into counselors at the school. We've got two available for community members, free of charge. But if these kids don't reach out, if we don't know they're hurting, how are we supposed to help?"

I sighed. "I'm not trying to criticize. It's just...it's been a long week."

He untucked a hand and put his arm around my shoulders. "Sorry."

"Do you think there's a chance they aren't suicides?"

"I wish I could say yes. I wish there was another explanation. But each of those deaths was investigated. Most came with notes."

"Lily didn't leave one."

"Or maybe you just haven't found it yet."

"I'll keep looking."

"I know you will. I don't like thinking of you dealing

with this. It's heavy and hard. But someone has to carry it, and I trust you above anyone else to do the right thing."

"Thanks." I leaned into his side. His faith in me was unwavering. I'd earned it. I'd keep earning it. Starting with giving Melina Green whatever answers I could find about her daughter.

"Change of subject," he said. "I stopped at Willie's on Saturday."

"Um…okay." *Shit.* Willie hadn't struck me as a bigmouth. He wouldn't have talked about Griffin and me, right?

"He saw your picture in the paper," Pops said.

"You mean the gossip rag?" In the one and only newspaper I'd read, there hadn't actually been much news. Not that I'd read the whole thing. I'd had to stop after the front page.

The article on my position as chief had basically called me a child cop and stated the only reason I'd gotten the job was because of Pops. But the paper had come out on Wednesday. I'd been at Indigo Ridge, then with Melina Green.

Pops had called and left me a voicemail, fuming and cursing the Nelsen name. By the time I'd listened to his message, then stopped by the grocery store to buy the paper, it had been after dark. When I'd finally sat down to read the article, I just hadn't had many fucks to give.

"Willie mentioned that you and Griffin Eden were there together last week."

Damn it, Willie. "Yeah," I muttered.

"Want to tell me what's going on there?"

"Nope."

"I thought lunch was a little awkward."

"Awkward is an understatement."

He laughed. "Then I'll assume I don't want to know."

"You really don't."

"Well, just be careful. Griffin is a good man, but he's been known to break a few hearts."

"No need to worry about mine. I have no interest in Griffin Eden."

That wasn't entirely true.

One night with Griffin and he'd become a constant on my mind. Maybe if I stopped kissing him, it would help. But he was too good-looking for his own good—certainly for mine—and my God, could he kiss.

The chemistry was off the charts. The man was magnetic. Never in my life had my body responded so strongly to a man's touch, not even Skyler's.

Replaying our night together had become an escape. When everything else in my head became too loud, I'd think of his kiss. Of his hands and his tongue, roaming across my skin.

It was alarming to think so much about one man. But since I had no plans of seeing him anytime soon, what was the harm of a few errant thoughts when I was alone in bed?

Pops and I finished our walk, mostly in silence. The streets of Quincy held a peace unrivaled. I hugged my grandpa good night to drive home, hoping to unpack at least one box before bed.

Except the minute my gray house and red door came into view, I spotted a familiar truck.

Two trucks, actually.

One was coated in dust. The other was gleaming black and freshly waxed.

"Damn it." I really didn't have time for this. He was going to ruin my night, wasn't he?

I parked in the driveway, climbed out and slammed the door.

Two handsome faces waited for me on the front porch. One stood, arms crossed, legs in faded jeans planted wide. The other was in a suit. He hadn't even loosened his tie.

They exchanged a wary glance, then focused on me as I stopped on the bottom stair and crossed my arms over my chest.

"What are you doing here?"

# CHAPTER 6

## GRIFFIN

**W**as she talking to me?

Those deep blue eyes narrowed, though not in my direction.

The suit stood taller. "Hey."

"Answer my question, Skyler." Winn marched up the porch steps, arms still crossed. "What are you doing here?"

"I tried calling you."

"Me not answering should have been the first clue I didn't want to talk to you."

*Or was it because she'd lost her phone?* I kept my mouth shut, watching as this guy withered under her stare.

Winn had the death glare perfected. It was sexy as hell to see such a fierce woman, especially knowing she could throw it all away and let her guard down to flirt and laugh like she had at Willie's. And beneath it all was another layer, the professional, sharp-witted woman who'd come to my home bearing her notepad and pen.

Complex. Confident. Compassionate. Each of Winslow Covington's facets was attractive.

I fought a grin as she stood unmoving, waiting for the suit to speak.

"I was worried about you, Winnie."

She patted the Glock holstered to her belt beside her gleaming badge. "Unnecessary."

He glanced in my direction, his mouth flattening. *Skyler* had been glaring at me since the moment I'd parked on the street and walked to Winn's porch.

Before I could knock on the door or ask who he was, he'd informed me that she wasn't here. He'd probably thought I'd leave. Why hadn't I left? Maybe because I'd instantly disliked this guy and the arrogance wafting off his tailored jacket.

"Who is this guy?" he asked, jerking his thumb at me.

She ignored his question. "How did you find my address?"

He looked to me again, inching closer to her. "Can we talk in private? It's about the house."

"What about the house? I told you ten times, I don't want it. If you do, then you can buy me out. Otherwise, quit stalling and put it on the market."

"Winnie."

"Skyler." She uncrossed her arms and flicked a wrist like he was a fly that she was brushing away. Then she turned to me, and for a moment, I expected that same glare and dismissal. But then her expression lightened so suddenly it made me blink twice.

Gone was the glare. Gone was the set jaw and furrowed brow. A stunning smile transformed her face, showcasing her beauty, and damn it, I wanted to kiss her again.

"Hey, babe."

*Babe?* Before I could make sense of that, she closed the gap between us, stood on her toes and pressed her lips to the corner of my mouth.

When she dropped to her heels, she shifted, giving Skyler her back. Her eyes widened and she mouthed, "Please."

Pretend to be the boyfriend.

Fine by me as long as she knew I wouldn't ever *be* the boyfriend.

"Hi, baby."

"How was your day?"

I bent down, unable to help myself, and brushed my lips against hers. "Better now."

And damn it, that wasn't a lie. Every time I saw her, she was more beautiful.

"Are you staying tonight?" she asked.

"Was planning on it."

"Good." She stepped past me and inserted her key into the lock. Without a glance at Skyler, she disappeared inside the house.

"Winnie," he called.

She was already gone.

I chuckled and followed her into the house, closing the door behind me. After navigating a maze of boxes, I found Winn in the kitchen, standing against the counter, silently fuming.

"Friend of yours?"

"My ex."

"Ah. Now the fake-boyfriend play makes sense."

"Thanks for going along with it."

"Welcome." I leaned against the wall.

"Wait." She gave me a wary glance. "Why did you go along with it?"

I shrugged. "He irritated me."

"He irritates me too," she muttered.

"Want me to hang out until he disappears?"

"If you wouldn't mind."

"There something I should know?" Because if that bastard was harassing her, I'd march outside and make sure he understood the rules had just changed.

"No." She shook her head. "He's harmless unless you count him being a royal pain in my ass."

"What's the story there?"

She shrugged. "We were together for eight years. Engaged for six. We called it off four months ago and he moved out of our house. Which he refuses to sell."

Eight years was a long damn relationship. Six years was one hell of an engagement. Why hadn't they gotten married? "Is that why you moved here? Your breakup?"

"Part of the reason. It was time for a change. When Pops mentioned that the former chief was retiring, I decided to at least apply. I honestly didn't think I'd be considered."

"Even with Covie as the mayor?"

"Pops loves me, but he loves this town too. He wouldn't put someone in the chief's position who wasn't capable of doing the job. And I am capable, Griffin."

The more I learned about her, the more I suspected she was. "I heard you went to visit Melina Green yesterday."

"How'd you know that?"

"Conor. He went to see her. Apparently he just missed you."

"That was nice of him."

"That was nice of you."

She dropped her gaze to the floor. "The least I can do is show her that she's not alone."

That act, in and of itself, set her apart from the former chief. He'd always kept his distance from the community. Maybe it had been intentional. It had to be difficult to bust friends or family members. It was likely easier to remain apart than punish a buddy for breaking the law.

Or maybe he was just a cold bastard. That was Dad's impression.

Winslow was anything but cold.

I studied her as she stood there, the silence of the house growing louder. There was a weight on her shoulders. An exhaustion in her eyes.

"Hell of a week, huh?"

"That's one way to put it." She looked to a box set on the counter, then trudged over, opening the top with a sigh. "As you can see, unpacking hasn't been a priority."

She'd put her life on hold to ask questions about Lily Green and visit a grieving mother. "This is a nice place. Good neighborhood too. One of my buddies in high school lived in the green house three down."

"Is that how you knew where I lived?"

"No, I asked my mom. One of her best friends was your realtor."

"So much for privacy," she muttered.

"Small town. Privacy is relative."

"I guess that's true." She pulled a glass from the box and put it directly into the dishwasher.

"Want some help?"

"No, but thanks." She finished with the glasses, and because it wasn't in my nature to stand around when there was work to be done, I collected the empty box from her and folded up the packing paper, then broke down the box.

"Where do you want this?"

"There's a stack of empties outside my bedroom down the hallway."

"Got it." I strode that way, taking the box and paper along.

My boots seemed twice as loud as normal on her hardwood floors. There were two rooms down the narrow hall. On the right was her bedroom. The mattress rested on the floor, the blankets unmade. Three suitcases were pushed against the far wall, open and overflowing.

Winslow seemed so put together. Did it bother her living in a mess? Because it sure as hell would have bothered me.

Opposite her room was another crammed with boxes. I added mine to the short stack of flattened cardboard, then returned to the kitchen.

The dishwasher was running. Winn had retreated to the living room. Beside her, on the center cushion of the leather couch, was the purse she'd carried in earlier and a stack of files.

The couch was the only piece of furniture in the room, maybe in the whole house. It sat at an odd angle beneath the center light fixture. Beside it was an unopened box that Winn had shoved beside an armrest to use as a makeshift end table.

Had her ex taken the other furniture? Was it still being moved? I was about to ask when a manila file folder caught my eye from beneath her purse. Walking closer, I read the name on the tab.

*Harmony Hardt.*

The girl I'd found at the base of Indigo Ridge.

There were likely photos in that folder. Photos of the

images forever burned into my brain. The dark hair matted with blood. The limbs askew. The blood. The death.

"You're looking into the suicides," I said.

"Yes."

"Why?"

"Because I need to."

"They're suicides, Winn."

She stayed quiet, not agreeing or disagreeing.

"It's sad," I said. "Horrific. I get why you want to find a different explanation. Most outsiders do."

"You know, you keep reminding me that I'm new in town. But I'm not all that new. I've spent a lot of time here, especially when I was a kid. This was my father's hometown."

"There's a difference between visiting Quincy and living in Quincy."

"Well, I live here now."

"Yes, you do." And that made this insatiable attraction to her exponentially more complicated.

Winn rose up and leaned over the back of the couch, peering toward the window that overlooked the porch. The ex was still there, his face glued to his phone and his fingers flying over its screen.

"He's still here," she grumbled with an eye roll. "What are you doing here, anyway?"

I plucked her phone from the back pocket of my jeans. "This was at my place."

"Damn." She stood and crossed the room, taking it from my hand. Then she tossed it in the general direction of her purse, like she didn't care if it vanished again. "It must have fallen out of my pocket. I'm a bit scattered right now, but I would have tracked it down eventually."

"You don't need it?"

"Not really. It's my personal cell, the one Skyler's been calling." She went to the couch, plopping down in the same seat. "You're welcome to sit down. But if you need to go, it's fine."

The only thing waiting for me at home was a stack of bills to pay. This woman was far more entertaining than hours spent in my office, so I took the seat beside her, leaving enough space to keep my dick from getting any ideas.

"So what was the reason you called it off? Your engagement?" It was none of my business, but I was asking anyway. Maybe if I understood her better, I'd get her off my mind. That, and go a few years without kissing her.

Days later and the temptation of her lips was as powerful as ever.

She was as captivating as she was dangerous.

"He's not the man I thought he was," she said.

The asshole had probably been fucking someone else. *Idiot.* "Sorry."

"It's better now than if we'd actually gotten married."

"True."

Like Skyler knew we were talking about him, the doorbell rang.

Winslow's nostrils flared. "He's stubborn."

"Why's he here?"

"Your guess is as good as mine. He didn't speak to me after he moved out. Then he heard through some mutual friends I was moving to Quincy and he had *concerns.* He might claim to be here about our house, but the ball's in his court. And our realtor knows the best way to reach me is email."

"What were his concerns?"

"Skyler is used to getting what he wants. I think he

expected me to pine after him. Maybe he thought I'd forgive him. Maybe beg for him to come back. Hell if I know. He probably doesn't like the fact that I won't give him any more of my time. He had eight years. And I won't beg any man."

That wasn't exactly true. She'd begged in the backseat of my truck when I'd had my finger on her clit and she'd wanted to come.

My cock twitched.

"Want to mess with him some?" I asked.

"What do you have in mind?"

I grinned. "Be right back."

Skyler's face whipped to mine when I opened the front door. He'd been on his phone again.

I jerked up my chin, passed him for the stairs and walked to my truck. Earlier today I'd stopped by the grocery store for a few things. Winslow had been on my mind when I'd passed the condoms, so I'd grabbed a box on a whim.

Or maybe a wish.

With the condoms in my hand, I shut the truck door and returned to the house.

Skyler spotted them instantly. His jaw clenched.

"Still here? Have a good night." I shot him a smirk, then walked through the door and flipped the dead bolt.

Winn sat up straighter as I rejoined her on the couch, both of us listening.

Footsteps descended the porch stairs. Moments later, a truck's engine started.

"That was entirely too satisfying." She laughed. "Thanks."

"Welcome." This was the moment when I was clear to leave, but instead, I relaxed deeper into the couch, tossing an arm over the back.

Winn's eyes landed on the box of condoms in my hand. "Can I ask you something?"

"If I said no, would you ask me anyway?"

"Yes."

I chuckled. "Shoot."

"You thought I was a tourist at Willie's. Is that your thing? Tourists?"

"My thing is beautiful women. But yeah, it's less complicated if they don't live here. Fewer expectations."

She hummed. "Why'd you kiss me at your house?"

"Why'd you kiss me back?"

The corner of her mouth turned up. "Who are the condoms for?"

"You." There was no point in lying. She was stuck in my head.

Winslow was a woman apart. In beauty. In brains. In sex appeal.

Her confidence was as alluring as those freckles across her nose.

In one graceful move, she lifted and closed the gap between us. Her leg swung over my lap, her knees settling outside my thighs. Her hands, dainty but powerful, slid up the smooth cotton of my charcoal T-shirt. Then she pressed her center into my swelling cock, rubbing her core against my belt buckle.

"Give me your mouth," I ordered.

She bent, her lips grazing mine.

I clasped a hand around her head, holding her to me as I surged, my tongue sliding between her teeth.

Winn gasped, her hips banging into mine.

Any hope of me walking out of here before dark evaporated.

# CHAPTER 7

## WINSLOW

A cry lodged in my throat as I jolted awake. Sweat beaded at my temples.

I squeezed my eyes shut, dragging in a breath to calm my racing heart, using every fragment of mental fortitude to shove the nightmare from my mind.

My parents used to say, "It's just a bad dream, Winnie."

This wasn't a dream.

The blood, the mutilation, was real. The lifeless eyes. The scream, my own, that still rang in my ears five years later.

Would these nightmares ever stop? They'd been worse since moving here. They'd haunted me almost every night.

Beside me, Griffin shifted. The sheet he'd pulled over us after the last tumble dipped lower, revealing the sculpted contours of his muscled back. The broad shoulders. The dimples just above his ass.

I slipped out from beneath the cotton and stood from the mattress, still on the floor. On tiptoes, I padded out of the room, easing the door closed behind me.

My clothes from work were strewn alongside Griffin's in the living room. I snagged his T-shirt, pressing it to my nose. It smelled of laundry soap and the masculine, natural spice of the man who'd made me see stars last night. I breathed it in again, drawing comfort from the scent, before pulling it over my head. The shirt hit me on my upper thighs and skimmed below my bottom, but at least I was covered in case one of my neighbors was awake too.

A favorite part of this house was the living room's bay window. A narrow bench seat was built beside the glass, not wide enough for lounging, but enough to sit and stare into the night. There was comfort in the tranquility of this street. Peace in the silence of sleepy homes and glowing porch lights.

The nightmare tapped at my temple, begging for attention. I pushed it away and studied Griffin's truck instead, tracing the Eden ranch brand on the passenger door with my gaze. Then I closed my eyes and pictured him on my couch. Naked. His washboard abs bunched. His hips thrusting. His cock like velvet and steel.

Focusing on sex probably wasn't the right way to cope with my past, but for tonight, I didn't care about right. I just wanted the nightmare gone. So I imagined Griffin's face as he came, the clench of his stubbled jaw and the bulge of his biceps as his body shook through its release.

We'd fucked hard on the couch. Afterward, I'd expected him to leave, but he'd carried me to my bedroom, and if I'd thought the sex had been good before, with a little space to move, he'd shown me the power of that large body.

Orgasm after orgasm, I'd practically blacked out after the last round.

A smile tugged at the corner of my mouth.

Sleeping with him was undoubtedly a stupid decision. An addicting, toe-curling, stupid decision. Self-control was typically my specialty, but when it came to him, the rules didn't seem to apply.

Griffin Eden was tantalizing. Magnetic. Rugged and bold.

And naked in my bed.

I pulled my knees up, stretching his shirt over my calves. Three yawns were my body's way of reminding me just how tired it was, but I didn't want to sleep. The dream would come back. It lingered too close to the surface. So with my temple to the window, I stared into the darkness. Alone.

The nightmare—a memory—always left me feeling alone.

My breath fogged the glass and the chill from the house brought goose bumps to my forearms. I was about to give in, to sneak into my bedroom for a hot shower, when the shuffle of bare feet filled the room.

Griffin emerged from the hallway, the sheet wrapped around his narrow waist. His steps slowed when he spotted me in the window wearing his shirt. "You okay?"

"Just couldn't sleep," I lied.

No one knew about my nightmares. Not even Skyler. He'd never asked why I woke up in the middle of the night, only that when I did, not to turn on a light. It might wake him up and he had work.

Griffin nodded and walked to his jeans, dropping the sheet to pull on his pants one thick, strong leg at a time.

He left the top button undone and the belt hanging open as he strode my way, dragging a hand through his disheveled chocolate hair.

I'd tousled it myself earlier, holding on to it as he'd sucked my nipples into his talented mouth.

"I'd better get going." His deep voice was fogged with sleep and the rumble sent a shiver down my spine.

"Okay." I nodded, taking in his bare chest. The dusting of hair on his pecs was too tempting and I raised a hand, my fingers brushing through the coarse strands. His heartbeat was so solid and strong, like everything else about this man.

"Are you going to give me my shirt?"

"Are you going to take it?"

His hands went to the hem, lifting it up and over my head. Then he smirked as he put it on his own body, covering up the hard stomach and the sculpted V at his hips.

This man was better than any fantasy. Better than any romance novel hero or movie star. Better than any lover who'd ever taken me to bed. Not that I'd had many.

The cold air from the window skated over my naked skin, but I didn't move from the bench. I waited while Griffin grabbed the sheet and brought it over, wrapping it around my shoulders before finding his boots amid the boxes.

An awkward quiet settled in the room. Casual hookups were completely out of character for me. Even in my early twenties, the only men I'd been with had been boyfriends. Then Skyler.

I wasn't sure what to say. I wasn't sure what to do. So I stayed put, listening to Griffin buckle his belt. It had been easier at the bar to simply get in my car and drive away.

Mom had told me once that I wasn't the sleeping-around type. I was like her, a woman who loved. Did it make Mom wrong that I liked this fling with Griffin? There was no love between us, simply lust.

I didn't want Mom to be wrong about anything. I wanted her to remain a perfect memory, the beautiful woman who'd loved me before the nightmare.

"Hey." Griffin's hand came to my shoulder, his thumb drawing a circle on top of the sheet. "Are you okay?"

"Yeah." I swallowed the lump in my throat. "Tired."

"You sure?"

I nodded and slid off the bench's ledge. "Thanks for staying. When Skyler was here."

"Is he going to be a problem?"

"I don't know." But after Griffin's display with the condoms, I doubted I'd see Skyler again.

"So, um…this." He gestured between us. "Probably not a great idea if it becomes a regular thing. I'm busy."

*Busy.* That term grated on my nerves but it didn't matter. I was *busy* too.

"Agreed." The orgasms had been out of this world but I was too raw for any sort of relationship, even if it was only for sex.

"Good." He breathed, like he'd expected me to argue. "Lock up behind me."

I was the chief of police, I had a black belt in karate, and I knew my way around a pistol, yet this man wanted to assert his protectiveness.

I hated that I liked it.

"See you around, Griffin."

"Bye, Winn." He waved once, then headed for the door.

I waited beside the window, watching until his truck disappeared down the block, then I locked the door and went to the bedroom. The air smelled like Griffin and sex.

The fitted sheet on the mattress was rumpled and my comforter had been kicked to the foot of the bed. The black alarm clock on the floor beside a discarded pillow showed it was three thirty. There was no way I'd get back to sleep, not now, so I dropped the sheet and went to the bathroom for a scalding shower.

Dressed in jeans and the black button-down shirt that every officer wore as part of their uniform, I headed to the station.

The night shift was just a skeleton crew, so it was quiet when I parked in my reserved space. The dispatcher at the desk jerked in surprise when I walked through the door.

"Oh, uh, hi, Chief."

"Good morning." I smiled. "Hope you guys have some coffee on."

"Just brewed a fresh pot." He nodded, then buzzed me in so I wouldn't have to use my key.

With a steaming mug in hand, I retreated to my office, where stacks of files from yesterday were waiting, and I wasted no time diving in. The shift change at six was a bustle of activity and more than one officer gave me a wide-eyed look when I emerged from my office to join them in the bullpen.

Conversation was stunted. Laughter limited. I listened in as the night shift gave their summary report, then returned to the solitude of my office so they could have a few minutes without the boss eavesdropping.

Maybe one day, they'd welcome me into their huddle.

Maybe one day, it wouldn't bother me that they didn't.

"Knock, knock." Janice poked her head inside my office. "Good morning."

"Hi." I smiled and waved her in.

"You okay?" she asked, studying my face.

I opened my mouth to lie but a question came out instead. "Can I confess something?"

"Sure." She took a seat across from my desk, the folder she'd brought along resting on her lap.

"This is my first job as the boss. You probably know that already."

She nodded. "Yes."

"Is it that obvious that I haven't done this before?"

"No, but we all read the paper."

My lip curled. The reporter had completely omitted my résumé, making it seem like my only qualification was the last name Covington. "I'm used to being in the bullpen, not in an office. I'm used to being in on the conversations, not on the receiving ends of the official reports. I'm used to being included. I didn't expect it to be so jarring, the difference between being an officer and being the chief."

"That's understandable." Janice gave me a soft smile but didn't offer any advice.

There was none to give. I wasn't an officer. I was the chief.

The line between the two was necessary, even if that put me on one side, alone.

"Anyway." I waved it off and pointed to the folder. "What do you have for me?"

"The autopsy came in from the medical examiner for Lily Green. I thought you'd want to see it before I put it on Allen's desk."

"Yes, please."

Allen was the officer officially assigned to Lily Green's death, though he hadn't seemed to mind my interference. In a way, he'd almost seemed relieved when I'd told him I was going to be taking an active role. And when I'd offered to tell Melina Green of her daughter's death, he'd instantly agreed.

Janice handed over the report, then went through a short list of items that needed to be addressed. Afterward, she left me to the autopsy.

It was almost exactly as I'd anticipated. The cause of death was extreme bodily trauma due to a fall. There'd been no substances in her blood. No marks or wounds beyond those caused by the impact.

The only note of interest was Lily's sexual activity. The examiner noted that she'd likely had sex within twenty-four hours prior to her death because there'd been lubricant residue on her skin, though no semen.

"Huh." I pulled out my notepad for the case, flipping through my notes.

Melina had told me that Lily hadn't had a boyfriend when I'd asked. Maybe she hadn't known? If Lily had been seeing someone, would her boyfriend have insight into her mental state? Had he been with her before her death, driving her car? Had he taken her to those deserted gravel roads along the Eden's ranch?

As much as I wanted to hunt down answers to those questions, they'd have to wait. My day was filled with meetings and phone calls. Another unexpected side effect from being the chief. I hadn't expected the meetings, and transitioning from investigations to management was going to take some getting used to.

Whatever grace the staff and community had given me during my first week was gone, because the administrative work came in a flood.

Finally, around four o'clock, I hit my first lull of the day.

My calendar was clear until tomorrow, and though there were emails to return, I needed to get away from this desk. So I grabbed my purse and escaped the station.

The route to Melina Green's house was familiar, and when I parked in front of her white picket fence, she was kneeling on the grass beside a flower bed.

"Afternoon," I called.

She looked over her shoulder, her blond hair tied in a braid beneath a straw hat. She gave me a shaky smile and stood, coming over as I opened her gate. "Hi, Winnie."

"How are you?" I opened my arms and she walked right into my embrace.

"Minute by minute. That's what you told me, right?"

"Minute by minute."

It was something Poppy had told me after my parents had died. I'd asked her how to deal with the sort of pain that tore through every heartbeat.

"What are you working on?" I asked, letting her go.

"Weeding. I was tempted to stay in my pajamas all day but..." Unshed tears glistened in her eyes. "I need to do something, anything, but cry."

"I can understand that. Why don't you put me to work?"

We spent the next thirty minutes cleaning two flower beds. The afternoon sun was hot on my black shirt, but I sat beside Melina, plucking shoots of grass and baby thistles as sweat dampened my brow.

"I need to ask you a question about Lily. Would you mind?"

"No." She shook her head, her eyes focused on the trowel in her hand and the weeds she chopped at the root. The blade sank into the earth with a gritty slice. She'd get through this loss by keeping busy. I'd done the same. Because when you were busy, there was less time to think. Less time to hurt.

Until the night, when the memories crept into your sleep.

"You said she didn't have a boyfriend. But could she have been seeing someone new? Maybe a first or second date with a guy?"

"Not that I know of. Why?"

"I'm just trying to find out who she spent time with." Normally I believed in full transparency, but until I had more answers about Lily and whoever she'd been with before her death, I didn't want to leave Melina with unanswered questions.

"Lily liked to head downtown on Friday and Saturday nights with her friends. They usually met up at one of the bars. I always felt like I was walking a fine line. She lived here and I loved that she lived here. But she was an adult, so I tried to keep my mouth shut about the partying."

If Lily was like most twenty-one-year-old women, she'd probably met a guy at the bar. Hell, I was thirty and had done the same with Griffin.

"I didn't ask too many questions," Melina continued. "I tried not to pester her about coming home before two. Maybe that was my mistake. But she was young and once, a long time ago, I was young too."

The tears began to fall and Melina did her best to wipe them dry with her garden gloves, leaving streaks of dirt on her cheeks.

"I, um…" She pulled off her gloves. "I'd better wash up."

"Of course."

When she excused herself to go inside, I saw myself out of the yard. Any other questions would have to wait, but Melina had given me a place to start.

I'd spoken to many of Lily's friends but I hadn't asked

about her at the local bars. They would be my next stop. But first, before the sun went down, I wanted to pay Indigo Ridge one more visit.

Leaving Melina's house, I drove toward the mountains, navigating the gravel path to Indigo Ridge. My shoes weren't the best for hiking, but I parked at the base of the trail and started my climb anyway. Step by step, I made my way up the dirt path. I was panting and sticky by the time I reached the top. The breeze that threaded around the rocks cooled the sweat between my shoulder blades.

Inching to the edge of the trail, I leaned forward to stare over the cliff. Her body wasn't on the jagged rocks below, but I could still picture it there. Her blond hair. That blood-soaked dress.

One jump. One step. That was all it would take. One trip. One fall.

And a life shattered.

"What the fuck are you doing?" A hand clamped over my elbow and dragged me away from the edge.

I whirled around, my heart in my throat as I threw a fist toward Griffin's nose. I managed to stop the punch before it landed, but just barely. My knuckles grazed his skin and his eyes widened that I'd moved that fast.

"Jesus, Winn." He released my elbow. "What the fuck is wrong with you?"

"Me? What the fuck is wrong with you? You scared the shit out of me. I could have fallen."

"Then don't stand so goddamn close to the edge," he bellowed, dragging a hand through that thick hair. "Fuck. We don't need you having an accident."

"This should be blocked off," I barked, pressing a hand to my thrashing heart.

"That's what I'm doing here." He jerked his thumb toward the trail. "I came up here to build a fence along the path and spotted your rig. Followed you up here just in time to see you leaning over the edge."

I frowned up at his scowl. "I was just looking."

"Look from back here." He grabbed my arm again, hauling me back against him. "I can't find your body down there too."

The plea in his blue gaze, the fear in his expression, chased away any anger, and my shoulders slumped. "Okay. Sorry."

He blew out a long breath, shaking away his frustration. "It's all right. Why are you *looking*?"

"I don't know," I admitted. "I know you think it was suicide. I don't even know what to think myself, I just... something feels off. And I need to figure out what. For Lily. For her mother. Sometimes when I can't make sense of something, I start at the end and work my way backward to the beginning."

So I'd stand here until I could retrace her steps.

Which was what I did. I stood there, staring out to the nothing beyond the trail.

Griffin stood beside me, unspeaking. Unmoving. He simply stood at my side while I thought.

She'd come up here, terrified. Desperate. Likely alone.

I took one step closer to the edge.

Griffin grabbed my hand, holding it tight.

I let him be my tether as I glanced over the cliff, putting myself in Lily's place.

She'd had a good job. She'd had loving parents. She'd had friends in Quincy. Something had pushed her over this edge.

"A broken heart?"

"What?" Griffin asked, pulling me away from the edge once more.

"Nothing," I muttered. The autopsy was confidential, and Griffin hadn't earned the details. "I'd like to know what Lily was doing up to the time of her death. If she'd been hanging out with friends. A boyfriend. Where would someone her age hang out on a Sunday night?"

"Willie's," he answered.

"Would you have noticed her if she'd come in?"

"You and I were the only people there."

"Anywhere else?"

He rubbed that strong jaw. "The bars downtown. The younger crowd usually hangs there in the summers with the tourists. And you're in luck."

"Am I? Why?"

He took my arm, tugging me yet another step away from the cliff. "I was just thinking about heading downtown myself."

"Oh, were you?" I raised my eyebrows. "I thought you were going to put up a fence on this trail."

"Change of plan."

# CHAPTER 8

## GRIFFIN

"You don't need to come with me." Winn paused outside Big Sam's Saloon. "Aren't you busy?"

Yes, I was busy. But I grabbed the door's handle and opened it for her anyway. "After you."

She frowned but walked inside, then I was forgotten as she soaked in every detail, from the wagon-wheel chandeliers to the seams in the wood-paneled walls.

The owners had done a major remodel about ten years ago. They'd moved to Quincy from Texas and the longhorns they'd brought along were hanging behind the bar. The tables were whiskey barrels with glass tops. The stools were upholstered in black and white cowhide.

They were playing up the Western theme for the tourists, and country music crooned from the jukebox in the corner.

I loathed Big Sam's.

"It's packed," she said, scanning the room.

"Most days are in the summer."

A few familiar faces jumped out from the crowd, and as we walked to the bar, I lifted a hand to wave at one of the guys who worked at the hardware store.

I jerked my chin to the bartender as he came over, his bald head catching the glare from the light that reflected off the mirrored liquor shelves. "Hey, John."

"Griffin." He reached over the bar to shake my hand. John had trimmed his white beard since the last time I'd stopped in about a month ago. It brushed against his heart instead of his protruding beer belly. "What brings you in?"

I nodded to Winn. "John, this is Winslow Covington."

"The new chief." He held his hand out to Winn. "Welcome to Quincy."

"Thanks." She shook his hand, then slid onto a stool. "Mind if I ask you a few questions?"

"Depends on the questions."

I took the seat beside her, and before she could launch into her questions, I ordered a beer. "Bud Light for me, John. Vodka tonic for the chief."

"I'm on duty," she muttered as he walked away.

"Then don't drink it."

She shot me that stern frown again. It, like everything else with this woman, was frustratingly sexy. "This is quite the place."

"It used to be one of the Eden family businesses. My great-uncle was Big Sam." The new owners hadn't changed the name, probably because it went with their cheesy theme, but that was about the only thing left from the bar it had once been.

"Used to be?"

"Sam was more about the drinking than he was about running a business. He sold it to the current owners before it went under."

"Ah. Is John one of the owners?"

"No, the manager. But if Lily was here Sunday night, he's your best bet at getting information. He works most weekends."

"Can't I just ask him? Why did you order us a drink?"

I leaned in closer, my shoulder brushing hers. "Bartenders in small towns always know what's going on. They hear the gossip. They see the excitement. But they also protect their own. John's a good guy but he doesn't know you, and he doesn't trust outsiders."

She gritted her teeth. "Do you have to keep calling me that?"

"It's what you are. Want to fit in? Sit here with me. Order a drink. Leave him a decent tip. You want to stop being an outsider, then get to know the community."

"Fine." She sighed as John returned with our drinks. "Thank you."

He nodded as she lifted the glass to her lips, sending me a glare over the rim.

I grinned and sipped my beer.

"So what are these questions?" John asked, leaning a hip against the bar.

"I'm trying to learn more about Lily Green. She was—"

"I know who she was."

Winn stiffened at his sharp tone. "Do you remember seeing her here on Saturday or Sunday night?"

"No, she wasn't here."

"Did she come in often? Her mother said that since she turned twenty-one, she came to the bars often on the weekends."

John shrugged. "No more than any of the other kids around here. They come down. Have a few drinks and play pool. Mix with the tourists."

"Was there anyone in particular you saw Lily with more than once?"

"Yeah." He nodded. "Her regular group of friends."

Who Winslow would have known had she been from here. It was a dig on John's part. He could have just as easily rattled off the list of friends' names.

But he didn't need to. Because Winn did it for him.

"Frannie Jones. Sarina Miles. Conor Himmel. Henry Jacks. Bailey Kennedy. Clarissa Fitzgerald. Those friends?"

I took a drink to hide my smile as the smug expression vanished from John's face.

"Yeah," he muttered.

"Did you notice Lily with anyone else?" she asked. "Like a boyfriend?"

"No. She wasn't that sort of girl. She'd come down, have a drink or two. Always responsible about calling a cab or catching a ride with a designated driver. I can't think of a time when she left here with a guy."

A crease formed between Winn's eyebrows, like she was disappointed in that answer. What was she after? Conor would know if Lily had been seeing someone. So would Melina.

"Anything else?" John asked. "I need to check on the other tables."

"No, thank you. I appreciate the help and it was nice to meet you."

"Same." John tapped on the bar, then left to take another order.

"What are you after?" I asked, keeping my voice low.

"Like I said on the ridge, I just want to retrace her steps and figure out what she was doing before she died. But sounds like she wasn't here."

"John would know."

Winslow took another drink, then dug through her pocket, pulling out a twenty. "Bye, Griffin."

She slapped the cash on the bar and headed for the door.

I ditched my beer and followed, catching up to her before she'd even stepped outside. "Let's head to the Old Mill. Maybe she went there."

"I don't need an escort," she said but fell in step beside me down the sidewalk.

"The two bars on Main bookend the touristy section of Quincy." The Eloise Inn was almost exactly in the middle. "Want to know why?"

"Because there's an ordinance that requires at least four hundred yards between any establishments with a liquor license."

I grinned at the sassy smirk on her pretty mouth. "You've done some research."

"No, I've just been here many, many times. Pops has lived here his entire adult life and loves to tell stories. I know a lot about Quincy. Even if I don't know the people yet. Even if I'm an outsider."

Oh, did she hate that word. I guess in her shoes, I'd hate it too.

"The ordinance was my great-great-grandmother's idea," I told her as we made our way across those four hundred yards toward the Old Mill. "My great-great-grandfather founded Quincy. Our family has lived here ever since. The running joke in town is that you can't throw a rock without hitting an Eden."

With aunts, uncles and cousins, I had countless relatives living in town. My parents had taken the unofficial helm of the family. Most of the businesses that had been started by my great-great-grandfather and his descendants had funneled down to my grandfather. He'd then passed them to my father.

Some of my other relatives were entrepreneurs in town, but for the most part, my parents, my siblings, or I owned and operated most of the businesses with the Eden name.

"Old Mill was the first bar in Quincy," I said. "Started shortly after the town was founded. The story goes that my great-great-grandmother allowed my great-great-grandfather to open the bar but only if the bartender was employed by her. That way, she could set the rules."

"The rules? Like how many drinks he could have?"

I nodded. "And how late to serve him. But she was worried that someone else would come in and open another bar. According to family rumor, she was a fairly shrewd businesswoman herself, so she suggested the ordinance, and since the Edens were pretty much in charge at the time..."

"It passed."

"Exactly. The town was only two blocks at that time. She figured it would take a hundred years for it to double in size. A four-hundred-yard radius not only gave her control of the alcohol in town, but control over her husband's drinking habits."

Winn smiled. "And it hasn't changed."

"Nope. The town grew but that ordinance stuck around."

"Which makes sense why Willie's isn't on Main."

"It's not long enough, so they established it five blocks off Main and it became the locals' hangout."

And the place where I'd never expected to meet this intriguing creation.

We passed two men, tourists based on their polo shirts, jeans and unscuffed boots. They both looked Winn up and down. It wasn't subtle and her mouth pressed into a line as she ignored them, her eyes aimed forward.

Brave men, not only because she was wearing a gun, but because I was a possessive bastard. With one glare from me, they each dropped their eyes to the sidewalk.

That would always be a problem with Winn.

She was too beautiful. You didn't expect to see a woman so stunning walking down the streets of Quincy. Her hair was down today, straight and long as it draped down her spine. Without sunglasses to shield her eyes, those blue irises sparkled beneath the afternoon sun.

We reached an intersection and she checked both ways before crossing the street and marching to the bar. Her shoulders were square and her serious face in place as she opened the door.

Old Mill wasn't the over-the-top scene that was Big Sam's. It was more of a sports bar, and if I wasn't up for Willie's, I came here to catch a game and have a drink. Flat screens were mounted between neon beer signs. Three keno machines hugged the wall just inside the door. Above them hung a framed Quincy Cowboys jersey. Two different baseball games were playing tonight, the announcers' voices muted through the bar's sound system.

"Does your family still own this place?" she asked as we walked toward the bar.

"Not anymore. My parents sold it to Chris when I was a kid."

"Who's Chris?"

I pointed to the bartender.

"Is there another ordinance in Quincy requiring all bartenders to have bushy white beards?"

"Not that I know of." I chuckled and pulled out a stool for her at the bar before taking my own. "Hey, Chris."

"Griff." He nodded to me, then held his hand out to Winn. "You're Covie's granddaughter, right?"

"I am." She fit her delicate hand into his meaty grip. "Winslow. Nice to meet you."

"Same. What brings you two in?"

"Winn's got a few questions for you. But how about a beer first? Whatever's on tap. Surprise us."

"You got it." Chris wouldn't be gruff like John—who, compared to Willie, was as welcoming as a doormat. Of the regular three bartenders in town, Chris was the nicest guy.

Winn didn't need me here, but I was having a hard time walking away.

Her questions for Chris were the same ones she'd asked John.

*Was Lily here on Saturday or Sunday? Do you remember seeing her with the same guy more than once? Did she have a boyfriend?*

Chris's answers were the same as we'd gotten at Big Sam's. Neither of us finished our beers, and when she went to pay, I beat her to it. With a wave goodbye to Chris, we retreated to our vehicles on the opposite end of Main.

"You talked to all of Lily's friends, didn't you?" I asked.

"I did. I hoped that one of them might have noticed something wrong. But they were all as shocked as Melina."

"Conor's broken up about it. I think he might have had feelings for her."

"Really?"

"I don't think she returned those feelings. He got shoved into the friend zone a long time ago."

"Hmm." Her shoulders fell.

"You think she had a boyfriend, don't you?"

She stayed quiet.

That was a yes. Maybe Lily had hooked up with the mystery guy before she died. But who? Now my own curiosity was racing down the block. If Lily had been seeing someone, Conor would have known about it. Unless Lily had hidden a relationship to spare his feelings.

"Maybe she was sleeping with someone who worked at the bank with her," I said.

"I never said she was sleeping with anyone."

I gave Winn a knowing look. "You didn't have to."

"Why did you come to town with me?" She crossed her arms. "You told me to back off. You told me to drop this, remember?"

"I remember. But for Melina's sake, for Conor's, I respect that you're trying to give them more of an explanation."

"Oh." Her arms fell to her sides. "Thank you."

"You're welcome."

"Bye, Griffin."

Before she could climb into her SUV and disappear, I walked to the passenger side of her Durango.

"What are you doing?" She narrowed her eyes through the window.

"Might as well drive together to Willie's."

"How did you know I was going to Willie's?"

I chuckled. "Do you want me to drive instead?"

"No." She huffed but unlocked the doors.

The five blocks to Willie's was too short. The inside of her car reminded me of her bed. The moment we pulled into the parking lot, the temperature in the cab spiked. Attraction crackled between us like a spark.

Would I ever come to Willie's and not picture her in my truck? *Probably not.*

Winslow parked and was out of the car so fast she practically jogged to the door. Her cheeks were flushed when I caught up.

"Shuffleboard?" I nudged her elbow as I opened the door.

"No." That pretty flush deepened. "I'm here on official business. And you said it yourself this morning. Not a good thing to repeat. You're a *busy* man."

I said a lot of stupid things.

"Griff." Willie stood behind the bar, his scowl fixed firmly in place as we walked in.

"Hi, Willie." Winn didn't bother taking a seat, and what I'd told her about making nice at the other bars had been forgotten. Or maybe she knew ordering a drink and making pleasantries with Willie would be a waste of time. She launched into her questions about Lily, and when she received a series of grunted *no*s, she thanked him for his time.

Winn turned, ready to leave, when the door opened and a familiar face walked into the bar.

"Harrison." My uncle Briggs walked over, his hand extended. "What's going on, brother? I didn't know you were coming into town tonight."

*Fuck.* My stomach dropped.

Winn looked between the two of us.

"Griffin." I clapped my hand on his shoulder. "I'm Griffin, Uncle Briggs."

He studied my face, confusion clouding his eyes. He

looked normal in jeans and a red shirt. But he was wearing two different boots, one round toe and the other square. A set of keys dangled from one hand.

"What are you up to?" I asked.

"Thought I'd grab a beer." His forehead was furrowed, still trying to figure out how I wasn't my father.

"I'll buy." I nodded for Briggs to head to the bar, then faced Winn. "I'm going to stay here with him."

"Sure." She looked to my uncle, her eyes softening. "Have a good night, Griff."

"Bye, Winn."

As she walked to the door, I joined my uncle at the bar. He called me by my father's name three times in the hour we sat and sipped a beer. He remembered Willie just fine, but kept giving me strange looks.

"I'd better get home," I told him. "Mind if I hitch a ride with you? I haven't seen your place in ages."

"You were just there last week."

Huh? "That's right. My bad."

I paid Willie, then snatched Briggs's truck keys. "How about I drive? I didn't finish my beer."

"Okay." He shrugged and led the way to the parking lot where his old Chevy truck waited.

I climbed behind the wheel, cringing at the scent in the cab. There was a coffee tumbler in the cup holder and my guess was that the creamer he'd added had long since curdled.

With the windows rolled down, I drove to the ranch, passing the gravel road that I'd been on earlier today. The place where I'd found Winn's car. The next turnoff led to the back side of Indigo Ridge, and as we made our way up the mountain foothills, I stole a few glances at Briggs.

He looked older today than I'd ever seen. The skin on his cheeks sagged slightly. The whiskers were white. Briggs was five years older than Dad and had lived his entire life on this ranch.

He'd been there to help Dad build us kids a tree house. He'd helped me break my first horse.

When my grandfather had been ready to pass down the ranch and his business holdings to his sons, Briggs had chosen to let Dad take over. Management had never been his passion. He was content to have a bank account healthy with money he rarely spent and a simple life living on the land that owned his heart.

Briggs's cabin was nestled in a grove of evergreens in arguably the prettiest meadow on the ranch. A stack of unevenly chopped firewood was scattered around the porch. An ax was propped up against the steps.

"Chopping wood?" I asked.

Briggs nodded. "Getting a head start before winter."

"Good plan." Though I wasn't too keen on him running the stove if he couldn't manage to put on a matching pair of boots.

I parked and picked up the travel mug, dumping the contents as we made our way to the house. With no idea what I'd find, I braced as I followed him inside. But the cabin was as clean and tidy as ever.

"How are things going on the ranch, Griffin?" he asked, taking the cup from my hand and carting it to the sink.

That was the first time he'd called me by my name tonight.

"Good. Busy. We're about done with fence repairs for the year."

"That's always a good feeling." He chuckled. "Want to

stay a while? Join me for dinner?"

"No, but thanks." I gave him a smile. "I'd better get on."

"Appreciate you swinging by."

"You're welcome." Did he remember even coming to the bar?

Goddamn, this was hard. My heart clenched. His blue eyes were the same as those I met in the mirror each morning. He was the very best uncle a boy could have wished for. He'd treated Dad's children—me—like one of his own.

Briggs had been married once, briefly, until she'd left him after their third anniversary. My siblings and I, my parents, had been his family. He hadn't missed a single one of my basketball or football games. He'd been present at every graduation.

Seeing him like this... fuck, but it was hard.

"I'll see you soon." I waved goodbye, then let myself out.

I was more than ready to go home.

Except I didn't have a vehicle. It was downtown.

"Shit." I pulled out my phone and called Dad. "Hey, can you come pick me up and run me into town?"

"Now?" He sounded like his mouth was full.

"Yeah. Now. I'm at Uncle Briggs's cabin."

"Where's your truck?"

"In town. And I need to talk to you."

"All right." There was the shuffling of feet and a muffled exchange with my mother before the line went dead.

I started walking down the road, making it about a mile before I heard the rumble of an engine and Dad's new pickup emerged from a bend in the trees.

He had a drop of barbeque sauce on his shirt.

"Sorry to interrupt dinner."

"It's okay." He turned the truck around, heading toward

home. "What's going on?"

I blew out a long breath, then told him about Briggs.

"Damn," he cursed, his hands tightening on the wheel. "I'll talk to him."

"You need to do more than talk."

"I'll handle it."

"Maybe we should call Grandpa's doctor. See if we could get Briggs into a home or—"

"I said I'd handle it, Griffin," he snapped.

*Christ.* I held up my hands. "Fine."

Tension crept through the truck's cab, and when Dad pulled in beside my rig on Main, he didn't say a word as I climbed out. He reversed out from his spot and drove away before I'd even fished the keys from my pocket.

I unlocked my truck and hopped in, slamming the door too hard. "Damn it."

Briggs had had a few episodes like this over the past year. It had started with mixing up a name at family dinner. But that happened all the time, right? Mom used to run through all our names before landing on the one kid in trouble.

Except for Briggs, the small mistakes were becoming habit. He'd driven into town this winter and Knox had stumbled upon his truck on Main. Briggs had forgotten where he was. Six months ago, Talia had bumped into Briggs at the grocery store and Briggs's shirt had been backward.

But tonight...tonight had been the worst. He'd actually thought I was Dad. The entire time we'd been at Willie's.

Maybe if my grandfather hadn't suffered from dementia, I wouldn't worry as much. But I'd been a teenager when Grandpa's mental health had deteriorated. I'd watched him become a ghost of the man I'd known.

It had crushed Dad. Briggs too.

Now our family would go through it again.

My stomach growled, forcing me out of my head. Leftovers waited for me at home. So did a pile of work. But as I drove down Main, my truck steered itself toward a little gray house with a red door.

There was no time for this. The ranch didn't run itself and I had shit to do. But I parked on the curb, spotting Winn through the front window.

She'd shed the black shirt she'd had on earlier for a plain white tank top. The straps of her black bra peeked out at her shoulders. Her hair was tied up in a ponytail, the ends swaying across her shoulders as she dragged a tall cardboard box down the hallway.

When I rang the doorbell, I heard a loud thud and then a pair of muted footsteps before the door flew open.

"Hi." She shoved a tendril of hair off her sweaty forehead. "How's your uncle?"

"Not great," I admitted. "My grandfather had dementia. Alzheimer's. It didn't set in until he was in his seventies. It's happening earlier with Briggs."

"I'm sorry." She waved me inside, closing the door behind us.

I inspected the living room, as full of boxes as it had been this morning. "Are you unpacking?"

"Sort of. My bedframe arrived today."

"So you aren't planning on sleeping on the floor forever."

"It was on backorder. My mattress arrived before I moved, but not the frame."

"What about the one you had in Bozeman?"

"It was Skyler's." Her lip curled. "I left all of the furniture to start fresh."

"Ah." I nodded. "So where's the frame?"

"In the box. I just hauled it to the bedroom."

"Got tools?"

"Um...yes?" She tapped the top of a box. "I have a screwdriver. Somewhere. It's in one of these. Or maybe a box in the office."

She'd spend an hour just finding her tools.

Without a word, I strode outside to my truck, grabbing the small toolbox I kept under the backseat. When I came inside, Winn was in the bedroom beside the frame's open cardboard box.

"Instructions?" I asked.

She pointed to the hardware pack and attached pamphlet. "I can do it."

"I'll help."

"Why?"

I grinned. "So I can help you break in the bed."

"I thought you didn't want to do that again."

"I can make time for one more night. What do you say, Chief?"

She picked up the instructions and handed them over. "One more night."

# CHAPTER 9

## WINSLOW

Griffin's tongue swept inside my mouth, fluttering against mine before he broke away. Then he bent to pull on his boots.

I stood back, watching as he trapped his hair beneath the faded black baseball hat he'd been wearing last night. The ends I'd been toying with before he'd climbed out of my bed curled at his nape.

It took effort not to go to him. Not to run my hands up his wide chest and beg for one more kiss. But I stayed on the armrest of the couch because if this was going to work, boundaries were key.

"See ya around." Griffin walked over and leaned in like he was about to kiss my forehead, but at the last second, pulled away, adjusting the brim of his hat.

I shouldn't have been disappointed. Sweet gestures and

forehead kisses weren't part of this relationship. We were enjoying casual sex, nothing more.

*Boundaries.*

"Bye." I followed him to the door and waited by the threshold as he went outside, his boots thudding on the porch stairs before he stepped onto the sidewalk, taking it with those long, easy strides.

Watching him walk away had become part of my daily routine.

He'd been coming here each night for a week. Each morning he'd leave before dawn and I'd wonder if he'd come back. Or if last night had been the last night.

Some nights, he'd come over early, not long after I'd gotten home from work. Other nights, it would be after dark and he'd find me unpacking a box. He'd interrupt my progress and carry me to the bedroom, which was why my living room was still full of cardboard and I continued living out of suitcases. The kitchen was unpacked, but little progress had been made elsewhere.

The sex was...distracting. Brilliantly distracting. This fling had no chance of lasting. So the boxes could wait until Griffin and I fizzled out.

He glanced over his shoulder as he rounded the hood of his truck, and even in the dark, I saw the sexy smirk on his lips. Yeah, he'd be back tonight.

I wasn't the only one enjoying this.

Closing the door, I waited for the rev of his truck's engine before retreating to my bedroom. The sheets were rumpled and his scent, spice and leather and earth, clung to the air. I'd fallen asleep to that smell last night as I'd lain on his chest, my body limp and utterly sated.

We'd gone wild last night. He'd worn me out so

thoroughly, I hadn't had a nightmare all week.

If this new bed of mine could talk, it would scream *Oh, God, Griff.*

What was it about him that had made it so easy to shed my inhibitions? With Skyler, I'd always felt reserved with sex. It had taken years to truly relax when we were in bed, and he hadn't been the most creative lover.

Maybe it was different with Griffin because there were no strings. No pressure for a long-term commitment. Maybe because my own pleasure had become a priority. Maybe because Griffin made it a priority too.

Damn, that man. Griffin had a body built to please. His hands turned me into putty. His lips, a shivering mess. His cock, a wanton slave to his command.

I smiled as I walked into the bathroom and turned on the shower. The warm water soothed some of my aching muscles.

Since I'd moved to Quincy, I hadn't gone on one of my regular morning runs. I hadn't worked out, period, because sex had taken exercise's place. Maybe tomorrow, if I had the energy, if Griffin didn't keep me up until one or two, I'd find my tennis shoes and run a few miles through my neighborhood. Or maybe I could try out the small gym at the station. It wasn't much more than an elliptical and a set of free weights, but a couple of the officers used it regularly. Maybe we could bond over cardio.

Doubtful, but at this point, I'd try anything.

After tossing in a load of laundry and reading through the case files I hadn't last night—a drunken disorderly, a petty theft and a vandalism of a Santa display last Christmas—I headed to the station.

Officer Smith was ready and waiting at his station in the

lobby to give me his standard cold welcome.

"Good morning, Officer Smith."

Nothing.

Asshole.

His first name was Tom, but he and I were sticking to last names. He seemed to hate me more and more with each passing day.

Eventually he'd have to get to know me, right? Maybe that attitude would thaw when he realized I was here for the long haul. Or...early retirement. He was getting a few more weeks to shape up, then I was pitching him an early retirement.

My desk was its usual disaster but I'd blocked off the morning to tidy up. I spent hours putting files away, going through emails and my long to-do list. And finally, by noon, the brownish gray wood was visible.

"I really need to do this at home." Settle in. Clean up.

I swiveled my chair to the window at my back, taking in the forest beyond the glass.

The station was nestled between a grove of pine and fir trees, their trunks so wide I wouldn't be able to wrap my arms around them. The branches provided a canopy over the building that kept the sun from streaming inside. I'd been so busy sinking into this job, I hadn't spent time looking out the window.

A mistake I'd remedy in the future.

Like my quiet street under the moonlight, there was peace to be found in those trees.

Now that I was settling in, piecing together a routine, it was time to put my house in order so that when I walked through the door at night, I could simply breathe.

A knock at the door had me turning from the window.

"Whoa." Pops's eyes widened as he came into the office. "You've been busy."

"Productive morning." I smiled. "What are you doing here?"

"Thought I'd invite my favorite chief of police to lunch."

"Good, I'm starved. And afterward, I need to head to the courthouse. Get my vehicle registration switched over. Change my driver's license."

More steps to making this move official.

Once the Durango was registered, it would be in the garage the majority of the time. I'd been hesitant to use the former chief's unmarked Explorer because it smelled like cigarettes, but after a thorough detailing, the stink was beginning to fade.

"Meet you downtown?" Pops asked.

"Where to?"

"Eden Coffee."

Griffin's sister's business. A spike of nerves hit, but I nodded and followed Pops out of the station. Like our last lunch date, we had to park off Main and walk.

"It's cute," I said, taking in the green building.

*Eden Coffee* was emblazoned in gold letters on the coffee shop's front door. The black-paned windows gleamed in the June sunshine. A chalkboard sandwich board stood on the sidewalk, the swirly lettering outlining today's specials. Even from beyond the door, the scent of coffee, vanilla, sugar and butter filled my nose.

"Now I'm really hungry."

"You haven't been here yet?" he asked.

"I've been sticking to coffee at home or at the station." Hoping a few encounters with the officers in the break room would give us a chance to bond. "And I didn't realize they had lunch."

"Lyla makes amazing food. Sunday morning, let's meet here for breakfast. Her pastries are the reason I'm getting a gut."

I scoffed and smacked his barrel of a chest. "Please."

He chuckled, opening the door for me. A bell jingled overhead, and the moment we stepped inside, I nearly collided with Frank.

"Hey there." Frank beamed, pulling me into a quick hug. "How's it going, cutie?"

"Good." I smiled. "Pops and I were just going to eat lunch."

"Same here. I just walked through the door and was searching for a table."

"Join us," Pops said, motioning toward the counter.

I moved to follow them, taking in the restaurant. The interior was painted the same shade as the exterior, giving it a moody, modern feel. Beside the counter were glass cases of pastries and muffins and other baked goods. There were a handful of wooden tables along the walls, all but one of them occupied.

My steps faltered as I spotted a handsome face at the table closest to the counter.

Griffin was wearing the same clothes he'd been in this morning at my house. His faded hat still covered his unruly hair. He was sitting with two beautiful women. One had brown hair the same shade as Griff's, twisted into a knot. She wore a green apron. *Lyla.* I recognized her face from the family picture at his house.

The other woman's long blond hair hung in straight, shiny strands over her shoulders. Her strappy tank top showcased her lean arms and her jeans were skintight. She placed her hand on Griffin's forearm and a zing of jealousy raced through my veins.

I tore my eyes away, forcing my feet across the room. We were casual. We were temporary. But we hadn't talked about being exclusive. I'd just assumed that since he'd spent each night in my bed, it was the only bed. Was he dating her? Was this why he was so busy? I kept my gaze aimed forward, refusing to look.

My stomach twisted and whatever hunger I'd had earlier vanished as I followed Pops and Frank through the cafe.

"Hey, Covie." Lyla stood from the table, rounding the corner to stand behind the counter.

"Hi, Lyla." Frank waved.

"Frank." She said his name but kept her gaze on Pops.

"Lyla, it's a special day." Pops gave her a wide smile. "I'd like you to meet my granddaughter, Winslow Covington. She gets to experience the magic of your food today."

"Hello!" Lyla smiled, her blue eyes sparkling as she extended a hand. "It's nice to finally meet you. My dad's been talking about you constantly."

But not her brother. Because I was a secret. The blonde was not.

"It's nice to meet you too." I shook her hand, doing my best to pretend her brother wasn't at the table within earshot.

Pretending was pointless.

Griffin's gaze burned into my spine.

"What are you having today?" Lyla asked.

The three of us ordered the special, and after Pops paid, we turned from the counter with a numbered table card.

Griffin stood and dropped some cash on the table.

The blonde stood too, cozying up to his side.

Their arms brushed.

A green haze spread across my vision and my jaw clenched so tight I doubted I'd be able to unlock it and eat the chicken salad sandwich I'd ordered. I had no right to be jealous, yet here I stood, fuming. Not just at Griffin and the fact that clearly he had some sort of relationship with that woman and hadn't bothered to mention it. But with myself.

Once again, fooled by a handsome man.

"Hi, Griffin." Pops walked over. "How are you today?"

"Fine, Covie. You?"

"Famished. Lyla can usually fix that problem though."

"I came here for the same reason." Griffin grinned, but the smile didn't reach his eyes. His gaze flicked to Frank and his expression flattened. "Frank."

"Eden," Frank muttered, then walked away to claim the last remaining empty table.

What the hell? What was I missing?

"Here's your coffee, Covie." Lyla came over carrying a cup balanced on a saucer. "Want me to put it at your table?"

"Oh, I'll take it." He lifted it from her and smiled, his attention completely on Griffin and Lyla.

The blonde glared daggers at Pops like Griffin had at Frank.

Definitely missing something.

Silence stretched awkward and thick as Pops lifted his coffee cup to his lips, ignoring the blonde's existence.

Finally, Griffin cleared his throat and met my gaze for the first time. "Winslow Covington, this is Emily Nelsen."

*Emily Nelsen.*

The reporter.

Well, damn. This just got better.

"Hi. Nice to meet you," I lied with a fake smile.

"Same." She leaned in closer to Griffin.

He stiffened but didn't move away. *Bastard.*

"We'd better claim our table," Pops said. "Have a good one, Griff."

"You too." His gaze met mine for a split second, then darted away as he headed for the door.

Emily scurried after him.

*Don't stare. Don't stare.*

Griffin was just a hookup. A casual fling. A fling that was very, very over now.

I'd mourn the loss of sex and distraction later, so I followed Pops to join Frank.

The front wall of the coffee shop was made entirely of windows and beyond the glass was the sidewalk and Main. It was impossible to miss Emily walking to Griffin's truck.

"The goddamn reporter," I muttered. "Really?"

Why, of all the people, did Griffin have to be with the fucking reporter who'd smeared my name before even meeting me? I gave up any attempt not to stare and watched their every move.

Griffin said something to her, his expression stern. That didn't mean much. He often wore a serious face. It was rare that he'd smile and laugh. But he had a few times. With me.

He leaned in closer to Emily, speaking low. The pout on her face said she didn't exactly like what he had to say.

She crossed her arms over her chest and gave him pathetic, pleading eyes.

He shook his head, his shoulders slumping. Then he gave her a small nod before walking to his truck and climbing inside.

She hurried to the passenger door, getting in with a smug grin aimed toward the coffee shop. No doubt she could see me staring through the glass. Bitch.

What was the joke he'd made the other night? You can't throw a rock in Quincy without hitting an Eden. At the moment, I wouldn't mind throwing a boulder at the man.

I tore my eyes away from Griffin's truck as he reversed out of his space and rolled down Main.

"Those goddamn Nelsens," Pops said.

"Those goddamn Edens," Frank muttered.

Lyla chose that moment to appear, her hands full with three water glasses. Her cheeks were flushed, and I was sure she'd heard both Frank and Pops.

Frank didn't notice but Pops gave her an apologetic smile. "Thanks, Lyla."

"Sure, Covie." She walked away, returning to the counter.

"You don't like the Edens?" I asked Frank. Then why was he at Eden Coffee?

"Oh, I like Lyla just fine. And Talia and Eloise. But no, I'm not exactly fond of Harrison or Griffin. They think they own the whole town."

Envy crept through his voice. There had to be more to it than just dislike but I didn't care to hear it. Not today.

Griffin hadn't once given me the impression that he *owned* Quincy. Then again, he also hadn't given me the impression that he was cozy with another woman, so clearly, when it came to that particular Eden, my judgment was impaired.

Oh God. My stomach churned. On Monday, he hadn't come over until ten. Had he been on a date with her first? Had he visited her bed before coming to mine?

"You okay, Winnie?" Pops asked.

"Yeah." I nodded and took a sip of my water. "Just been a hectic week."

"How are things going at the station?"

"Good." They would be good. Eventually.

Maybe this run-in with Griffin was what had needed to happen. Hadn't I just been thinking about how I needed to get my life at home together? Griff had been a constant on my mind and a regular intrusion during my evenings.

I had a life to establish in Quincy. I had a house that needed to become a home. Building lasting relationships with my staff was more important than a fleeting one with a hot cowboy.

I'd moved here to heal. To build a new life. To repair the heartache from my split with Skyler. Jumping into bed with Griffin wasn't going to help me achieve any of those goals.

It had to end. Tonight.

When he showed up tonight, I'd call it off.

• • •

I shot out of bed, my heart racing. My stomach lurched. The bedroom was bathed in gray but my mind was swimming in red. Blood red.

I ran to the bathroom, tripping on the shoe that I'd kicked off in the middle of the room earlier. I managed to catch myself before I smashed into the wall, righting my feet as I slapped a hand over my mouth.

My knees cracked on the tile floor as I landed by the toilet, retching until my stomach was empty. Tears streamed down my cheeks as I shoved the hair from my eyes.

"Damn it," I cursed to the empty room, burying my face in my hands.

This was the worst nightmare I'd had in months. Maybe years. It was like the versions I'd had early on. The ones where I was at the scene of the crash.

It was the nightmare where I found my father's mangled

arm outstretched on the pavement. The dream where I saw my mother's head severed from her body.

I squeezed my eyes shut, willing the smell of torn flesh and burnt rubber and scraped metal out of my nose. *Think of something else. Anything else.*

The first image that popped into my mind was of Lily Green. Her disfigured body shattered on the rocks below Indigo Ridge.

My stomach roiled again but there was nothing left to puke.

"Fuck." I pressed my fingers into my eyes until the black became white.

Shoving myself off the floor, I stood on shaking legs and shuffled to the sink. After splashing water on my face, I brushed my teeth, then turned on the lights.

All of the lights.

I flipped every switch as I made my way from the bedroom to the kitchen. The clock on the oven showed it was just past midnight.

The house was still and quiet. My heartbeat filled each room with a resounding *boom, boom, boom.*

I brewed a pot of coffee. There was no way I'd go back to sleep tonight. With a steaming mug in hand, I went to my bedroom and began organizing. I threw myself into the task, refusing to think of the nightmare. Refusing to think of Griffin.

For the past week, each night he'd slept in my bed, I'd slept all night long. Chances were, if he'd been here tonight, I still would have had the nightmare. Or maybe the dreams had been waiting for me to be at my weakest.

Sometimes, it was like the images had a sick mind of their own. The harder I fought them, the harder they struck. Every nightmare I'd had since moving here had been brutal. It was like they'd crept their way into my new pillows, waiting to pounce.

Of course it would be the night of Griffin's absence.

Maybe he was with his reporter tonight.

Maybe not.

It didn't matter anymore.

He hadn't shown up for me to end it tonight. I guess that was end enough.

So I worked alone to unpack my house. Because that was what I was.

Alone.

# CHAPTER 10

## GRIFFIN

The restraint it required to stay away from Winslow was crippling.

For the past two nights, I'd practically barricaded myself at home. My email inbox was empty, my desk clear. Last night, after dinner, I'd wanted to go to her so badly that I'd spent three hours cleaning stalls in the barn.

Keeping busy.

Keeping my distance.

My skin craved the heat from hers. My fingers twitched, desperate to thread through her hair. My arms ached to hold her as she fell asleep.

I missed her blue eyes. I missed the freckles on her nose.

The nights had been brutal. Sleepless. But even the days were difficult. It was noon and all I wanted to do was turn my truck around, head into town and track her down.

I refused to let myself break.

The ranch and my family needed my full attention. There was no time for anything else.

It shouldn't be like this. Never in my life had I struggled so much to let go of a woman. Especially when there'd been no commitment involved. Hell, I'd had girlfriends in college easier to erase from my mind, despite dating them for months before calling it quits.

So why the hell was Winslow Covington stuck in my head?

Her beauty was unmatched, her intelligence as attractive as her slender body. Her responsiveness in the bedroom and the way our bodies came together were like nothing I'd felt before.

This had to be a physical thing, right? Chemicals and hormones fucking with my rationality. One thought of her bare, creamy skin and I was hard again. Like I'd been for the past two days.

"Goddamn it," I muttered.

"What?" Mateo asked from the passenger seat of my truck.

"Nothing." I waved it off. "Thanks for coming out today."

"Sure." He shrugged those broad shoulders.

At twenty-two, he hadn't quite filled out his frame. But he would. If he kept eating Mom's cooking and working on the ranch like he had been this summer, breaking a sweat and testing those growing muscles, soon he'd be as big as me.

Of all my siblings, Mateo and I looked most alike. We all had the same brown hair and blue eyes, but Mateo and I shared the same nose, the small bump at the bridge. Like mine, his Adam's apple was pronounced, a feature I hadn't thought much about until Winn.

She loved to drag her tongue up my throat, especially while I was buried inside her body.

*Fuck.* Why couldn't I stop thinking about her?

"What's the plan for today?" Mateo propped a forearm on the open window. The smell of grass and earth and sunshine clung to the air.

There weren't many places I'd rather be in life than rolling down a Montana dirt road in June.

Winslow's bed was threatening to take that top spot.

"I'd like to check the fence along the road to Indigo Ridge. Conor started on it but...you know." I hadn't had the heart to send anyone back there since Lily Green.

"Yeah," Mateo mumbled. "How's he doing?"

"We're working him hard." On the other side of the ranch and as far from here as possible.

"He always liked Lily. Even after their breakup. I always thought they'd eventually get together."

"I'm sorry." I glanced over and gave him a small smile.

Lily had been a year younger than Mateo, but the size of Quincy High meant they would have known each other well.

"I hadn't really talked to her in a while. But every time I bumped into her, she'd smile. Give me a hug. She was sweet like that. Like you were this long-lost friend she hadn't seen in years. Not someone you saw once a month at the bank. I had no idea she was struggling. No one did."

*Because maybe she wasn't.*

That knee-jerk thought hit so fast and hard that I flinched.

The doubts were Winslow's doing. She'd put them in my brain, and now, whenever the topic of Lily came up, any previous assumptions had been tossed in the trash.

Was there more to her death? What if she hadn't committed suicide?

Winn had been searching for a boyfriend or hookup during our stops at the bars. Maybe Lily had slept with someone recently. Maybe that guy had done something to mess with her head. Or maybe she hadn't been alone on Indigo Ridge.

Maybe there was more.

"Was Lily dating anyone?" I asked.

"Not that I know of. Whenever I saw her at the bar, she was usually with other girls."

Probably the same girls Winn had rattled off to John at Big Sam's. Local girls. And knowing Mateo, he wouldn't have paid them much attention.

My little brother took after me in that regard too. He wasn't interested in a relationship and tourists wouldn't be there to harass him for more come morning.

It was advice I'd given him.

Advice I wasn't following myself.

"Heard you're hooked up with Covie's granddaughter. Winslow." Mateo grinned. "I got a speeding ticket last week. Think you could get her to fix it for me?"

This idea that Winn and I would be able to keep our tryst under wraps had disintegrated like wet toilet paper. "It's not like that."

"Fuck buddies?"

That term grated on me and my hands tightened on the steering wheel. It was the right term but it was like nails scraping chalkboard in my ear. "Where'd you hear that?"

"Bumped into Emily Nelsen at Old Mill last night. She asked where you were. I told her you were probably at home and then she made some comment about how you could also be at Winslow Covington's place."

"Goddamn Emily." I shook my head.

She was the reason I'd avoided Winslow's place the past two days. Apparently, that had been pointless.

On Wednesday, I'd gone into Eden Coffee to grab one of Lyla's sandwiches for lunch. She'd been talking to Emily, making nice. Lyla always made nice. Maybe because she was smarter than me. She kept her friends close and her enemies in the folds of her green apron.

Emily had never been mean to Lyla and they'd graduated at the same time. For a while, I'd thought they might have been friends but I hadn't paid much attention. Then I'd screwed up and fucked Emily one night a year ago, and ever since, all she'd done was linger around Lyla.

My sister was smart. She knew why Emily was kissing her ass.

I'd made the mistake of sitting at their table to visit with my sister. It had been...informative. Not only had Emily gossiped about every person in the coffee shop, but she'd also commented that she'd seen my truck at Winslow's house three nights in a row.

I knew better. Damn it, I knew better. How could I have been so stupid as to forget that Emily lived in that neighborhood? Of course she'd recognize my pickup. The last thing I needed was to have rumors spreading around Quincy. It was the last thing Winn needed too.

So I'd stayed away.

It was the smartest decision. For both of us.

Winn was fighting enough battles at the moment. At the station. With the community—no thanks to Emily's article. She didn't need to wage war with the gossip mill too.

"She's a good cop," I told Mateo. "I think she was the

right choice."

For all the shit I'd given Winn for being an outsider, she fit here. She took the job seriously and had decent connections. Though I wasn't thrilled about her friendship with Frank Nigel.

That asshole could go fuck himself. He'd had a problem with my family for no reason my whole life. He'd buy a latte from Lyla's coffee shop, flirt with her until she was uncomfortable, then leave a shitty review on Yelp. He'd swing by Knox's restaurant at The Eloise and tell everyone who'd listen that the food was mediocre.

He'd talk about us all behind our back—to me and Dad, our faces. At least he'd stopped trying to fake it when we bumped into each other around town. I'd made it clear the last time he'd tried to shake my hand that I had no use for the son of a bitch.

Frank's friendship with Covie was the one black mark against our long-time mayor. I never did understand how they'd become such good friends. Neighbors bonded, I guessed. Hopefully Winn didn't listen to Frank's poison.

Mateo and I reached the edge of the ditch along the road. A loose wire dangled at the corner post. I parked the truck, grabbed a pair of leather gloves from the bench seat and pulled on my ball cap, letting it shield my face. Then my brother and I got to work repairing the strings of barbed wire.

Two hours later and we'd made it halfway down the line.

"More junk." Mateo picked up a hubcap lying on the tall grass.

"Just toss it in the back of the truck. I swear the previous owners of this place took apart an entire car dealership and left the pieces scattered around here just to irritate me."

I'd been picking up rusted scraps and old parts since I'd bought this property. It had taken us a month of regular trips to Missoula to haul away all of the old cars they'd left scattered around the barn.

"I hate fencing," Mateo muttered as he picked up his fencing pliers.

I chuckled. "It's part of ranching."

"It's part of *you*."

This ranch was all I'd ever wanted. From the time I was a kid, I'd known that I'd live and die on this place. My heart belonged to the land. My soul was tethered to the earth. A day of honest work gave me peace.

I considered myself a lucky man that happiness came easiest when my boots were in the dirt. This wasn't a job. This was a passion. This was my freedom.

My siblings loved the ranch but *ranching* hadn't been their dream.

"Any thoughts on what you want to do?" I asked Mateo. Being nine years older, I often felt more like an uncle than a sibling. He came to me for advice, much like I'd done with Briggs.

"No." He groaned, crimping a clip to hold a fresh wire to a steel fence post. "I don't know. Not this."

"There are other things to do on the ranch besides fencing."

"This has always been yours."

"It doesn't have to be just mine."

"I know. If I wanted to be part of it, you'd make it happen. But I just...don't. And I don't know what I want yet. So I'll just work here and at the inn until I figure it out."

"The offer always stands."

"Thanks." He nodded and stepped back from the section

we'd just fixed. He looked past my shoulder as the sound of tires crunching gravel filled the air.

I turned as Briggs's truck rolled our way. My uncle was behind the wheel and behind him, against the glass window, his gun racks were loaded with two rifles.

"Why's he decked out in orange?" Mateo asked.

"Hell." I shoved the top wire down to swing my leg over the fence, then walked to the road, Mateo right beside me, as Briggs pulled over.

"Hey, boys."

"Hey, Briggs." I leaned against his door. "What are you up to today?"

He jerked a thumb at his rifles. "Thought I'd hunt the base of Indigo Ridge. I saw a herd of mule deer yesterday. Would be good to get more jerky made before the snow flies in the next couple of weeks."

"What the fuck?" Mateo mumbled.

I sighed, wishing like hell my father would stop ignoring this. The incidents were getting more frequent. "Briggs, it's not quite hunting season yet."

"It's October."

"It's June."

"No, it's not." He frowned. "What the hell is wrong with you? It's October."

"It's June." I dug out my phone from my back pocket, opening up my calendar for him to see.

"You know I don't trust those goddamn phones." He huffed. "Stop messing around, Griff."

*Christ.* "You can't go hunting right now, Briggs. It's not the season."

"Don't tell me what I can and cannot do on my own ranch." His voice rose along with the color in his face.

"Damn kids. Running all over this area like you own it. How many years have I worked here? This is my place. Owned by me and my brother. You don't get to tell me what to do."

"I'm not trying to tell you what to do." I held up my hands. "Just take a look around. Does it look like October to you?"

His forehead furrowed as he faced forward, taking in the green grass and wildflowers in the meadows. "I, uh…"

Briggs trailed off, staring over the wheel. Then, in a flash, he brought his hand up and slammed it into the dash. "Fuck."

I tensed.

Mateo flinched.

"Fuck!" Briggs roared again with another strike to the dash.

The outburst was so unlike him, so unlike his gentle, calm nature, that it took me a moment to react. Never in my life had I seen him shout. Not once. He and Dad were a lot alike in that way. Both had always kept a firm grip on their temper. It was the reason they were both so good with horses and kids.

This man was not my uncle.

This furious, angry man had realized that his mind was slipping.

And there wasn't a thing to do about it.

I put my hand on his shoulder. "Archery season will be here before you know it. Probably just had your days mixed up on your calendar at home. Happens to me all the time."

He nodded, his eyes unfocused.

Mateo and I shared a look, and when he opened his mouth, I shook my head. Now was not the time for questions. Those would come later. Along with yet another conversation with my father about Briggs's mental health.

"We're getting thirsty and we forgot water today," I lied. The canteen in my truck was full. "Mind if we come on up to your place for a quick drink?"

Before Briggs could answer, Mateo rounded the hood and climbed in the passenger side of our uncle's truck. "Meet you up there."

I nodded, waiting until they'd flipped the truck around and headed down the gravel road before returning to my side of the fence and getting into my own pickup. I caught them about halfway up the mountain to Briggs's cabin.

When we arrived, Briggs stepped out of the truck and shed his hunter's orange. He shook his head, like he was confused about why he'd had it on in the first place, then waved Mateo and me inside.

Whatever anger he'd had earlier seemed to have vanished.

"How are things on the mountain?" I asked as we settled into our chairs at Briggs's round dining table.

"Good. Retirement gets monotonous. But I've been hiking a lot. Trying to stay in shape."

"Which trails?" Mateo asked, taking a sip of water.

"Mostly around Indigo Ridge. It's challenging, but you can't beat those views from the top."

It was the second time he'd mentioned the ridge today. Ten years ago, I probably wouldn't have thought much of it. But now, after those three girls...not many of us went to Indigo Ridge.

Tragedy had its way of tarnishing beauty.

"Have you seen anyone else up there?" My question came courtesy of Winslow's doubts.

"No. It's always just me. Why?"

"Just curious."

If Briggs had seen someone, would he even remember?

We finished our waters and I took the glasses to the sink, looking out over the yard.

Briggs had been busy, keeping the grass around the house trimmed. He'd put in a small raised garden bed. The beginnings of vegetables sprouted from rich, black soil. Around it was a tall deer fence, seven feet high in hopes they wouldn't jump it and eat his crop. There was a pair of cowboy boots next to the fence, each filled with dirt and a ruby red flower.

"Love the boots, Briggs. Clever idea."

He chuckled and stood from his seat, walking over to stand beside me. "Thought it was pretty clever myself. Pretty nice pair of boots but way too small for my big feet. Found them on a trail a while back. Felt like a waste to throw them away, so I decided to turn them into my flowerpots."

My stomach dropped. "You found them?"

"Yeah. Was out shed hunting."

"Where?"

"Oh, I don't know. Some trail not far from here."

A trail on Indigo Ridge most likely. Because there was pink stitching along the brown leather shaft. There were plenty of men's boots with pink stitching, but the delicate square point of the toe box and the arch of the heel...those were women's boots.

Winslow had been looking for Lily Green's shoes.

The sinking feeling in my gut said I'd just found them.

"We'd better get going," I told Mateo. "Thanks for the water, Briggs."

"Stop by anytime. Gets lonely up here."

I nodded, my throat thick. "Hey, do you mind if I borrow

those boots for a spell? Mom might like to do something like that herself."

"Not at all. If she likes 'em, she can keep 'em."

"Thanks." I left the house and grabbed the boots.

They were dusty but on the newer side. The leather on the vamp and instep was stiff. I put a finger through each of the pull straps, hoping not to leave a bunch of fingerprints behind, then hauled them to my truck.

"Uncle Briggs is messed up." Mateo blew out a long breath as we started down the road. "The whole drive up here he kept calling me Griffin."

"I'll talk to Dad." *Again.*

"Think he's got what Grandpa had?"

I nodded. "Yeah, I do."

"What's going to happen?"

"I don't know." But if Dad didn't act sooner rather than later, I'd step in and do what needed to be done.

Briggs needed to see a doctor. We needed to know what we were dealing with here. Maybe medication would help. Maybe not.

I drove us back to Mom and Dad's place, dropping Mateo off at the shop.

"Are you coming in?"

"No, I've got to head to town." I could blame Briggs for shattering my resolve to stay away. But really, it had only been a matter of time before my resolve shattered.

"Okay." Mateo pointed to the boots in the backseat. "Want me to take these inside?"

"No. They aren't for Mom."

They were for Winn.

# CHAPTER 11

## WINSLOW

"What are you doing here? And why do you have flowers in your boots?"

Griffin walked into my office with the boots, each with a geranium poking out of the top. He eyed my desk, searching for a clear space to set them down. There wasn't one.

"This was clean," I mumbled, shuffling folders and papers out of the way. The mess I'd wrangled had returned. Story of my life.

The moment I thought I had something under control, it snuck up on me.

Sort of like Griffin.

I'd spent the past two days making peace with the end of our relationship. It was fine. Good, even. The right decision. It had been time to put Griffin behind me and focus on this job.

That was the reason I was in Quincy, right? I should be spending my evenings out and around town, not locked in my bedroom with a gorgeous man who knew how to deliver an orgasm. I'd tucked my weeks with him away on a shelf in my mind where they'd collect dust for the next decade.

Except then he'd walked through my office door with flowers and suddenly all I wanted was more.

More nights. More weeks.

More.

He set the boots down on the desk, then took an empty chair, leaning his elbows on his knees. Looking up from under the brim of his hat, those blue eyes didn't have their normal glint. He looked worn, like the world was propped against those broad shoulders.

This visit wasn't about me, was it? This was not an apology and whatever these flowers were, they weren't a gift to work his way back into my bed.

I waited, giving him a moment. People usually told you the most when you lent them a minute to breathe.

"My uncle. Briggs."

"The one from Willie's with dementia."

He nodded. "He had these boots at his place. Said he found them on a hike around Indigo Ridge."

My body tensed. "When?"

"He wasn't sure. I didn't press. He found them and turned them into flowerpots."

A unique idea, except he'd probably erased any evidence I might find. They were women's boots, the intricate pink and coral stitching in the leather a pattern of paisleys and swirls.

"I did my best not to touch them," Griff said.

I grabbed my phone from the desk and took a few quick

pictures from all angles, then I left Griffin in his seat as I went to the bullpen. "Allen."

He looked up from his desk and I waved him into the office.

"What's up, Chief?" He dipped his head to Griffin. "Griff."

"These boots were found on Indigo Ridge," I said. "Without the flowers. Would you mind taking the flowers out and then cataloging these into evidence? We'll want to dust for prints and see what we find. But I'm guessing these are Lily Green's."

"You got it. Want me to check with her mother to see if she recognizes them?"

"Please."

Allen walked out of the office, coming back with two evidence bags. I helped him put a boot in each, then closed the door behind him as he left.

"I'll be visiting your uncle," I told Griffin, returning to my chair.

"Figured you would." Griffin stood and walked to the bookshelf in the corner.

I hated how good it was to see him. His faded jeans draped over his strong thighs. They molded to the curve of his ass. The T-shirt he wore today was dusty, like he'd been out working all morning.

The scent of his soap and sweat filled the room. I'd washed my sheets yesterday, erasing him from my bed. I regretted that decision now because that smell was intoxicating.

He picked up a framed photo on the middle shelf. "Who's this?"

"Cole."

"Cole." His eyes narrowed. "Another ex?"

"A mentor. We worked together in Bozeman. And he was my sensei."

In the photo, Cole and I were standing together, each wearing white gis at the dojo in town where I'd taken karate. When I'd been promoted to detective in Bozeman, Cole had suggested I learn martial arts. Not only as a way to keep in shape but as a way to protect myself.

"You have a black belt."

"I do," I said.

"And these are your parents." He pointed to the photo on the next shelf. Not a question, but a statement, like maybe he'd seen their picture before.

Mom and Dad stood beside me on the day I'd graduated from the police academy. I was wearing a black uniform and a hat. The smiles on all three of our faces were blinding.

"Your dad looks like Covie," he said. "I've seen him around town before. And you look like your mom."

He couldn't have known what a compliment that was. My mother was the most beautiful woman I'd seen in my life, inside and out.

For a while after they'd died, I'd put their photos in storage. It had been too hard to see them frozen in time, laughing and smiling and happy. I'd walk into my bedroom, see their photo on a shelf and burst into tears. But then the nightmares started, so I'd put the photos back, because even though it hurt to see them, to miss them, I'd take their smiles a million times over their deaths.

Griffin moved to the last picture on the shelf, one of me and Pops fishing when I was a teenager. "You had more freckles."

"Summers in the sun. That was before I wore sunscreen every day."

He hummed, then resumed his seat, leaning forward once more. His eyes stayed glued to the edge of my desk, and once again, I waited until he was ready. "Do you still think that Lily's death might not have been a suicide?"

"I don't know," I admitted.

As the days went on, the uneasy feeling hadn't faded, but the logical part of my mind had begun to yell. There was no evidence pointing to anything but suicide. At some point, I'd have to let this go.

Maybe the boots would help.

Maybe not.

Griffin looked up and there was desperation in his eyes. Like he needed me to give him a different answer.

"It's still not sitting right," I said. "Every time I talk to someone who knew her, they are shocked. Friends. Family. No one had a clue that she was struggling."

"Yeah, that's pretty much what I'm hearing too."

"It doesn't mean she wasn't hiding it. Mental health is usually a well-kept secret. But I would have expected to find one person she'd confided in." Either there wasn't that person. Or I hadn't found them yet.

If he or she did exist, I suspected it was probably whoever had been with Lily before her death.

Maybe those boots would provide a clue, assuming they were hers and if any fingerprints hadn't been erased while they'd been turned into garden décor.

"Thank you for bringing in the boots."

"I'll get out of your hair." He stood and took a step for the door.

"Griff," I called, waiting for him to turn. Then I squared my shoulders and straightened my spine.

I hated the question I was about to ask. "Are you sleeping

with another woman?"

"Excuse me?" His jaw ticked.

"That woman on Wednesday. Emily." The reporter. "Are you sleeping together?"

He fisted his hands on his hips.

"We used protection but it's not foolproof. I'm on birth control but I'd like to know so I can get tested if necessary."

Griffin raised his eyebrows, then with two long, stomping strides, he planted his hands on the desk, leaning so far down that the fury in his gaze hit me like a heat blast. "I don't fuck two women at the same time."

The air rushed from my lungs. Thank. God.

Ending this relationship was for the best, but that decision hadn't exactly translated to my emotions. Every time I pictured Griffin and blond *Emily*, jealousy would eat at me for hours.

"That's not the type of man I am," he said through gritted teeth.

"Okay."

"It's not fucking okay. You shouldn't have had to ask me that question."

"Well, you seemed rather cozy at Eden Coffee."

"Did I touch her?"

"Um…" She'd touched him. But he hadn't touched her, had he?

"No, I didn't fucking touch her. Did I kiss her?"

I swallowed hard. "No."

He was pissed. Really pissed. I liked that he was mad. His character was in question, and for good men, they'd stop at nothing to set the record straight. "No, because I don't play with women. Understood?"

"Loud and clear."

"Good." He shoved off the desk and stormed out of the office. His footsteps down the hallway pounded as hard as my heartbeat.

It wasn't until I heard the exit door open and shut that I breathed. Then a smile tugged at my mouth.

There was nothing going on with the reporter. I sighed, sinking into my chair. The days I'd spent being angry at Griff had been for nothing. Maybe I should have trusted him.

It was Skyler's fault I'd jumped to this conclusion. Being betrayed by the man who'd promised to love me, to be my companion, to be my friend, had left its mark.

Griffin wasn't Skyler. There was no comparison.

Griffin was honest and true. And he knew his way around my clitoris.

The smile was still on my lips as I shook the mouse on my computer and got back to work. Maybe tomorrow I'd see the surface of my desk again.

And maybe the next time I saw Griffin around town, I wouldn't want to hit him with a rock.

· · ·

The cork in my wine bottle popped free at the same moment someone pounded on my door. Not a knuckle tap. A full-fisted hammer.

Only one person in this town beat on my red door.

I poured a glass, then carried it with me as I went to answer. "I have a doorbell."

Griffin's scowl was fixed in place. Clearly, an afternoon and evening hadn't made him any less angry than he'd been at the station. "What about you?"

"What about me?" I took a sip of my cabernet, letting the dry, robust flavor burst on my tongue as he glowered.

"Are you fucking anyone else?"

I nearly choked on my sip. "No."

"Good." That large body forced me out of the way as he strode inside.

I closed the door behind him and followed as he walked into the living room and glanced around.

"You unpacked."

"For the most part."

"Where's your furniture?"

"On backorder." Just like my bedframe had been.

Everything I'd ordered was delayed, so all I had was the couch and an end table. The books that had been in boxes were stacked against a wall. The television was on the floor, waiting for its stand. The knickknacks and artwork I'd collected over the years had been unwrapped and set aside, ready to be placed on the bookshelf that had been shipped yesterday.

Besides my bed, the only piece of furniture that had arrived was my desk. I'd put it together last night after I'd woken up at two. Then I'd spent the early morning hours setting up my home office.

Griffin inspected it all, then he went to the couch and sat down.

"Want a glass of wine?"

"Sure."

I handed him mine, watching as he put the rim to his lips. Then I went to the kitchen and poured myself another glass.

He'd taken off his baseball hat when I returned to the living room and was dragging his fingers through the dark strands of his hair. "Emily saw my truck parked outside."

"What does that mean?" I took a seat beside him on the

couch, curling my legs beneath me. After work, I'd put on a pair of leggings and a tee, having every intention of going for a run. Instead, I'd opted for this bottle of wine.

"We hooked up about a year ago," he said. "She wanted it to be more. I didn't. It was my mistake, but it happened. She knew the score. It was a one-time thing. Said she was good with it. Turns out…"

"She wasn't."

"Emily's got a big mouth. Her family doesn't like your grandpa much."

"He told me." Because of some small-town drama years ago. "It was fairly obvious from her article about me."

"If she's talking about us, other people will."

"Ah. And you don't want people to know." Awesome. As if my ego hadn't taken enough hits since I'd moved here. First from the station. Now from Griffin.

"It's not that, Winn."

"It's fine." It wasn't fine. Not even a little bit. I took a long, necessary gulp of wine, wishing I'd gone for that run after all and missed this entire conversation.

"Hey." Griff reached over and pulled the glass away from my mouth. "I don't give a fuck if people talk about me. Hell, they already do. But I don't want them talking about you. I don't want them saying that you're screwing around with me and not concentrating on your job. Or that our relationship was the reason my dad pushed to hire you. I want people to see you as the chief of police. As a capable cop. Not as the woman warming my bed."

"Oh." My heart swelled so much it hurt. I had no idea he cared about my reputation. Me, the outsider. "I've never slept in your bed."

"No, you haven't. But that doesn't matter. People will

talk. They'll make up their own version of the truth."

This was the small-town life that Dad had always cussed. It was the reason he'd moved away from Quincy after high school.

People would make up their own minds based on fact or fiction. They'd believe the Emily Nelsens of the world simply because Emily Nelsen's gossip was the most entertaining. There was nothing I could do to stop it, and living in fear of the rumor mill wasn't in my five-year plan.

"I don't care." I shrugged. "Besides, I'm guessing she's already running her mouth."

"Pretty much."

"Then it's done." I raised my glass to take another drink, but before it reached my lips, Griffin took it once more, this time out of my hand entirely.

He set my glass with his on the floor, then he wrapped a hand around my wrist and hauled me off the couch.

"What are you doing?"

His arms banded around my back, pulling me flush against his chest. "If people are going to talk about us having sex, we might as well have sex."

I smiled, and when he dropped his lips to mine, I welcomed him into my mouth, moaning at his taste. Oh, how I'd missed him. More than I wanted to admit.

Clinging to his broad shoulders, I wrapped my legs around his hips when he lifted me off the floor.

With tongues tangled, he walked us to my bedroom, pausing when he stepped through the threshold to tear away. "This is not the same room."

I unwound my legs, my toes easing to the floor. Gone were the suitcases shoved against the walls. They were neatly stowed in my closet along with the clothes they'd carried, either hung on a hanger, folded on a shelf or tossed in a hamper. "I unpacked."

"The whole house?"

"Yes."

He studied me, like he knew there was more to my answer. It took effort not to squirm under the intensity of his gaze. But tonight was not the time to discuss the reasons I hadn't been sleeping.

I lifted a hand to his hard chest, letting it run up his smooth cotton shirt.

Griff trapped it beneath his wide palm. "Miss me?"

"Did you miss me?"

"Yeah." His free hand came to my breast, skimming the swell before moving to my neck. He had such large hands and long fingers that his touch started at my throat and wrapped around my nape.

One tug and I was crushed against him again, his mouth closing over mine, wet and hot.

I reached for his jeans, slipping my hand from beneath his so I could undo the button and zipper. Then I dove for his cock, finding it hard and thick beneath the fabric of his boxer briefs.

The moment I wrapped my hand around his velvety shaft and gave him a stroke, Griffin surged, picking me up from beneath my thighs to toss me on the bed.

He came down on top of me, giving me his weight as his mouth left a trail of hot, open-mouthed kisses across my jaw. Then he tugged and pulled at my leggings, stripping me bare.

"Take your top off," he ordered as he stood, reaching behind his head to grab a handful of his shirt and yank it free.

Griffin's body was a masterpiece of rugged lines and masculine strength. The dusting of hair on his wide chest. The sinewed forearms, tanner than his washboard abs. This was a man who worked to keep his body strong. Who didn't believe in waxing or spray tans.

"Winn. Top off. Now."

"Bossy." I loved his bossy side. I pulled off my top as he undressed.

His boots dropped with two distinct thuds on the carpet, followed by the plop of his jeans as he shoved them down his bulky legs. He stared at me as I stared at him, drinking in every single inch.

"You asked me if I've been with anyone," he said. "I haven't. Got checked up a few months ago."

My mouth watered as he fisted his cock, giving it a hard pull. "I'm on the pill."

"I want to fuck you bare, Winslow. But only if you're good with it."

*Winslow.* The name I'd always loved. It was a masculine name, but in his deep voice, it sounded so smooth and soft. If he kept calling me Winslow, it would be hard to let him go. "I'm good."

The words were barely out of my mouth when he came at me, dragging me deeper into the bed. His mouth latched on to a nipple and my eyes drifted closed, my fingers threading through the dark strands of his hair.

He tormented me with that tongue, sucking at my breasts, licking across my skin, until my core was throbbing.

"More," I whimpered.

He slipped his hand between us, trailing those calloused fingers down my belly. The heel of his palm pressed against my clit as two of those long fingers stroked through my wet folds, toying with me until I trembled.

"Griff."

He nipped at my earlobe. "Do you want to come on my fingers or my cock?"

"Cock."

His hand between us disappeared, then he was there, thrusting inside with one fast, skilled drive of his hips.

I cried out as I stretched around him, my nails clawing at the taut skin of his shoulder blades. "Oh, God."

"Damn, you feel good."

"Move, Griff. I need more."

He obeyed, pulling out to slam back inside. Without the condom between us, I felt every. Single. Inch. Over and over, he brought us together until my limbs trembled and my back arched, my body giving in to the most intense orgasm of my life.

Stars burst behind my eyes. My nails tore into his shoulders. Tremors racked my body as I clenched around Griffin, unable to breathe. Unable to think. Unable to do anything but feel.

"Fuck, Winn," he growled against my skin, his movements never slowing. He drew out my orgasm, pulse after pulse, until I finally came down. And then he let go to pour his own inside of me, coming on a roar that echoed through my house.

He collapsed on top of me, giving me his weight. I wrapped my arms around him, holding him for a moment before he spun us, keeping us connected as we shifted positions so I was draped over his chest. His arms never let me go.

Our hearts thundered together, each at different rhythms.

"It's so good," he said through panted breaths. "Every damn time. That should scare me."

"Me too."

But if it did, it wasn't enough to make him leave. By the time darkness settled beyond the windows, he'd exhausted me thoroughly.

And for the first time in days, I slept through the night.

# CHAPTER 12

## GRIFFIN

"**M**orning." I bent to kiss Winn's head, hesitating before my lips could touch her hair.

She wasn't my girlfriend. Other than her passing out on my chest after sex, we didn't cuddle. We didn't hold hands or go on dates. This wasn't the first time I'd gone to kiss her good morning or goodbye, only to remember that we'd put lines in place.

Except in the past week, I'd spent every night at her place. There wasn't an inch of her body I hadn't tasted.

Maybe the lines needed to be redrawn.

*Fuck it.* I brushed my lips against those silky tresses and moved to the coffeepot.

She looked up at me from beneath those long lashes. "Morning."

I poured myself a cup, standing beside her as she leaned

against the cluttered countertop. "What's on deck for today?"

"Work. My day is slammed with meetings at the courthouse. You?"

"We're moving cattle today."

These were usually my favorite days on the ranch, when I was in the saddle all day. I'd be up at dawn, itching to go. But I was already late to get started. The sun was up and I was sure the guys were already at the barn, saddling horses. Meanwhile, I was still in yesterday's clothes and bare feet. Every morning I lingered here, in Winn's kitchen, for just a bit longer than the previous day.

"What are you doing this weekend?" I sipped from my mug.

"I'll probably go and spend some time with Pops. Maybe do some work, and hopefully a piece of furniture or two will show up today."

This was how our mornings for the past week had gone. We'd wake up early and she'd come out here and make a pot of coffee while I rinsed off the scent of sex with a quick shower. Then we'd stand in the kitchen, talking about our upcoming days, delaying the inevitable exit when I went my way and she went hers.

We had an unspoken understanding. She had her plans. I had mine. But later, we'd come together.

"I ran into Frank yesterday at the grocery store," she said, glancing up.

"And what did the asshole have to say?"

"Be nice." She elbowed my ribs. "He was not overly happy to hear that we were sleeping together."

"People are talking." Just like I'd expected they would. Whether it came from Emily or someone else, it had only been a matter of time. "You good?"

"I'm good." She nodded. "He asked if we were a couple. I reminded him that I was an adult, it was none of his business, and I could make my own decisions."

I grinned and took another sip, wishing I could have seen Frank's face when she told him to butt the fuck out. She might be one of the few people in this town not rattled by gossip.

Eventually it might wear on her. I'd dealt with it my whole life, but this was new to Winn.

"I'm not big on labels, but if you need one, if that would make it easier to field questions..."

She lifted a shoulder. "I just got out of an eight-year relationship. I think the only label I need right now is single."

"Fair enough." I'd gladly enjoy the hell out of the sex.

"But maybe we should put a limit on it. Just to keep the boundaries in place. Keep talk to a minimum."

A limit? I hated this idea already. "To what?"

"I don't know. Once a week?"

I scoffed and took a drink. "How about you come out to the ranch tonight? There's a lot less traffic going past my house than there is yours."

"So that's a no on the limit."

I set my mug down, took hers from her hand and picked her up, earning a little gasp as I set her on the counter. Her legs were bare and the sleepshirt she'd pulled on this morning rode up those lean thighs.

"That's a hard no." I pressed in close, dragging my hands up her legs before pushing them apart so I could settle between them. My cock, in a constant state of arousal when it came to her, strained against the zipper of my jeans.

"What time do you have to leave?" She brought her hands to my cheeks, pulling my lips to hers.

"Later," I murmured, letting her control this kiss.

Yes, I was busy. But somehow there always seemed time for this.

Her tongue dragged across my lower lip. Her taste, infused with coffee, broke on my tongue when she slid hers past my teeth.

My hands left her legs to unfasten my jeans. Then I pushed her panties to the side and drove into her tight body. "So. Damn. Good."

Winn wrapped her arms around my shoulders and raised her legs, her heels digging into the small of my back. She clung to me as I drove into her again, skin slapping skin the only sound other than our ragged breaths.

We went for it. Hard. Whenever I thought to ease up, her heels would dig in deeper, urging me on. A whimper escaped her lips before her inner walls fluttered. Then she came on a cry, pulse after pulse, her orgasm triggering my own, and we flew over the edge together.

I held her in my arms as the rush subsided, my nose buried in her hair. Her scent clung to my skin, and for a moment, I forgot what life had been like before this.

The sex. The heat. The woman.

Maybe we did need a limit. Every time we were together, I wanted two more. And one day, I was going to have to cut this off. Before feelings got tangled and we had a mess to unravel.

Maybe it was too late to avoid the mess.

I pulled free and tucked myself away, and this time when I met her brilliant blue eyes, I didn't let myself lean in to kiss her goodbye. "Tonight."

"Bye." She shoved a lock of hair out of her face as she hopped off the counter.

I showed myself out of the house and the cool morning air felt crisp against my overheated skin. The drive home was quiet, the streets mostly deserted at this early hour. But when I got to the ranch, there was a bustle of activity waiting.

Five vehicles were parked in front of my house. Four belonged to hired men. One was my mother's Cadillac.

I parked and hustled to the front door. The smell of coffee greeted me from inside, and I followed my nose to the kitchen, where Mom was staring out the window that overlooked the backyard.

"Morning, Mom." I put my arm around her for a sideways hug.

"You smell like a woman."

"Because I was with a woman."

She sighed. "From what your father says, Winslow Covington is a good cop and is good for Quincy."

"I would agree." I let Mom go and moved to the cupboard to pull out my own coffee mug and fill it from the pot.

"Are you—" She held up a hand before she could finish her question. "Actually, never mind. I don't really want to know. I promised myself when you kids graduated from high school that I'd stay out of your love lives. And frankly, I prefer it that way."

I chuckled. "What are you up to today?"

"Hiding."

"From?"

"Your father. He's mad at me." She blew out a deep breath. "We got into a fight about Briggs."

"Uh-oh. What happened?"

"I went up to the cabin yesterday afternoon. I made a couple of pies and thought he'd like one. Griffin..." She shook her head. "When you told us about him, I believed you, but I didn't think it had gotten that bad. I knocked on his door and he had no clue who I was. Not a damn clue."

"Shit. Sorry, Mom."

She sniffled and dabbed at the corner of her eye. "He's my brother too. Has been since I married your father. Seeing him like that is heartbreaking."

"I know." I pulled her into my side.

"Don't take your mind for granted, Griffin. Or your heart. They are your gifts. And they are not guaranteed from one day to the next." She sniffled again, then held up her chin. Because that was my mother. She walked through life with her chin held high. "Your dad is in denial. When I told him what happened with Briggs, he didn't believe me. He made an excuse that since I had my hair up, I looked different."

"Yeah, he didn't seem to believe me either."

"When his father's mind began slipping, it was devastating. To see it happen to his brother... I think he worries that maybe he'll be next."

That was my fear too. I wasn't sure if I could handle it if my father looked at me and didn't remember my name.

"We can't leave this alone," I said. Not only because he might cause himself harm, but because he might cause harm to others.

Over the past week, since I'd delivered those boots to Winn at the station, I'd thought a lot about this situation. Briggs had most likely found those boots while he was hiking. He'd always been disconnected from events in town, and even if he had heard about Lily Green's suicide, I doubted he would have put the pieces together.

I'm sure he would have expected that she'd died with shoes on her feet. Winn had told me they'd confirmed the boots as Lily's.

But that outburst in the truck, when we'd argued over the month, had plagued me daily. Briggs wasn't a violent man. Except there were times when he simply wasn't Briggs.

Could he have stumbled on Lily? Could he have found her on Indigo Ridge and done the unthinkable?

No. Never. He wouldn't have taken the time to remove her boots. No, she had to have done that. She had to have jumped.

Lily Green and Briggs Eden had nothing to do with the other.

"Give Dad time. He'll make the right decision."

"He will." She pulled away and poured the dregs of her coffee into the sink, rinsing it clean. "What are you doing today?"

"Moving cattle to the forest service."

"Then I'll get out of your hair. I just wanted to see your face. You've been scarce lately."

"I saw you Tuesday."

"For a whole five minutes to drop off the mail." She turned and walked out of the kitchen, pausing before she could disappear down the hallway to the front door. "Bring Winslow around for dinner one night."

"That's not really our kind of relationship, Mom."

"Oh, I've got a pretty good idea of your kind of relationship. But you can bring her by regardless. Your father speaks highly of her and I'd like to meet her. I suspect she'll be part of this community long after you two quit one another. Covie is her only family left now that her parents are dead, and I'd like her to know that she's got more than her grandfather pulling for her to make Quincy home."

"Hold up." There was a lot there to appreciate. My mother's warm and inviting heart. But my head was wrapped around something else. "Her parents are dead?"

"For a couple of years now, I think. They were killed in an accident in Bozeman."

But I'd just seen their photo in her office last week. I'd met them years ago at Willie's when they'd been here to visit Covie. How had I been sleeping with Winn and not known that her parents had been killed? "I didn't know."

"Covie didn't talk much about it. He didn't tell many people in town that they died."

"Really? Why?"

"He lost his son and his daughter-in-law. I believe they were very close. We all handle our grief differently. I think Covie went through a period of denial. Pretending life was the same was his way of coping. And he spent a lot of time in Bozeman with Winslow. He mentioned to your dad once that she was having a hard time."

What the actual fuck? I hated that my mother knew more about this than I did. Why hadn't Winn told me? Maybe she'd suspected that I already knew. Still, not a hint that they were gone. In fact, she hadn't spoken much about her parents other than to remind me that her father had grown up in Quincy.

I opened my mouth to ask Mom more about it, but the doorbell rang.

"I'll get it." She disappeared down the hallway, and when the door opened, I recognized Jim's voice.

"I think he was just grabbing a cup of coffee," Mom said. "Griffin?"

"Coming." I chugged the rest of my cup, then strode down the hallway and out the door, where my men were waiting.

After grabbing my favorite Stetson, I waved goodbye to Mom and headed for the barn. Everyone had saddled their horses, so while they visited, I made my way to Jupiter's stall.

"Hey, fella." I ran my hand over his buckskin cheek, letting him nuzzle me for a moment before I went through the motions I'd done a thousand times, combing him off before strapping on his saddle.

Jupiter had been my horse for the past decade. He was the best I'd ever had. Strong and confident with a tender heart. On days I needed to clear my head, he'd do it with me. We'd ride off through the valley or into the forest and I'd unload the burdens with the steady sway of his canter.

I led him from his stall, snagging my favorite pair of chaps from a hook on the wall, then together we walked into the sunshine. "Ready for a long day?"

Jupiter answered by nudging my shoulder.

I grinned, ruffling the black tuft of hair between his ears. "Me too."

As promised, the day was long. We rode for miles, moving the cattle into their summer grazing home in the section of the mountains that we leased from the forest service. The animals would have more grass than they could consume, and with them there, they'd help alleviate the risk of a forest fire.

On the return trip, I broke apart from the guys. They headed to the stables at Mom and Dad's place, where they all kept their horses. It was a benefit of working on our ranch—

free boarding. While I continued on alone to my place.

Home was a happy sight.

So was the woman standing beside her Durango in my driveway.

I swung off Jupiter, my legs stiff as I walked to Winn. Wearing a pair of jeans and a simple sage-green blouse, she was breathtaking.

"When I show up here, I'm going to need you to be wearing that." She pointed from my hat to my chaps to my boots. "Every time."

I chuckled as she moved into my space. "I've been in the saddle all day. I smell like a horse."

"I don't care." She stood on her toes, going for my lips.

I bent, ready to take her mouth, when my horse shoved his nose between us. "Do you mind?"

Winn laughed. "Who's this?"

"Jupiter."

"Jupiter. Interesting name for a horse."

"Eloise named him. Dad bought eight horses ten years ago. She was into some science project for school about the solar system, so she named them all after planets."

"I like it." She reached up, hesitating for a second before touching his cheek. "Hey, Jupiter."

He nuzzled her palm. My horse was as smart as they came. He knew quality attention when he got it.

"Let me get him put away. Head on in. Make yourself at home." I took the kiss I needed, then winked and escorted Jupiter to the barn. After getting him settled, I returned to the house, finding her on the porch, rocking in one of the chairs.

She had a beer in her hand and another ready for me.

What a sight she was.

Most days like this, I'd come home to an empty house and pray that no one showed up at my doorstep. I craved the time alone, the time to decompress. But I hadn't had a night alone in a week. And at the moment, I didn't want one.

"I figured you'd want one of these." She motioned to the beer as I walked up the porch.

"Yeah." I sat down, tipping the beer to my lips and quenching my thirst.

She took her own drink as her eyes raked over my legs. "You are sexy on that horse, cowboy."

"What's it going to earn me?"

"Take a shower and you'll find out."

I laughed, leaning over the arm of my chair and waving her closer. Then I fit my lips to the corner of her mouth before I left her on the porch and went inside to shower.

With a towel to my hair and wearing only a pair of jeans, I came out of the master bedroom and checked my phone.

I'd missed seven calls, and a dozen texts waited to be read. They were all from family members, and though I should find out what was happening, put out whatever fires had started today, I ignored it all and went in search of Winn.

I'd expected to find her inside, but through the glass windows in the living room, I saw her sitting in the same porch chair, rocking gently as her eyes stayed glued to the trees and the mountain peaks rising beyond.

She looked at peace. Maybe more at peace than she'd ever been, even in sleep.

My heart skipped. The towel fell from my hand. My hand came to my sternum.

She was perfect in that chair.

So beautiful I wanted this view every night.

*Fuck.* We were supposed to burn out. We should have burned out already. I *needed* it to burn out. My focus had to stay on this ranch. On my family.

Yet it didn't stop me from walking outside, picking her up out of that chair and carrying her to my bedroom.

We would burn out.

Just not yet.

# CHAPTER 13

## WINSLOW

"**D**id he give you any trouble?" Mitch asked.

"Not unless you count him crying the whole ride here." I glanced through the jail cell's steel bars to the man I'd hauled in for drunk driving.

He sat on the cot, his head in his hands, still crying. *Dumbass.* Maybe this would teach him a lesson.

Oh, how I hated the Fourth of July.

"Hopefully he'll be the last," I said.

Mitch sighed. "It's still early. I bet we bring in one or two more."

"But we're out of space." All five cells were occupied by other dumbasses.

"We'll double up if we have to. Last year on the Fourth we had to triple a few cells."

"Let's just hope no one gets hurt."

"Agreed." He nodded. "But hey, on the bright side, no bar fights this year. Two years ago we busted up a brawl at Old Mill. That was a cluster. And last year we had six girls who got into it at Big Sam's. That was even worse. Girls fight mean."

I laughed, following him out of the holding area. "Yes, we do."

The bars in town were closed. The rodeo was over. Now, hopefully, we just had to deal with the idiots who hadn't gone home. The ones who'd decided to take the party elsewhere and cause trouble.

Mitch would be here to lock them up when the other officers brought them in.

The keys attached to his belt jingled as we walked. Of the officer team, Mitch was my favorite. His tall and stout frame made him an intimidating man, but I'd learned in my time here that he was gentle and kind.

Smiles aimed my way were rare in the station. They normally only came from Janice. And Mitch. He always had one waiting when I walked into the station in the early-morning hours before the shift change.

As we passed the last cell, the man who'd been hauled in first was on his cot, snoring louder than a bear.

Mitch simply shook his head and hit the button on the wall to signal we were ready to come out.

Allen was waiting on the other side to buzz us through the secure door. He'd swapped out of day shift to help tonight on patrols.

Every member of my staff had been on duty today, even the office crew. The county sheriff and his team had come into town to help manage the crowds and patrol the streets. The Quincy Independence Day celebration had been a whirlwind of activity. We'd been prepping for it all week, and in just a few more hours, it would be over.

*Thank God.*

I yawned and dug a set of keys out of my pocket. They belonged to the cruiser I'd taken out for a two-hour patrol shift.

"It's all yours." I handed them to Mitch. He and Allen would be taking the next patrol shift together.

"Thanks, Chief."

"Winslow," I corrected.

He nodded but I suspected he'd keep calling me Chief. "Heading home?"

"Yeah." I yawned again and glanced at the clock on the wall. Three in the morning. I'd come in at four, yesterday morning. "Call me if you need anything."

He nodded. "Will do."

"Night, Allen."

"Night, Chief," he said. "See you Monday."

"That's technically tomorrow, isn't it?"

"Guess so." He scrubbed a hand over his face. "I'm not cut out for the night shift."

"Me neither." I waved, ducking into my office to collect my purse before heading outside, where my Durango had been parked for nearly twenty-four hours.

Sliding behind the wheel, I let my shoulders slump. "What a day."

The festivities had started with a parade on Main. My team had barricaded the road and put out detour signs for the traffic needing to pass through Quincy. Officers had been stationed at both ends of the street to guide pedestrians and wave through cars. I'd missed most of the parade—floats and horses and classic cars—too busy walking the sidewalks and surveying the crowd.

Cleanup had followed, and I'd found thirty minutes to scarf down an early lunch at my desk. Afterward, while half of the officers had set out in cruisers on patrol, the rest of us had made our way to the fairgrounds to prepare for the evening rodeo.

During the barrel racing, I'd visited with the county sheriff, learning more about him and his team. During the steer wrestling, I'd escorted a drunken cowboy who'd been vomiting behind the porta-potties off the grounds to sleep it off in the back of his horse trailer. And during the team roping, I'd helped a little girl who'd gotten separated from her family find her parents.

But toward the end of the night, as the sun had set and with it the temperature, I'd found a quiet moment to stand against the fence and breathe. The overhead lights had cloaked the arena in their blinding glow and obscured the stars above. Bull riding had been the final event, and as young men had climbed on the back of massive beasts, hoping to make it eight seconds, I'd focused on the stands, searching for Griffin.

He'd sat toward the bottom rail, and even from the opposite end of the fairgrounds, his smile had made my heart skip. Every row had been crammed, the space around Griffin no different. I'd recognized his family sitting close by.

The Edens had drawn nearly as much attention as the bull riders. People had passed, waving and stopping for a quick hello. Like he'd known I was watching, Griff had searched the fence line and found me.

In a sea of people, above the noise and below the lights, one look from him and the world had melted away.

The Fourth of July meant trouble.

In that moment, with that single look, I'd known I was in trouble.

Casual was becoming a craving. We'd sailed past uncomplicated weeks ago. Whatever boundaries we'd erected had been destroyed. I'd peeled my life away from Skyler's after eight years together. Eight *years*. Yet the idea of letting go of Griffin seemed impossible and it had only been a month.

As he'd stared at me and taken a sip from his beer, that sexy grin had widened. Griff had shifted to dig his phone from a pocket, and mine had dinged moments later with a text.

*Come over when you're done tonight.*

That text had been hours ago. After the rodeo, my team had migrated to the park by the river, where the county firemen had set up a fireworks show. We'd had the area prepped earlier in the week, making sure there were ways for our cruisers and an ambulance to get in and out.

Like the parade and rodeo, I hadn't gotten to watch much of the show. I'd caught the tail end of the finale, but that was only after chasing a group of teenagers away from the water, where they'd been vaping.

I hadn't seen Griffin at the park, not that I'd had time to search him out. Soon after the park had emptied, I'd returned to the station and taken my scheduled patrol shift.

Apparently this was not something the former chief had done. When I'd rattled off the schedule at our prep meeting, including my name in the rotation, every officer but Mitch had given me a strange look.

So...no different than most days.

By rights, I should go home and crash. I hadn't slept in

my own bed for a week, opting for Griffin's instead. But as I pulled out of the station's parking lot, I aimed my wheels toward the Eden ranch.

The porch light was on when I parked outside Griff's house. My eyelids were heavy and my footsteps leaden. I trudged up the stairs, expecting to find him in bed and asleep, but before I could touch the door handle, it opened.

"Hey." His arms opened.

I fell into them, sagging against his strength. "Hi."

"Everything go okay?"

"For the most part."

"Any accidents?"

"No." And I prayed when I woke up in the morning that would still be the case. Work had been my savior today. It had kept me from thinking of a summer night not unlike this one.

"Come to bed." He kissed my hair.

"Okay, but you have to do all the work tonight."

He chuckled, then bent and swept me into his arms.

Too tired to overthink it, I curled into his chest and let him carry me to the bedroom.

He stripped me out of my clothes but left my panties on. Then he yanked the T-shirt from his body and pulled it over my head. "Sleep."

"Okay."

I wanted sex. Tomorrow.

Tonight, I burrowed into the pillows, drawing in his scent, and only stayed awake long enough to feel his warm chest curl into my back. Then I crashed, grateful that tonight of all nights, I wasn't alone.

· · ·

I gasped awake. A silent cry tore at my throat. My eyes were open, but I couldn't see Griffin's dark bedroom. The blood was too thick.

I squeezed my eyes shut. *Please. Stop.* The blood oozed.

Griffin shifted behind me but didn't wake as I slid out from beneath his heavy arm and padded across the hardwood floor, closing the door to escape his bedroom.

I should have expected it. Tonight, I should have known there'd be a nightmare. But foolishly, I'd thought sheer exhaustion would win. That I'd sleep those last few hours of the day away.

The microwave clock showed 4:32. I'd slept an hour, at most. The faint rays of dawn lit up the horizon but stars still clung high in the sky.

Grabbing a throw from the couch, I made my way to the front door, easing it open to slip outside. The porch's boards were cold against my bare feet, the rocking chair damp from the night's dew. I wrapped the blanket around my shoulders, then sank into the seat, letting the fresh morning air chase away the scent of death.

Griffin's house sat in the center of a clearing. Trees surrounded it on every side, but they were far enough away that from the porch, I could see the mountain range in the distance. It jutted into the horizon, the peaks glowing with sunlight and snow. At their tips, the sky was a yellow so clear it was almost white.

Sunrise. A new day. The fifth of July. The mark of another year alone.

I missed them. I hoped I'd never stop.

"Hey." Griff's rugged voice cut through the quiet.

"Hey." I turned, finding him at the door I hadn't heard open. "You should go back to bed."

He shook his head, his hair a mess, and stepped outside wearing only a pair of boxer briefs. He waved me out of the chair.

I couldn't go back to sleep, not now. But he hadn't slept any longer than I had, so I'd go back to bed and lie there until he drifted off, then sneak out to the porch again.

But when I stood, he didn't lead me inside. Instead, he took the blanket from my shoulders, tossed it around his own, then stole my chair.

"Sit down." He patted his lap. The fabric of his boxer briefs strained at the bulk of his bare thighs. The circles under his eyes said he'd had a long day yesterday too.

"You don't have to stay out here."

"Sit. Keep me warm."

I sighed but settled into his lap, letting him circle me in his arms and snuggle us beneath the blanket. Then he started to rock the chair with slow, measured nudges of his foot. "Sorry to wake you."

"You need to get some rest. You were on your feet all day yesterday. What's going on?"

"Just a bad dream."

"Want to talk about it?"

*Yes. No.* The nightmares had been my secret. My pain. Even when Skyler and I had lived together, I hadn't told him why I'd woken up late at night. Though he had to have suspected what was going on, he hadn't asked.

Because the dreams were real. They were massive. And he hadn't been one for heavy lifting.

"I don't want to burden you," I said. "It seems like you carry a lot already."

He tensed. The rocking stopped.

When I looked up, a crease marred the skin between his

forehead. "What did I say?"

The tension on his face melted away. His arms held me tighter. "You might be the most intuitive person I've ever met."

"I don't know about that." I leaned my forehead against his shoulder. "Just an observation."

He started rocking us again, and for a few minutes, the only sounds were his heartbeat and the birds in the trees, chirping their morning song. "I'm the oldest of my siblings. That's always put me in a different position with my sisters. My youngest brother too. As little kids, they'd take their problems to Mom and Dad. The older they get, the more those problems come to me. Especially after I took over the ranch. I'm the role model. The mediator."

"Does it bother you?"

"No."

Because Griffin was the type of man who stood at the ready, always willing to heft the load.

"But it is a weight. I need to be here for them. I don't want to let them down. And I don't want to fail the ranch."

"Is everything okay with the ranch?"

"Yeah, it's good. Just a lot of work."

"Do you enjoy it?"

"I do." He nodded. "I can't imagine doing anything else."

"I feel the same way about being a cop."

He tucked a lock of hair behind my ear. "How'd you get into it?"

"My senior year in high school I worked as an office aide. The officer stationed at our school was this beautiful woman. She was personable and gracious. Gorgeous, but you also knew not to fuck with her."

"Sort of like you."

I smiled. "I asked her once how she became a police officer. I'd been struggling to decide if I should go to college or a trade school. All of the other kids at school seemed to know exactly what they wanted to do and I came up blank every time. One day, I was in the office and she was there too, so I asked her why she decided to be a cop."

That conversation had changed my life. She'd given me ten minutes of her time, just ten minutes, but it was ten minutes that had set me on this path.

"She told me that when she was a teenager, she didn't know what she wanted to do either. And while she was debating her options, her dad gave her a piece of great advice. In the absence of a clear ambition, serving others is a mighty purpose. She didn't want to be a nurse or a teacher. So she went to the police academy. I went home that evening and told my parents I wanted to find out what it would take to be a cop."

"And here you are."

"Here I am."

"How did your parents react?"

"As you'd expect. They worried. Rightly so. It was hard, really hard. Men don't always take me seriously. It's a dangerous job. But I believe in my heart that I'm in the right place. That because I'm a woman, I'm able to handle some awful situations differently than a man." Like rape. Domestic abuse. I'd worked with plenty of incredible male cops, but there were times when a woman would only talk to a woman. Those cases, as horrific as they'd been, had only solidified my decision.

"Is that what wakes you up at night? The awful cases?"

"No." I blew out a long breath. "But like I said, I don't

want to burden you."

"It's no burden to listen, Winn."

Talking about it hurt. The few times Pops had wanted to discuss the accident, every word had scraped and sliced across my tongue. That had been years ago, and since, I'd always change the subject. Ignoring the pain was easier. Wasn't it?

Something had to give. Something had to let go. These nightmares couldn't go on forever, and maybe because I'd kept it inside for so long, the bad dreams were my heart's way of screaming for relief.

"My parents died five years ago." One sentence and my chest burned.

"My mom mentioned something about that the other day."

"It was on the Fourth of July. They were driving home from a party at a friend's house in the mountains. They were hit by an oncoming car. The driver was texting."

"Damn." Griffin dropped his forehead to my temple. "I'm sorry."

I swallowed hard, pushing past the ache. "I was the first officer on the scene."

His body stilled. The rocking stopped again.

"It was my last year as a patrol officer. I'd already put in my application to be promoted and my parents were so excited that I wouldn't be on the streets as much. When the call came through my scanner, I just...I can't describe it. This pit formed in my stomach and I knew that when I got there, it would be bad."

Bad was an understatement.

"When you got there, were they..."

*Dead.* "Yes. I found the other driver first. He'd been

thrown from his car. His body was on the center line."

The blood had pooled around his slackened face. He'd only been eighteen. A child. It was hard to hate a child, but I'd managed it for five years.

"It was a head-on collision at forty miles per hour. My parents..." My chin quivered and I slammed my eyes shut.

What people said about time healing wounds was bullshit. No amount of time had made it easier to relive that night. Not an hour. Not a day. Not five years. Because each day that passed was a day we had missed together.

Mom and Dad would have been so proud to see me in Quincy. Dad would have warned me about the gossip mill and done his best to shield me from it, like Griff. Mom would have insisted on visiting each and every weekend until my house was set up and perfect.

"That's what you see in your dreams," Griffin whispered.

I nodded.

Both of them had been wearing seat belts. They'd been trapped in their seats, their bodies destroyed after their car had rolled six times, landing on its roof.

"Dad's eyes were open. Mom, she, her body..." My eyes flooded. The words burned too much. "I can't."

"You don't have to."

I studied the trees, taking a few minutes to breathe as Griff began to rock us again.

"They didn't suffer," I whispered. "It was instant."

"I'm so sorry, Winn." Griffin's arms banded tighter, and when the first tear dripped down my cheek, he just held on. He held on as I buried my face in his neck and cried for the people I'd loved more than anything in this world.

By the time I pulled myself together, the sun had risen above the mountain peaks.

"Thank you for listening." I wiped my cheeks dry.

"Anytime."

"You're good at it."

"Practice. I've got five siblings."

"No." I put my hand over his heart. "It's just who you are."

He kissed my hair, his arms never letting go as we stayed stuck together in the chair. "What are you doing today?"

"I don't have anything planned." Sleep. At some point, I'd have to attempt sleep.

He picked us both up, setting me on my feet. Then he traced a fingertip across the freckles on my nose. "Spend the day here."

We'd never spent the day together. That had always been a boundary. And like the others, crossing it was as natural as breathing.

"Okay."

# CHAPTER 14

## GRIFFIN

One morning spent in a rocking chair, and the world had shifted. Like going for a ride and veering off the main path to get a look from a different angle, and then discovering that the trail you'd been on was lacking in every way imaginable.

I was in it with this woman.

So fucking in it.

The shift had happened weeks ago. Or maybe there'd been small turns along the way. Yesterday, during the annual Quincy activities, I'd realized just how different life would be with Winn. The Fourth had always been fun. Busy, but fun. Except I'd struggled to relax and enjoy the day.

I spent most of my time searching for her, finding her in the crowd at various events. When I spotted her at the parade, walking up and down the sidewalks, her expression was one of concentration and awareness. Once the street sweeper passed, she disappeared, probably back to the station, and it took effort not to call and check in.

Instead, I rushed around to help my siblings. Knox needed a hand at the restaurant for the lunch rush, so I stopped at The Eloise to haul in supplies. There'd been a ninety-minute wait for a table—which hadn't seemed to turn many people away.

I left Knox hustling around his kitchen, in his element and exactly where he wanted to be, then headed to the coffee shop because Lyla had been slammed too. Some asshole had clogged one of the toilets, so I plunged it, then cleared the overflowing garbage cans.

It was all hands on deck for the Eden family. Dad was the gopher, running around town to the hardware store or the grocery store for whatever anyone needed. Mom and Talia were helping Lyla behind the counter making coffee. Mateo was at the hotel, working with Eloise to make sure guests were taken care of for the sold-out weekend.

As the community migrated off Main and to the fairgrounds, my family managed to get together. We gathered in our family's regular seats for the rodeo. The coffee shop was closed. So was Knox's restaurant. Eloise's staff at the hotel was on duty, so we could come together for a few beers and hot dogs.

The Quincy rodeo was a standing tradition, much like Christmas or Thanksgiving. It was one of the few events we always made sure to attend together, even if that meant closing shop. Except that evening, surrounded by my family, a piece was missing.

I hadn't realized until late in the evening, when I'd glanced across the arena and found Winn at the fence, that the missing piece was her.

Another shift.

She belonged by my side, not standing alone.

Especially not yesterday.

I wished I had known about her parents. She'd probably worked all day yesterday as a distraction. Today, if all I could do was keep the distractions coming, then I'd bust my ass to make it happen.

"Your hair dryer is nicer than mine. I might have to steal it," she said, coming down the hallway from the master bedroom.

After we'd come inside from the rocking chair, I'd taken her to the bedroom for a couple of orgasms before hopping into the shower. While I'd dressed and come to the kitchen to brew coffee, she'd gotten ready too.

Normally she went home to shower. Not today. Today, she wasn't leaving my sight.

"The hair dryer is Talia's doing." I chuckled and handed her a steaming mug. "Sometimes my sisters will crash here if we have a family function at the ranch. Saves them from driving into town if they've gotten into my parents' liquor cabinet. Talia decided that since they're the only people who use the guest bedrooms, they might as well have stuff here to get ready the next morning."

Winn sipped her coffee. "That's sweet that you let them stay."

I shrugged. "I'm a lot like my dad when it comes to my sisters. Twisted around their little fingers."

"Also sweet."

"How about eggs for breakfast?" I walked to the fridge. "Bacon or sausage?"

"Either. Can I help?"

I shook my head and took out the sausage. "Have a seat."

She slid into a stool at the island, watching while I made a quick scramble. With it plated, I sat beside her, the two of us eating quietly. I wasn't one to talk much when there was food in front of me. I liked that she didn't either.

Wait. Was this the first meal we'd shared? I stopped chewing and glanced at her profile.

"What?" she asked, grabbing a napkin to wipe her lips.

"We haven't eaten together before."

"There was lunch my first day at work."

"That doesn't count."

"Then, no, I guess we haven't. We usually skip the dinner dates and go straight for the bed."

Sex had always come first. But it felt like we should have been sharing meals for weeks. That I should have taken her out on a proper date, like dinner at Knox's restaurant or my favorite steakhouse outside of town. "Maybe we should toss in a dinner date."

She held my gaze for a minute, like she was trying to decide if I was teasing.

"I'm serious."

Her eyes softened. "Okay."

"How about we do some exploring today?" I asked after we'd both finished eating.

"Sure." She nodded, motioning to her clothes. They were the jeans she'd had on last night and one of my black T-shirts, which dwarfed her, so she'd tied it into a knot at her hip. "Do I need to run home and change?"

"You'll be fine. Have you ever ridden a horse?"

"No."

"Want to learn?"

"Not especially." She smiled as I laughed. "Maybe one day."

If and when that one day came, I'd teach her. "We'll do another kind of ride."

So after our breakfast dishes were in the washer, we set out for the barn.

"How about a four-wheeler? Ever driven one of those?"

"Another no."

"Want to ride with me? Or drive your own?"

She eyed the machine as I filled the gas tank. "Ride with you."

"Good answer." I straddled the seat, patting the back for her to climb on behind me. Then I started the engine and set out on the road.

We rode for an hour, following old trails around the ranch. Winn's arms stayed tight around my waist, her head resting against my shoulder at times, as the sun warmed our skin and the wind blew her hair off her pretty face until I came to a stop along a fence.

"This is the far end of the ranch," I told her.

"This is all yours? From here to your house?" She pointed toward the direction that we'd just come from.

"And a bit beyond." I pointed left, then right. "This is the center point. How long we just rode? It goes twice as far in both directions." The Eden ranch was essentially a rectangle that stretched along the base of the mountains in some of the best country under God's blue sky.

"Are all ranches this big?"

"Very few." I stood from the seat, climbing off the machine to walk to the fence where a small cluster of wildflowers was tangled with the stalks of grass. I plucked a white one and a yellow one, bringing them to her. "We've expanded over the years. Bought new property."

"Like the one next to Indigo Ridge."

"Exactly. After a few generations of buying when land comes available, now we've got one of the largest ranches in this part of the state."

"It's beautiful." She pressed the flowers to her nose. "Thanks for taking me out today."

"Welcome." I propped a hip on the edge of the four-wheeler, looking out over the pasture. "It's been a while since I've done this. Just driven around. No task in mind."

"It's been a long time since I didn't fill a day with work of some kind."

"What about in Bozeman? What did you do there to relax?"

"Hung out with friends. Did some hiking around the area. I had a vegetable garden one summer. Skyler ruined that one for me though."

"How did he ruin it?"

"He complained that it was too time consuming. That instead of having our evenings free to meet up with friends or go to a movie or whatever else he wanted to do, I liked to stay home and work in the garden. Maybe I'll put one in at my house here. Not that I have a lot of free time."

"Maybe by this time next year you will."

"Yeah." She smiled and lifted the flowers to her nose again. "Maybe."

"Have you heard from him?" I asked.

"No. His phone calls stopped, at least I think. I forget to charge that phone all the time. But I haven't had any messages to talk about us or the house. I think his visit here was the end, but you never know with him. He can be unpredictable, which is part of why I stayed with him for so long. He'd act distant and rude for months. I'd swear we were done. Then it was like he knew I was about to call it off because he'd become this entirely different person. He'd make me laugh. He'd be affectionate and caring. When I look back over our eight years together, it was like living in a constant state of whiplash."

He sounded like a manipulative dick but I swallowed that comment because I suspected that Winn knew it already.

"He knew my parents," she said. "That's the other part of why I stayed with him. Because they knew him. Or I guess I should say that he knew them. Anyone else and they would just be photographs and stories. And they would have been a stranger to my parents. That's not a great reason to stick with someone but..."

"It's understandable." It was the reason why I hadn't brought anyone home to my parents. Because there hadn't been anyone I'd wanted to give them memories about.

But Winn...maybe it was time to take Mom up on her offer and take Winn over for dinner.

"Why'd you end it?" I asked. "You never told me that night he was at your house."

"He was sleeping with someone else." She huffed. "I found out because she called the house looking for him. Can you believe it? She thought I knew because her husband knew."

"She was married?"

"Yup." Winn popped the word. "Apparently they'd made this arrangement. Sex only. Her husband was good with it, but Skyler must have known that I'd say *fuck no*, so he'd hidden the affair."

"Prick."

"Pretty much," she muttered. "I'm just guessing, but I bet she dumped him and that's why he made his visit."

"He thought you'd take him back?" *Idiot.*

"Skyler got away with a lot. He must have thought that eventually I'd forgive him. That eventually I'd pick a wedding date. I don't know. After my parents died, I pushed him away. He didn't pull me back."

Because he was a fucking idiot.

"It hurt," she said, twirling the flowers between her fingers. "We'd made a lot of promises together. Eight years is a long time to live your life around someone. But then I realized that we lived around each other, not with each other. I couldn't count on him. The promises crumbled. When I started peeling my life away, making it my own, there weren't many threads to untangle. The house is all that's left and that's simply paperwork."

At the moment, I was thinking of tangling her up so tight she'd never get free.

"It worked out the way it needed to," she said. "I'm glad to be here in Quincy."

"I'm glad you're here too." I stood, returning to the seat and the handlebars. The moment I was settled, Winn's arms wrapped around me and the insides of her thighs pressed to the outsides of mine.

She fit me. Perfectly. In more ways than just riding on a four-wheeler.

"Keep going?" I asked over my shoulder. "Or head back to the house?"

"Keep going."

I grinned, glad she was enjoying this, and started the engine.

Another hour later and the sun was beating down on us. We'd worked our way past Indigo Ridge, crisscrossing through pastures and bouncing from one fence to the next. The ridge was behind us and the only reason I'd come this far was to show her one more edge of the ranch so she could get a better idea of the size.

The backside of the ridge was a massive rise, the hill covered in evergreens. But on the flats, there wasn't much shade. Without a hat, I worried she'd get sunburned, so I aimed the wheels for home.

I slowed at a gate, ready to get off and open it for us, when I glanced up to the forest and saw a plume of smoke rising from the treetops. It was in about the same spot as Briggs's cabin. "What the hell?"

It was July. Fires in July were not only unnecessary but goddamn dangerous.

"What?" Winn asked, following my gaze. "Aren't there fire restrictions right now?"

"Yeah." I turned the four-wheeler around, and instead of heading home, we tore through the landscape toward my uncle's cabin.

Winn clutched me tight as we wound through the trees and up the road. The scent of charred wood and campfire reached us as we crested the climb and pulled into the cabin's clearing.

Briggs was standing beside a pile of burning pine limbs, smoke billowing from its center. The orange and red flicker of the flames tickled the open air, sending sparks on the breeze.

I parked and flew off the four-wheeler, racing over to my uncle. "Briggs, what the hell?"

He had a shovel in one hand. A hose in the other. "Harrison? What are you doing here? Didn't even hear you pull up."

Harrison? *Fuck.* I yanked the shovel from his hand, slammed the end into the dirt, stepped out a scoop and tossed it on the flames.

"Hey! I'm—"

"Trying to burn down the whole fucking mountain."

"It's a slash pile burn. It's under control."

I ignored him, shoveling as quickly as I could. Then I snatched the hose from his hand, dousing the fire. Steam hissed and popped as it broke through the pile.

A small cough made me turn to see Winn behind me. "What can I do?"

I handed her the hose.

"Who are you?" Briggs asked her. "Harrison, who is this? What the hell do you think you're doing with another woman? Does Anne know?"

"I'm Griffin, Briggs. Griffin," I barked. "This is Winslow, and you're in her way. Move."

He flinched at the volume in my voice and shied away.

*Damn it.* At my age, Dad and I would have looked nearly identical. I should be patient. I should take it easy. But a fire in July? We waited until the dead of winter when there were two feet of snow on the ground before we burned slash piles.

The rumble of a truck's engine came from the road, and Dad's pickup skidded to a stop beside the four-wheeler. He flew out the driver's side, running our way. "What's going on? I saw smoke."

I waited until he was close enough to throw him the shovel, so pissed off I could barely see straight. "Talk to your brother. He thinks I'm you."

Without another word, I grabbed Winn's free hand and pulled her away from the hose. She followed, silently climbing on the back of the four-wheeler and holding on as I sped down the road and away from the cabin.

"Goddamn it." I shook my head, my heart racing.

Winn's hold tightened. She'd heard me.

We rode straight for home. I parked in the barn, letting the quiet settle after I killed the engine. Then I hung my head.

"It's getting worse. I didn't want to believe it. Yesterday, he was so...normal. At the parade. At the rodeo."

Briggs had seemed exactly like the man I'd known my entire life. He'd gone around town with Dad to help for a while. He'd been at the rodeo arena, talking to his buddies and drinking a beer.

"He was so normal that I thought maybe I was blowing this thing out of proportion. Maybe I've been taking it too far. But..."

"You weren't."

I shook my head. "Something has to change."

And either my father would push for that change, or I'd have to do it myself.

"I'm sorry," Winn whispered, dropping a kiss to my shoulder.

I twisted, taking her face in my hands. Those indigo eyes seared into mine. They saw the fears. The doubts. The frustration. They gave me a place to put it all. A place to just...be real.

She'd told me this morning that I carried burdens. I did. But right here, in this moment, she was there to help share the load.

I dropped a kiss to her lips, then helped her to her feet. "We smell like smoke."

With her hand clasped in mine, I led her to the house and straight to the bathroom, where I turned on the shower. We stripped out of our dirty clothes and stepped under the spray like two people who'd showered together a hundred times. Easy. Comfortable. And as the soap cascaded over our bodies, the smell of the fire and the stress of my family disappeared down the drain.

My hands found Winn's wet skin at the same time her lips found mine. The desire for her swirled with the steam, and when

I lifted her into my arms, pressing her back against the tiled wall to slide into her silky heat, nothing else in the world mattered.

No drama. No family. No fire.

Just Winn.

We came together with shaking limbs and frenzied moans, lingering until the water ran cold.

She yawned as I handed her a fresh towel.

"Tired?"

"I'll be fine."

"Want to try and sleep?" Because I could use a nap myself. Our conversation in the rocking chair felt like days ago, not hours.

"I don't know." She met my gaze in the mirror and the fear behind them was like a punch to the gut.

I stepped close and took her face in my hands, my fingers threading through the wet strands of hair at her temples. "I'll hold you. If you have a nightmare, I won't let go."

Her body sagged and her forehead fell into my chest. "Okay."

With a swift move, I picked her up, cradling her to my chest. Then I retreated to the bedroom, setting her in the unmade bed and drawing the blinds.

She fell asleep first. I wouldn't let myself sleep until she was under. And as I listened to her breath even out, I sank in with her.

Deeper and deeper. She pulled. I followed.

It had happened so naturally, this fall into Winn. Like I was out for a short drive, and when I looked back to where I'd started, instead of traveling yards, I'd gone miles.

Deeper and deeper, until there was no turning back.

I was in it with this woman.

So fucking in it.

# CHAPTER 15

## WINSLOW

"Are you coming over tonight?" Griffin was barefoot, one step down from where I stood on the top stair of his porch. He was still taller, but it gave me easier access to his mouth.

"Maybe." I leaned in and pressed my lips to his stubbled cheek.

His hair was disheveled, the strands sticking up at all angles from where my fingers had combed it earlier.

Griffin had woken up first and come to the kitchen to make coffee. Instead of eating breakfast, he'd hoisted me onto the counter and devoured me instead.

My man knew how to use his tongue.

"Want me to come to your place instead?" he asked.

"Let's see how the day goes." My own bed had been deserted for a week. I loved my little house, but I loved

Griffin's too.

It was relaxing out here on the ranch. Serene. I hadn't realized just how loud my thoughts were, how loud my life was—even the solitary moments—until I'd come here and spent a few hours in a rocking chair and cleared my mind.

My head was full of cases and stress from the station. Despite my best efforts to smother those feelings, I worried about fitting in and my reputation.

The moment I pulled onto the Eden ranch, the noise dulled. The worries faded. Or maybe it didn't have a damn thing to do with the property but with the man standing one step below me.

"Have a good day." I kissed him goodbye.

"You too." He propped a hip against the railing, his arms crossing over that broad chest as he watched me descend the stairs and head for my car.

It was early, the morning air fresh. The weather forecast promised it would be a scorcher, and as I started the Durango, I wished I had taken another day to enjoy the summer sunshine.

But there was work to be done, so I shoved the key into the ignition and headed into town.

Griffin had washed my clothes yesterday, and though I doubted anyone would notice I was in the same apparel as I'd worn on the Fourth, I made a quick pitstop home to ensure the place hadn't flooded and swap out my clothes for something fresh.

The shift change was over by the time I arrived at the station. The night-shift crew were likely in their beds while I filled a coffee cup and surveyed the quiet bullpen. Now that the Fourth was over, we were trimmed down for a few days to give everyone some added rest.

Except for me. I stifled a groan at the files scattered on my desk when I settled into my office. I hadn't earned vacation yet.

One file always seemed to rise to the top of the stack.

*Lily Green.*

I flipped it open, a photograph of her death on top. A month ago, this picture had made me cringe. But I'd stared at it long enough that now the only emotion I felt was soul-deep sadness.

"Oh, Lily." I turned the gruesome photo on its face, then skimmed the edge of the one beneath. It was the last selfie she'd posted on Instagram for Memorial Day.

Lily Green was a beauty, her blond hair like strands of spun sunshine. Her smile was as bright as the stars. Maybe it was all an illusion. Maybe the smile and the sparkling eyes had been the façade she'd put on for the world.

It was easy to force smiles. It was simple to lie and tell people you were doing great when the truth was that every heartbeat caused you pain.

I'd spent a month searching for signs that Lily might have been depressed. I'd questioned friends and family. I'd gone on an unsuccessful quest to find a boyfriend. I'd dug into all of her social media accounts and even pulled her text records and credit card statements.

But there'd been nothing to find.

Maybe because there was nothing to find.

No hidden confessions. No secret boyfriend. Chances were, she'd gone out with her friends to have some fun, then met a guy to hook up with. Considering I'd done the same with Griffin on my first night in town, it definitely wasn't out of the question.

Maybe he'd gone his own way and she'd stayed behind,

suffering in silence.

Until it had just been too much.

I touched the edge of her photo one more time, then closed the lid on the folder.

Obsessing over Lily's suicide wasn't getting me anywhere. Because of their age, there was a limit to the number of questions I was willing to ask about the other suicides. My job wasn't to reopen wounds unless absolutely necessary. If parents, friends and loved ones were healing, I respected that process.

I was living that process.

Some of my worst moments over the past year had been in Bozeman when I'd been going about my normal day only to have someone walk up to me on the street and tell me how sorry they were for my loss. Even if they meant well, each time was like a slap in the face.

People handled grief differently. Some welcomed the outpouring of affection and support. Others, like me, held it close to the heart and only let small pieces go when they were ready.

Yesterday, telling Griffin about Mom's and Dad's deaths, I'd let a piece go.

Lily Green deserved as much energy as I could give her. But Melina Green deserved space to heal. Today, that meant giving the case some room to breathe.

So I tucked the file into my desk drawer, adding the other suicides beside it, and I went about clearing my desk.

By the time I left the station at six, my inbox was nearly empty, I'd had three meetings, and every report that I'd needed to review and approve was finished. The officers had taken my critiques of their reports better than expected. The lack of detail was less noticeable now, though there was still room for improvement.

Two of the files I'd been given, both having to do with incidents on the Fourth, needed some revisions, so I left them with notes on the officers' respective desks. The bullpen was quiet again. The evening shift had clocked in, and besides the dispatcher at the phones, the other officers were out on patrol.

I had collected my purse and walked out, keys in hand to lock my office door, when I nearly collided with Officer Smith coming down the hallway.

"Oh, sorry."

"Watch it," he muttered, giving me a wide berth.

*This guy.* "Officer Smith," I called to his back as he walked by.

He huffed and turned, fisting his hands on his hips. He was in plain clothes, a pair of track pants and an athletic shirt. "What? I'm off shift. Just using the gym."

I stared at him, his ruddy cheeks and sweaty hair. For the month that I'd been here, I'd been kind. I'd been polite and professional, hoping that in time I'd win everyone over, including Tom.

Call it wishful thinking, but I'd been making progress with the staff. They didn't need to treat me like a friend, and it would be better if they didn't, but they were beginning to realize that I was the boss.

And I wasn't going anywhere.

As I looked at Tom Smith and the snarl on his lip, I realized I wasn't going to earn his respect. His loyalty. He'd made up his mind and it wouldn't change.

"Your report from Saturday is lacking. You'll find my notes on your desk. I'll expect to see the corrected version tomorrow."

His nostrils flared. "Whatever."

"Chief. The correct response is, *Yes, Chief.*"

Another nostril flare. Another snarl. Then he was gone.

I waited until I heard the door slam open and close. Then I blew out the breath I'd been holding. Tomorrow, I'd make sure I had a decent job description drafted for his position in case he quit. Or he pushed me far enough that I'd let him go.

Digging my phone from my purse, I sent Griffin a text.

*My place.*

As much as I wanted a quiet night at the ranch, I had a bottle of wine at home and it was calling my name.

Downtown Quincy was swarmed with tourists walking up and down Main as I drove home. There'd been a shoplifter this morning at the kitchen goods store. Two speeding tickets, one a local and one from out of state. Otherwise, life in my new small town seemed wonderfully simple.

Tonight, it felt like mine.

I'd heard from long-time cops in Bozeman that it was easy to get jaded toward the bad. That you searched for crimes around every corner. Maybe it would happen to me. Or maybe this little town, even with its faults, would keep the jagged edges away.

Quincy was home.

I turned onto my street, a lightness to my heart. It vanished when I spotted a familiar truck parked against the curb. And a familiar blond reporter standing on my sidewalk, talking to my ex.

"Shit," I muttered, pulling into the driveway. "Both of them? I should have gone to the ranch."

Skyler met me at the driver's side, opening the door for me.

"What do you want?" I asked, brushing past him and

heading for the house.

I ignored Emily Nelsen completely. Griff had mentioned she lived in this neighborhood. Judging by the leggings and tank top, she'd been out for a jog and must have spotted Skyler. She was probably looking for gossip to spread in her precious paper. Maybe that I was cheating on Griffin.

"Winnie." Skyler's hand touched my elbow as we took the porch stairs.

How ironic was it that just yesterday I'd told Griffin about Skyler? "What?"

"Let's talk. Please."

"About the house? Sell it. I don't care. But I don't want it."

"No. Let's talk about us."

"There is no us." From the corner of my eye I spotted Emily inch closer. Nosy bitch.

"I've been worried about you. Yesterday especially."

"Yet here you are, a day late."

"I figured you'd be busy yesterday and didn't want to bother you."

Or he'd had his own plans and hadn't wanted to cancel. "If you actually cared about the anniversary of Mom and Dad's accident, you wouldn't have planned a golfing weekend last year over the Fourth. Or maybe that trip was just an excuse to fuck your side piece."

He stiffened. "I've told you. That was just sex."

"Not to me."

"It wasn't a real affair."

"Oh, so you didn't really put your penis inside her vagina?"

"Jesus, Winnie." He flinched. "Do you have to say it like that?"

"Yes. Go away, Skyler." I leaned past him. "And you too."

Emily's eyes widened.

"Did you need something? A new story?" I asked her. "Because there isn't one here. Sorry to disappoint."

"I was just passing by and saying hello," she mumbled.

I waved. "Hello."

"Let's talk inside, where it's private." Skyler dropped his voice.

"No. You're not coming inside. We're done. We've been done for months. I don't understand why you're here and what it's going to take for you to disappear but—"

"Eight years. We were together for eight years. We had a house together."

"A house you refuse to sell."

"Because I can't." He tossed up his hands. "I walk through the door, and it still smells like you. I can still see you in the living room. I know I fucked up. I wasn't there when I should have been. I didn't realize it until I came home and it wasn't home anymore because you were gone. Don't we owe it to each other to try?"

"Try what? We wouldn't have made it, Skyler. There's a reason neither of us pushed for an actual wedding. There's a reason we never made that commitment. We wouldn't have made it." That was the truth I hadn't wanted to admit for those eight years.

There hadn't been enough loyalty, on either side. I hadn't made our relationship a priority. It had always been an afterthought to what was happening with my career. There was a reason I'd been promoted so quickly through the ranks. I'd given my job ninety-nine percent of my heart. Skyler had only gotten fragments.

He'd been just as dedicated to his own career, and there were couples like that who made it work. But we hadn't shared an urgency for one another.

I hadn't even realized what we'd lacked until I'd met Griffin. I hadn't understood what it was like to crave a person. To long for their voice, their scent, their taste.

Eight years with Skyler. One month with Griffin.

I'd choose Griffin every time.

"There's a reason you cheated," I told Skyler. "Because we wouldn't have made it."

"Winnie." He stepped closer, his hand moving from my elbow to my shoulder.

"If you want to keep that hand attached to your body, you'll take it off of her right now." The deep rumbling voice behind Skyler sent a shiver racing down my spine. The thud of boots echoed before Griffin stepped onto the porch and came to my side.

The glare he aimed Skyler's way brought a smile to my lips.

Jealousy on Griffin Eden looked incredibly sexy.

"I don't know who you are or what you're doing, but I'm having a conversation with Winnie," Skyler said, standing taller.

"And I'm here to give her an orgasm before dinner. Let's find out which one of us she'd rather have stick around."

My jaw dropped.

Emily's gasp was loud enough for us all to hear.

"Go home, Emily," Griffin barked over Skyler's shoulder.

She tensed but didn't move.

"There's nothing for you here," Griff told her. "Not a story. Not me. Go home."

She swallowed hard, her pride visibly dinged. That

might cost us later, but the sight of her scurrying down the sidewalk after he'd chosen me was reward enough.

"You too," I told Skyler. "Go home."

He shook his head. "I get it. You wanted to screw this guy for a while and balance the scales. Fine. I can look past him if you can look past—"

"You lost her." Griffin's voice had an edge unlike anything I'd heard before. An edge that made me glad I was standing on his side, not the opposing. "You fucked up and lost her. She's mine. And I won't fuck it up."

*Mine.* My heart melted into a puddle.

No man had ever claimed me before. Skyler, dressed in his signature black suit, had taken eight years and he'd never once said *she's mine.*

My ex looked at me and I ignored him, too busy holding myself back from hugging the angry cowboy. "Griff..."

"Unlock the door, Winn."

I fought a smile. And followed orders, but before I went inside, I gave Skyler one last glance. "Sell the house. Let it go. Let me go. Please."

He swallowed hard. Then nodded.

"Thank you." I took Griffin's hand, tugging him into the house.

He slammed the door shut, dragging a hand through his hair. "I really want to punch him."

"Don't punch him."

Skyler didn't wait around this time. As quickly as Emily had vanished, so did he. For good, I suspected.

"So that was, um..." Awkward? Incredible? Enlightening? *All of the above.*

"Yeah." Griff stalked my way, closing the distance between us in a single stride. Then his mouth was on mine, sending a flutter to my heart and a trembling to my knees.

He claimed me. One sweep of his tongue and those words he'd told Skyler raced through my body.

*She's mine.*

He was mine too.

It was dark outside by the time we emerged from the bedroom. As promised, Griffin had delivered on his orgasm before dinner. Three, actually.

"Are we calling in for food?" I opened my fridge. "Or do you want cheese and crackers?"

"Pizza." He wrapped an arm around my shoulders, his bare chest hot against my back. Then he closed the fridge. "Definitely pizza."

I sagged against him. "Are we going to talk about earlier?"

"Probably should," he murmured against my hair.

"We're not really casual, are we?"

He shifted, loosening his arm so he could turn me to face him. Those piercing blue eyes seared into mine. "No. We are not."

"Okay." That word seemed too small for this. I'd say *okay* to a latte. To a glass of champagne. Not to Griffin proposing, well...whatever it was he was proposing. Nothing at the moment. But the promise of a future needed more than a simple *okay.*

"You good with that?"

"Yes." Another word, too small. Or maybe it was the perfect word.

The two of us had started with a *yes*, whispered into his ear as we'd come together in the back of his truck.

"I want to take you to dinner," he declared. "On a date."

"All right." My head was spinning. "Tonight?"

"No." He grinned and dug his phone from his jeans pocket. After tapping the screen a few times, he pressed it to his ear.

My phone rang in the living room, so I brushed past Griffin as he ordered pizza and hurried to the floor where I'd dropped my purse earlier. I found my personal phone first, but it had been dead for days. I kept digging until I had my work phone in hand. The station's number flashed.

*Shit.*

"Hello," I answered.

"Hi, Chief," Mitch said, his voice tight. There was no smile.

"What's going on?"

"Got a call from Frank Nigel."

My heart galloped. Frank would only call if there was an emergency. He'd probably tried my personal phone, and when I hadn't answered, he'd called the station. "What happened?"

"It's Covie. He's at the hospital."

# CHAPTER 16

## WINSLOW

"I'm going to move in with you," I told Pops, his hand sandwiched between mine.

He scoffed. "No, you're not."

"I don't like that you were alone."

"I wasn't alone. I had Frank."

I shook my head. "It's not the same."

Because had Frank not needed to borrow a wrench, this entire situation might have turned out differently.

"I'm fine."

"You had a heart attack."

"A mild heart attack." He tried to pry his hand free, but I wasn't letting go. Not yet.

I frowned. "Semantics."

Pops sighed. "I love you, Winnie."

"I love you too." My chin began to quiver. It had been

a long night of sitting in this chair and my emotions were frazzled.

"Don't cry."

I nodded and swallowed the lump in my throat. There would be crying. Lots and lots of crying. But I'd save it for when I was home alone.

Pops was the only family I had left. Dad had been an only child. Mom had been too and her parents had passed away years ago. There weren't aunts and uncles and cousins who'd take me in for the holidays. Who'd tell me they loved me.

Pops was it. And this heart attack was a brutal reminder that he wouldn't always be here.

I'd spent most of last night watching him sleep. He looked so small in this hospital bed. The grayish-blue gown and the beige walls bleached the color from his face. The florescent lights brought out every line, every wrinkle.

Life was destined to end, but I wasn't ready to lose Pops. I wouldn't ever be ready.

The tears flooding my eyes didn't care that he wanted me to suck it up. One streaked across each cheek, leaving twin trails.

"Winnie. I'm okay."

I let go of his hand to dry my face. "I know."

"Like the doctor said, it's time to clean up my diet and reduce stress."

Pops was in such great shape for his age. He wasn't overweight and didn't get out of breath on our after-dinner walks. But I guess that didn't matter to his clogged arteries. His cholesterol was too high and he had a high-pressure job. "It would be easier for you at home if you had help to keep up the house."

"Pfft." He waved it off. "The house isn't a stress. But..."

"But, what?"

He studied the ceiling, his head sinking deeper into the pillows behind his shoulders. "Maybe it's time for me to retire."

"You love being the mayor."

"I sure do, sweetheart. I sure do." He gave me a sad smile. "But I'm old and being mayor is stressful. I feel like maybe I've done exactly what I needed to do. I've brought in the next generation to run this town. You included."

I sniffled, catching another tear before it could fall. "Let's start with your diet. I'm not ready for a new boss yet."

He chuckled. "Deal."

"Good morning." A knock came at the door as a doctor stepped into the room. She wasn't the same doctor who'd been here last night when Griffin and I had arrived, but I knew her face. "Hi, I'm Talia Eden."

"Hi." I straightened, standing to shake her hand. "I'm Winslow Covington."

"It's nice to meet you." Her blue eyes were the same bright blue color as her brother's. Talia was as beautiful as Griffin was handsome. Her rich, brown hair was pulled into a long ponytail that swished between her shoulder blades as she walked over to Pops's bedside. "How are you feeling today, Covie?"

"Good."

She swung a stethoscope from around her neck and fitted it against his skin, under the collar of his gown. "Deep breath."

He followed her orders as she delivered them until she was finished with her checkup. "How long do I have, Doc? Three months? Six?"

"That's not funny," I scolded.

Pops grinned. "I'll be fine."

"All of his vitals are strong," Talia said. "Have you had any more chest pain?"

"Nope," Pops answered.

"I'm going to keep you here for the day," she told him. "Just to monitor everything. But if everything looks good by tomorrow morning, we'll send you home."

He nodded. "All right."

"Do either of you have any questions for me?" she asked.

Pops shook his head.

I raised my hand.

"Oh Lord," Pops mumbled with an eye roll.

"Questions are my specialty." And I asked them without shame.

The first four had been in my head since arriving at the hospital last night. They came out of my mouth in a stream of word vomit. *How do we prevent this from happening again? Is there medication he can take? Last night, the doctor mentioned diet changes. Do you have a list of foods to avoid?*

Talia didn't even blink. She listened to them all and immediately answered each one. "I'll have the nurse bring in some pamphlets. They are fairly generic, but there are some good websites listed that provide much more information in detail."

"Thank you."

"You're welcome." She smiled. "It was nice to finally meet you."

"You too."

Talia walked to the door, and the moment she opened it, two angry male voices drifted in from the hallway. She cleared her throat and the voices stopped.

Pops and I shared a look. We knew both of those voices.

I followed Talia to the hallway, finding Griffin standing just outside the door.

His arms were crossed and his eyes narrowed. Fury radiated off that wide chest as he glared down the hallway to where Frank was walking away.

"What's going on? Why's Frank leaving?"

Frank disappeared through the door to the stairwell without a backward glance.

"Let it go, Griff," Talia said.

"It's not okay." Griff shook his head. "He undermined you. He went to your boss."

"What?" I looked between the two of them, waiting for the explanation neither was giving. Why would Frank go to Talia's boss?

"Please, drop it." She walked over and put her arm on his shoulder. "I appreciate you getting riled up on my behalf, but it's not necessary."

Griff's jaw clenched.

Talia laughed and punched his bicep. "I'll see you later."

"Fine," he mumbled.

"Bye, Winslow."

"Thanks for everything," I said, waving as she walked down the hallway toward the nurses' station. When she was out of earshot, I stepped closer to Griffin. "What's wrong?"

"Frank found out that Talia was going to be Covie's doctor today, so he went to her boss and requested someone else."

"What?" Talia seemed perfectly competent. Young, but how many people thought the same about me in my position as chief? "Why would he do that?"

"Because he's an asshole? I don't know. While she was in there, he got in my face. Told me she wasn't qualified to be his doctor."

"I don't understand. Why would he think that?"

"This is Talia's first year of residency. She got out of med school and the senior physicians here agreed to bring her on. Get her the experience necessary. Because unlike Frank, they realize that if they don't bring in some new doctors, there won't be anyone to take their place when they retire. Talia knows and loves the community. She's smart. She's a good doctor."

"You don't have to defend her to me." I stepped closer and put my hand on his forearm. "Frank was wrong to do that."

He uncrossed his arms, snaking one around my waist to pull me close. "I just don't want you to think that having her as Covie's doctor would put him at risk. She knows that she has things to learn. She'll call for help if she's in over her head."

"I'm not worried."

"Sorry." He blew out a long breath and wrapped his other arm around me. "How are you holding up?"

"Tired." I yawned.

As I leaned into his chest, giving him my weight, exhaustion crept through my bones, like it had been waiting on the floor, ready to weave its way up my legs like a vine around a tree trunk. I breathed him in, taking comfort from that smell. "You smell good."

He'd showered this morning and his clean soap lingered on his skin.

I probably smelled like antibacterial hand sanitizer and hospital air. "They're going to keep Pops here until tomorrow."

"Why don't you head home? Get some rest?"

"That's my plan. I wanted to wait and hear from the doctor—Talia—first."

He held me for a few long moments and I closed my eyes, letting him be my strength. At the rattle of an IV pole's wheels, I pulled away. A man in a hospital gown and robe emerged from his room next door in slippered feet.

"Want to say hi to Pops?" I asked.

"Definitely." He clamped my hand in his, holding it tight, like he had last night. Like he knew I needed it.

When we'd arrived, Pops had been in the emergency room. After the doctors had felt confident that the heart attack had passed, they'd whisked him away for a series of tests. It had taken hours, and Griffin had stayed by my side in the waiting room, holding my hand through every minute.

Frank had stayed too, and whatever animosity the two of them had for each other, they'd put away for the night. Clearly, the truce had ended sometime after they'd settled Pops into an overnight room and I'd insisted Griffin go home.

"Hey, Covie." Griffin didn't let go of my hand as we walked into the room. He just used his other one to shake Pops's hand. "How are you feeling today?"

"Better. I'm in good hands with your sister as my doctor."

"I couldn't agree more," Griff said.

I moved to sit on the edge of the bed by my grandfather's feet, but the minute my butt touched the white blanket, Pops pointed to the door.

"Out. Go. Now." He snapped his fingers.

"After you eat your breakfast."

He scowled, and when I didn't budge, he knew I wasn't

going to be swayed. I wanted to stick around to help with his meal and hopefully Frank would come back. I wanted to find out why he was so opposed to Talia. It didn't make sense and I didn't want him putting unnecessary doubts in Pops's head either.

"You guys need me to bring you anything?" Griffin asked.

"No." I yawned again.

"Go home, Winnie," Pops pleaded. "I'm fine."

"I will soon," I promised.

"I'm going to get out of the way so you can get some rest, Covie." Griffin clapped a hand on my grandpa's shoulder. "Glad you're doing okay."

"Me too," Pops said.

"I'll walk you out." I stood from the bed on heavy legs and went with Griffin to the hallway.

"Don't stay too long." He touched the freckles on my nose.

"I won't. I'm going to head home and shower and take a power nap."

"Then you're going to work before coming back here."

I cocked my head. "Am I really that predictable?"

"Yes." He bent to kiss my forehead. "Call me later."

"I will." I waited as he walked down the hallway, disappearing through the same door where Frank had bolted earlier. When it closed behind him, I gave myself a moment to feel worn down.

Three heartbeats. Four. Then the sound of footsteps forced me to turn around.

"Hey, Frank." I didn't force cheer into my voice because well... he'd irritated me. I was grateful that he'd found Pops on the couch. That when Pops had told him he was having chest pains, he hadn't delayed or waited to see if they'd pass. He'd simply loaded my grandfather into his car and driven him to the hospital.

But did he have to cause drama? Today?

He read the irritation on my face—I was too tired to do a decent job disguising it. "Griffin told you I asked for another doctor besides Talia, didn't he?"

"Yes, he did. Why? We met with her and she seems quite capable."

"She's not a real doctor."

"She's a resident."

"Which is basically an intern. Don't you want him to have the best?"

"Of course I do." But I was also trusting the hospital to know how to appropriately handle staffing. It was the same respect I appreciated with my own position.

"Then don't let the Edens fool you. I don't know what you've got going on with *Griffin*." Frank spat his name. "Just...be careful. Stay on guard."

I blinked. "On guard. Against what?"

Frank glanced over his shoulder, making sure we were alone. Then he inched closer and lowered his voice. "Griffin's worked his way through plenty of women in this town. And outside."

I frowned. This was not something I needed to think about today. Or ever. But before I could tell Frank that was my problem, not his, he kept talking.

"Briggs beat his wife. That's why she left him."

The wheels of my mind screeched to a stop. "What?"

"She was Rain's best friend. It took her a long time to confess that he was abusive. She came over one night crying. Told Rain everything. The next day, she was gone."

"Gone? Where?"

"I don't know, Winnie. She left. It was a long time ago, but that's why I'm telling you to be careful. Maybe she left him and needed to sever all connections to Quincy. But Rain was devastated. She lost her best friend. And there was nothing she could do to Briggs."

I pinched the bridge of my nose. "Anything else?"

"Other than the fact that he's losing his damn mind and no one seems to care that he drives around town with rifles in his truck window? No."

So Griffin and his family weren't the only ones who'd noticed Briggs's dementia. I kept my mouth shut because it wasn't my business.

Frank put his hand on my shoulder. "How are you holding up?"

"I'm all right. Tired."

"How about you head on home? I'll stick with Covie for a while."

"Are you sure?"

"Of course. But maybe charge your phone so I can actually get ahold of you if something happens."

I nodded. As of last night, I vowed to never let that phone go dead again.

The two of us walked into Pops's room, and after a long hug goodbye, I left him with Frank and headed for the parking lot.

Except the moment I slid behind the wheel, my brain decided to go into hyperdrive. There'd be no napping, not after what Frank had just told me.

Was Frank just out to create drama today? Or had Briggs abused his wife? Griff had been so forthcoming about Briggs's dementia. Why wouldn't he mention anything about Briggs's ex-wife? Unless maybe Griff didn't know. Depending on when Briggs had been married, that might have been when Griffin was a little kid.

But Briggs was the only person who lived anywhere near Indigo Ridge. His mental health was deteriorating, and if he had a history of violence, well...that changed everything.

I pulled out of the parking lot and drove to the station. Word around Quincy had traveled fast and I was inundated with questions about Pops when I walked through the door. Janice was practically in a panic.

After assuring everyone that he was fine, I retreated to my office, where I closed the door and logged on to my computer.

Pulling a background check on Briggs Eden felt like a betrayal. My skin crawled as it loaded and I squirmed in my seat. But the moment the report appeared on my screen, I began sifting through the information.

Birthdate. Addresses. Phone numbers. Known relations. And then the criminal record.

It was empty. No domestic abuse. No speeding tickets. Not even a parking ticket in the past ten years.

I closed the screen and stared, unfocused, at my desk. "Huh."

Maybe Frank had it wrong.

I picked up a pen for no reason other than to tap it. The steady click, like the sound of my fifth-grade piano teacher's metronome, grounded my thoughts. It let me block out the noise and just...think.

If there had only been a minor scuffle, no actual abuse, then it was unlikely the police would have been notified to arrest him. Or maybe if Briggs's wife had only told Rain. Maybe she'd kept it secret, fearing for her safety.

I grabbed my phone from my purse and pulled up Griffin's name, my finger hovering over the screen. But I set it aside.

This was his family. His life.

If he didn't know about Briggs, this was not how I wanted him to find out. Not from Frank's gossiping. If he did know, then there was a reason he hadn't told me about it.

*Tonight.* We could talk about it tonight.

After I made a visit.

Guilt plagued me as I drove out of town. A knot formed in my belly the closer and closer I got toward the ranch. By the time I turned onto the gravel road that led to Briggs's cabin, I was sweating, even with the air conditioner blasting.

Griffin had known for a while now that I'd planned on talking to his uncle. I'd told him as much the day he'd brought me Lily Green's boots. So why did I feel like I was breaking his trust? He couldn't come along. This was an official visit.

This was me doing my job.

I swallowed my doubts as I parked beside Briggs's truck. The spot where the fire had been on Sunday was now a circle of black grass. In its center remained a pile of gray ash. The charred limbs had been hauled away. Even days later, I swore I could smell the scent of burning pine.

I walked to the cabin, stepping beneath the overhang. Before I could knock, it flew open and Briggs Eden's broad frame crowded the threshold. Would Griffin look like him in thirty years? They had the same nose. The same shape to their lips. But Briggs had a rough edge, maybe from living alone for so many years.

"Hi." I held out a hand. "I'm Winslow Covington. We met the other day. I came up here with Griffin."

Briggs's gaze dropped to my outstretched hand, then back to my face. "Who?"

"Winslow Covington. I'm Quincy's new chief of police."

There wasn't a flicker of recognition.

"I was up here the day of the fire."

"Oh, uh...sorry." He shook his head, then fit his large hand over mine. "I just woke up from a nap and I'm a bit fuzzy. You know how that goes."

"Sure."

"Come on in." He stepped back to wave me inside. "Winslow, was it?"

"That's right."

"Can I get you some water?"

"That would be lovely. Thanks."

He moved to the kitchen and pulled two unmatched glasses from a cabinet.

The cabin smelled of bacon grease and fried eggs. My stomach squeezed—I hadn't eaten since lunch yesterday.

A cast-iron skillet sat on the range. There was a mason jar on the kitchen counter filled with picked wildflowers. The main room was one wide-open space with the kitchen and a dining table to one side. Opposite was a living room with two couches and a TV angled on a stand in the corner.

The coffee table had two books stacked neatly on the surface. The DVDs below the television were arranged in a perfect line. There was a bookshelf against the wall, but unlike the rest of the house, its shelves were chaos.

That bookshelf looked like it belonged in my home or office, not this tidy cabin. There was a bundle of rolled newspapers. Scattered paperbacks. A hammer that looked new. A jigsaw puzzle. A jar of pens.

The clutter was senseless. Where other people had a

junk drawer, Briggs had junk shelves. There was a pile of unopened bills. A pocketknife that had seen better days. And a purse.

Why would he have a purse? And why did it look so familiar? I took a step closer, inspecting the smooth, camel leather with exposed chocolate stitching at the seams.

"This is beautiful." I lifted it from the shelf, turning to hold it up to Briggs. "Your wife or girlfriend has exquisite taste."

"I'm not married." He chuckled, bringing me over a glass of water. "Not anymore. My wife left me ages ago. We, uh... we had some problems. Turns out, being a bachelor suited me just fine."

I smiled and sipped my water. It wasn't like I could ask him if he'd beat her and that was the reason they'd had *problems*. Today's visit wasn't to confirm or deny Frank's gossip. Briggs appeared lucid. Today was to feel him out. And maybe find out why he had this purse.

"Did you make this, then? Are you a leather craftsman?"

"Lord, no. I'm too impatient to master a craft. I was built for manual labor." His face changed as he chuckled. The rough edges softened. The crinkles at his eyes deepened. "I found that on a hike around Indigo Ridge. Thought it was too nice to leave on the trail."

There wasn't a smidge of dirt on the bag. Either he'd cleaned it after finding it.

Or...

I didn't want to think of the alternative. I didn't want to think that this purse hadn't been found, but kept as a souvenir.

"Would you mind if I looked at the lining and the inside?" I asked.

"Go for it." A phone chime came from the back of the cabin. "Let me go get that."

"Of course." I waited for him to leave, then took a quick video of the purse with my phone, swiveling it around to get a shot at all angles.

The purple silk lining was as clean and flawless as the exterior, and it smelled like new leather. The front flap was monogramed with an *H*.

The inside was empty except for a wallet, tucked at the bottom. A square, seafoam green wallet with a gold zipper. A wallet as feminine as this cabin was masculine.

I plucked it from the purse. The zipper was open. Inside was a folded twenty-dollar bill and a driver's license.

Lily Green's driver's license.

# CHAPTER 17

## GRIFFIN

"Are you decent?" Knox called from the front door.

"No," I lied.

He came inside anyway. "Are you alone?"

"Yeah."

"Damn. I was hoping to meet the chief. I'm feeling left out."

"Mateo hasn't met her either." I nodded to the plastic container in his hand. "What's that?"

"Breakfast." He set it on the counter before heading to the coffeepot. "Remember at Christmas when that baker from California stayed at the hotel? We've been emailing, exchanging recipes. I talked her into giving me her cinnamon roll recipe. I made some early this morning, took a batch to Mom and Dad's. Thought I'd drop some here too."

"Thanks." I popped the lid off the container and my

mouth watered at the scent of cinnamon and bread and sugar. Each roll was as big as my face.

Knox had brought two, probably thinking Winn was here.

"You look about as tired as I feel," he said.

"I am." I yawned.

The coffee I'd been drinking since four hadn't kicked in yet. I hadn't slept well last night, mostly tossing and turning. Each time my arm would touch the empty side of the bed, I'd wake, worrying that Winn had left after another nightmare. Then I'd remember that she'd stayed at the hospital, and not long after I'd fall back asleep, it would happen again.

Finally, as the faint rays of dawn had crept through my bedroom windows, I'd decided to get up and work in the office.

"How's Covie doing?"

"Better. Winn stayed at the hospital again last night." Against my pleading texts for her to sleep in a bed, not that damn chair. But if I was in her position, I would have done the same. "Sounds like Covie should get to head home today."

"Glad to hear it."

"Glad to say it." I didn't want that sort of loss for Winn.

"What's new?" Knox asked, taking a sip of coffee. "Feels like I haven't seen you in ages."

"You sat beside me at the rodeo."

"You know what I mean."

"Yeah, I do." Since Winn had invaded my life, she'd been the constant focus. Before her, I'd head to the restaurant and let Knox cook me dinner once or twice a week.

"You're serious about this one, aren't you?" he asked.

"I am."

"Damn." He blinked. "Thought you'd deny it."

"Not with Winn."

"Remember that time when we were, what, twelve and ten? We made a pact to never get married."

"I remember." I chuckled. "Girls are gross. Boys rule."

"We were going to build a tree house and live in it forever." Knox laughed. "Then we hit puberty and the tree-house plans were torched."

We'd both been fairly popular at Quincy High, and neither of us had gone long without a girlfriend. Though Knox had always dated more seriously, I'd been a typical teenage boy—in it for the sex.

Hell, that's how it had been my whole life. That's how it had started with Winn.

But if there was a woman to steal for the future, it was her.

I'd thought there wouldn't be time to add another person, another commitment, to my life. But being with her wasn't work. She fit. Seamlessly.

I wasn't getting any younger. My family was big and loud and exhausting more often than not. But the idea of building my own legacy, having my own children, grew more and more appealing each day.

I shook my head, getting ahead of where we were. First, we'd start with introductions to my family. And a date. She deserved a first date. "I'll bring Winn down to dinner. Tonight, if she's up to it."

"That would be great." Knox went to the island and slid onto a stool.

The normal stubble on his face had grown so thick it was almost a beard. His hair was longer than it had been in years, curling at the nape of his neck and as shaggy as mine. With the black tattoos on his biceps peeking out from beneath the sleeves of his T-shirt, he looked more like the bikers who rolled through Quincy each summer on their way to Sturgis than a successful businessman and chef.

Though I guess that's probably what people thought of me too. I wore dirty jeans and scuffed boots to run this multimillion-dollar ranch.

"Mom and Dad told me about Briggs this morning," Knox said. "Sounds bad."

"It is." I sighed. "And the worst part is how fast it's happening."

"He's been coming into the restaurant for lunch. Two, three times a week. Seems totally fine."

"I think most of the time, he is. But that doesn't matter if during the bad times he tries to burn the goddamn ranch down."

"Agreed. Dad said he was going to make some calls today."

"It's the right thing to do. You'd do it for me."

"I would." Knox nodded. "Just like you'd do it for me."

I waved it off, not wanting to talk about this today. Not wanting to think about my brother going through something like this.

Knox and I were the closest in age. At only two years apart, the two of us had been inseparable as kids. We'd explored the ranch, building forts and hunting invisible monsters with our BB guns.

We'd both been disgusted with our parents for having three girls. And by the time Mateo was born, nine years younger than me, we hadn't played much with him as a young boy. The times we had, it was as a babysitter.

I loved Mateo, but my bond with Knox went deeper.

He was the one I'd called my senior year when I'd gotten too drunk at a keg party and needed a ride. He'd called me to bail him out of jail after getting tangled in a bar fight years ago. A woman at the bar had been arguing with her boyfriend, and when the boyfriend had backhanded her, Knox had taught the son of a bitch a lesson.

Gone were the drunken nights. Anymore, the two of us would sit on my porch and have a few beers. Sometimes he'd crash here instead of driving to his place in town.

"Are you working today?" I asked.

"Always. You?"

"Every day."

Jim, Conor and the other hands had already stopped by to check in for the day. With all of them out working, I'd decided to stick closer to home. Mostly, I wanted to be around if Winn came out.

"Speaking of work"—Knox drained the rest of his coffee—"I'd better get going. Prep work is waiting. We've been slammed lately."

"That's a good thing, right?"

He grinned. "Wouldn't have it any other way."

Knox's dream was to run his own restaurant. He'd always loved being in the kitchen, working beside Mom, soaking up everything she could tell him. When he'd announced that he was going to culinary school, none of us had been surprised.

"I'll be in for dinner. With or without Winn. Maybe after, if you can get away, we can head to Willie's for a beer."

"You're on." He stood and, with a wave, headed for the door.

I finished my own cup of coffee, then found my work boots and went to the barn.

My plan was to spend an hour or two outside, then take

a shower and, if I hadn't heard from Winn yet, head to town. This was the longest I'd gone without seeing her in a week. With all she had happening with Covie, I was worried.

She hadn't replied to the last message I'd sent her this morning to check in. She was probably busy getting her grandfather out of the hospital and to his home. But still, I worried.

Mom had told me once that we worried for those we loved most.

For Winn, I'd always worry.

It was something I'd have to figure out. Get a handle on. She had a dangerous job, and though she wasn't out on nightly patrols, there were times when she'd be on the streets with the wackos. It was the reason I'd stayed awake on the Fourth. I'd known she was out and that had kept me up until she'd come over.

Those worries were a constant rattle in my head. Even an hour doing physical chores in the barn didn't clear my mind like it usually did.

I was in the middle of cleaning out Jupiter's stall when the crunch of tires came from the driveway. I strode into the sunshine, and the knot in my chest loosened as Winn stepped out of the unmarked Explorer she drove for work.

"Hey, baby." I walked right to her and pulled her into my arms. "How are you?"

She stiffened, shying away. "Fine."

"Oh, sorry." I brushed at my sweaty chest and the bits of hay stuck to my T-shirt. "How'd it go at the hospital? How's Covie?"

"He's okay. Home and settled for the moment." She met my gaze for a brief second, then her blue irises dropped to my shoulder. She stood stiff, her forehead furrowed. There were dark circles under her eyes and the normal flush to her cheeks was missing.

"Did you sleep at all?"

"Not really." She shook her head, then squared her shoulders and straightened. "I need to talk to you about something."

"Okay," I drawled. "About?"

"Your uncle."

"Briggs? Did something happen?"

She nodded. "I'm going to bring him in for questioning."

"Questioning? For what?"

"I went to see him yesterday."

I blinked, trying to wrap my head around this. I'd been worried about her, thinking she was at the hospital with Covie. Thinking about her at home alone, trying to get some sleep. But she'd been on the ranch. My ranch. "You went to the cabin. Yesterday, after the hospital. Without me?"

"I told you weeks ago I was going to talk to him."

"Yeah, but you could have warned me." Weren't we at the point where we shared this sort of thing?

"I needed to do this alone."

"Alone." What the hell? I took a step back and crossed my arms over my chest. "Why?"

"There's a rumor that he has a history of violence toward women."

"A rumor." I scoffed. "Now I get it. You were listening to Frank's poison. There was no abuse. Briggs's wife left him because she was a spoiled bitch. She thought he'd take over the ranch and get the money. When she realized he had no interest in running this place and was going to let my dad take it all, she skipped town—with all of his money, by the way. And before she left, she decided to fuck up his reputation first."

Everyone who knew Briggs knew the truth. He would never have hit his wife. He'd adored her, and when she'd left him, it had broken his heart.

"You should have come to me first," I snapped. "For the truth."

Winn tensed. "I'm coming to you now."

"To what? To tell me that you're going to haul my uncle in for questioning on a marital dispute from decades ago?"

"I'm bringing him in to talk about Lily Green and Harmony Hardt."

My heart stopped. "Why?"

"When I was at the cabin, I found a purse and a wallet. The purse was Harmony's. Her mother confirmed it for me yesterday afternoon. The wallet was Lily's."

"You searched my uncle's cabin." She might as well have slapped me in the face.

"No. He invited me in and I saw the purse on his bookshelf."

The bookshelf that was always so clustered and full of junk I hadn't really noticed what he'd kept on it. The contents changed constantly, and the only times I paid it much attention were when I'd go to the cabin and find the shelves organized.

"The wallet was inside," she said. "He gave me permission to look."

Was that supposed to make me feel like she hadn't betrayed me?

I shook my head, my molars grinding together so tight my teeth hurt. "I can't believe you'd do this."

"I'm doing my job."

"You're taking Frank motherfucking Nigel's opinion

over mine."

She flinched. "No, I'm not."

"I told you once that the bastard hates my family. I've known him my entire life and he's always treated me like shit beneath his shoe." If she was going to get pulled into the rumor mill, then she might as well get some facts to balance out the bullshit. "Did you know the reason he's such a prick to Talia is because he hit on her when she was eighteen and she told him to fuck off?"

Winn blinked. "I, um…no."

"Or how he goes into the coffee shop when Lyla is the only one working and makes her feel uncomfortable? Did he tell you how she's had to excuse herself into the back room twice to call Knox to come over so she's not alone with Frank?"

"No. He…" She shook her head. "What? Frank? I've known him my whole life. Maybe he's a flirt but he's harmless."

"So is Briggs."

She opened her mouth, then closed it, taking a moment to weigh her words. "I just wanted to give you a heads-up."

"A little too late, don't you think?"

While I'd been worried about her yesterday, thinking she was distraught over Covie's heart attack, she'd been on my property, talking to my uncle when she knew we had family shit happening with him at the moment.

"I didn't have to come here at all." Her expression hardened. "By all rights, I shouldn't have told you, but because of our relationship, I didn't want you to hear it from anyone else."

"Our relationship." I clenched my jaw. A relationship that I'd thought was serious enough that she'd come to me before believing Frank's bullshit.

Winn held up her hands. "I need to go."

"Fine."

I refused to look at her as she returned to the SUV, reversed away and disappeared down the road. When the sound of her engine was drowned by distance, I kicked a rock. "Fuck."

This was going to be a mess. A real fucking mess. What if Briggs said the wrong thing? Why would he have Harmony Hardt's purse? And Lily Green's wallet?

I wouldn't get the chance to ask him first. Winn was probably already on her way to the cabin. And the minute she brought him into the station, the entire town would know. One of the officers at the station would talk, and before my family and I had answers, Briggs would have earned yet another black mark on his reputation that would last the rest of his days. Just like the one his ex had delivered.

Decades later, there were those who still believed he'd beat her. And people like Frank, those who didn't like that our family was so ingrained in Quincy, only made it worse.

The rumor mill was about to spin out of control.

"Fuck!" I shouted, then spun and jogged for the house. I swiped my keys off the counter and hustled to my truck.

Its wheels left a trail of dust as I sped along the gravel road to Mom and Dad's.

We could have talked at the cabin. Winn could have questioned him there with one of us present. Why was she insisting on dragging him into town?

Briggs had most likely found the purse and wallet on one of his hikes. Much like Lily's boots. The day I'd taken those to her office, she'd told me she was going to talk to Briggs. As she should. But was it really necessary to bring him into the station?

I stomped the gas pedal.

If Briggs was having an episode, if he wasn't as sharp as he normally was, what would he say to her? It felt like she was handing the man a shovel and telling him to dig his own grave. All because she had questions to ask.

Her damn questions. Winn had been so against calling Lily's death a suicide. But we all knew it was suicide. The whole town. So why wouldn't she just let it go?

This was nothing more than a case of lost and found. A purse and a wallet. Hell, that purse had probably been out on a trail for years collecting dust and rain.

If I begged, would she take Briggs to the main house? Could we have this conversation at Mom and Dad's kitchen table, where he'd feel more comfortable?

I shifted and dug my phone from my back pocket, bringing up her name. The call went straight to voicemail.

"Shit." I drove faster.

The pit in my stomach doubled in size.

Maybe the reason I was so pissed wasn't because Winn was going to talk to Briggs. It was because I was fucking terrified that maybe there was a reason why.

She wouldn't haul him to the station if there wasn't something wrong. Right?

What had been in that purse? Why hadn't Briggs turned it in after Harmony Hardt's death? Why had he kept Lily Green's wallet? He knew where those girls had died.

*Fuck*. If he'd had something to do with those deaths...

No. Those poor girls had killed themselves. The former chief had investigated. Harmony Hardt had been depressed. She'd been struggling with mood swings according to her closest friends.

Her death had nothing to do with my uncle. My kind, gentle uncle who was losing his clear mind.

Mom was in the yard on her knees, pulling weeds from a flower bed, as I skidded to a stop beside Dad's Silverado. She must have realized something was wrong because she stood, tearing off her garden gloves and tossing them on the lawn as she met me by the porch. "What's wrong?"

"Where's Dad?"

"He's watching the news. You're scaring me, Griffin. Is it your brothers or sisters?"

I shook my head. "No, it's Briggs."

"Oh no," she breathed. "Come in."

I followed her inside. Dad was in his recliner in the living room with the news on the TV, his glasses on and the newspaper in his lap.

"Hi, son." His forehead furrowed as he looked between me and Mom. He kicked the footrest of the chair closed and sat straight. "What's going on?"

I planted my hands on my hips. "We've got trouble."

# CHAPTER 18

## WINSLOW

"Can I get you a cup of coffee or water?" I asked Briggs.

"No. But thanks." He shook his head, glancing around my office. His large frame consumed the chair across from my desk. It had looked just as tiny the day Griffin had sat there too.

"I appreciate you coming down here with me today." The smile I sent him was infused with as much warmth as I could muster.

Briggs motioned to the purse and wallet on my desk. "So you want to talk about these?"

"Yes."

Both articles were sealed in evidence bags. When I'd arrived at Briggs's cabin an hour ago, I'd simply asked if I could have them for an investigation. He'd agreed, saving me the trouble of requesting a warrant. Then I'd asked if he'd come to the station with me to discuss how he'd come upon them. Again, he'd agreed.

He was focused and sharp today. Like yesterday. When I'd knocked on his door this morning, he'd joked about having more police visits in the past week than he'd had his entire life.

It was easy to see why Griffin loved his uncle so much. Even riding in my unmarked Explorer—in the front passenger seat, because while I had concerns, I wasn't going to stuff him in the back—he'd talked to me the entire drive to town, asking me questions about how I was liking Quincy and telling me stories about his life spent on the ranch.

He seemed like a gentle man. A person who lived alone because he was content with his own company. A brother and a proud uncle—most of the stories he'd told had included one or more of his nieces or nephews.

It felt wrong to have him here, to be discussing ugly things. Or maybe it felt that way because of Griffin's reaction.

"Would you mind if I recorded this conversation?" I asked, reaching for the handheld recorder beside my phone.

"Not at all."

"Thank you." I put the recorder between us, then hit the red button. After a quick introduction, stating our names and the date, I described the purse and wallet for the record. "You said that you found both of these articles while hiking, correct?"

Briggs nodded. "I did."

"Where were you hiking?"

"Indigo Ridge. I've hiked around that area my whole life. It's a favorite spot. The views from the top are magnificent."

"I bet they are. Maybe one day I'll make it to the top myself."

"I'll take you." A genuine offer.

"I'd like that." A genuine reply.

If Briggs took me hiking, I doubted he'd push me off the cliff.

Wouldn't there be a twist in my belly if I feared this man was a murderer? Wouldn't there be a nervous zing through my veins? There was nothing. My instincts said that something about Lily Green's death wasn't right. Yet as I sat across from a man who shouldn't have had her wallet, a man who lived the closest to the place where she'd died, not a single cell in my body warned that he was dangerous.

Yet I wasn't paid to rely solely on instincts. I was here because we followed the evidence. The trail had led me here. I'd keep going until I reached a road block.

"Briggs, I'm sure you know this, but there have been three women found at the base of Indigo Ridge."

"Yes. It's awful. These kids…they're just kids." Heartfelt sympathy filled his voice.

"It is awful."

A crease formed between his graying eyebrows. "You don't think I had something to do with it, do you? I never even knew those girls."

"Tell me more about how you found the purse."

He cocked his head, staring at the object in question. "I thought you wanted the purse because it was stolen or something. Same with the wallet. Figured you'd tell me when we got here. I get it now. You think I had something to do with those girls, don't you?"

Instead of answering, I leaned forward, bracing my

elbows on the edge of the desk. "When did you find the purse?"

"I'm no killer." He gritted his teeth, not answering my question. "I'm losing my mind. I'm losing *myself*. That's a humbling realization for a man. To know that there's not a damn thing I can do to stop it. I'm facing my own mortality, Ms. Covington. Not murdering innocent girls." The color in his cheeks turned pink. His shoulders stiffened.

"Let's just talk about the purse."

"Whose was it?"

"Harmony Hardt."

He dropped his gaze. "Was that the woman Harrison found? Or Griffin?"

"Griffin," I answered. "When did you find this purse?"

"What day is it?"

"Wednesday."

"Sunday."

That was the day of the fire. "You're sure? This past Sunday?"

"Yes. I went for a hike early that morning. Came home. Put them on my bookshelf to sort out later. Went outside to do some yard work, and well…you were there."

Then he'd had an episode.

"Was the wallet inside when you found it?"

"No."

"Where did you find the wallet?"

"Same place on Sunday. Both were together."

Harmony Hardt had died years before Lily Green. Those pieces shouldn't have been together.

Unless Lily Green had kept a purse like Harmony Hardt's. I'd assumed at first that the H monogram had been for Harmony but maybe it was the designer's logo. When

I'd gone to identify the purse, I'd started with Harmony's mother. When she'd recognized it, I hadn't cross-checked it with Melina Green.

I'd be making a stop after taking Briggs home. And doing more research on the origin of this purse.

"Did you find the purse or wallet first?" I asked.

"The wallet. It was right in the middle of my usual trail. Nearly stepped on it."

"Where was the purse?"

"In a bush about thirty feet away."

"On the trail?"

He nodded. "Yes."

My mind was racing, possibilities and scenarios flashing like a strobe light. There was no reason that he should have found both articles so close together.

Briggs could be lying, though his admission only made it more suspicious. A more believable lie would be that he'd found the purse years ago and the wallet more recently, both on completely different trails.

Assuming it was the truth, why had they been together?

Could this be part of the suicide pattern? Maybe one of the kids had started it as a symbol, to leave something behind. But that didn't make sense at all. The purse was in too good condition if it truly was Harmony's.

And after Lily, we'd all gone around the area, looking for evidence. I'd spent hours up there searching for her shoes. The reason I hadn't found them was likely because Briggs had beaten me to it. But I hadn't found the purse or wallet either.

Who else had been up on that ridge?

"Is your trail well known?" I asked.

"Not really."

"Did you find the boots in the same area?"

"No. They were closer to my cabin in a field. I probably would have missed them except they were by a cluster of wildflowers and I stopped to pick a bundle."

I'd have to scout both locations. Maybe there was something else left behind. Maybe there was more. "The trail where you found these." I gestured to the purse and wallet. "Is it the trail that leads to the cliff? The one from the road?"

"No, they're separate. You can get to the cliff from my trail, but it's the long way around. There's a cut across to the one you're talking about that's about two hundred yards from the cliff. I rarely take it because I head up higher."

Paths swirled like spaghetti noodles in my head as I tried to visualize what he was talking about. "Is there a map that shows any of this?"

"No, but I could sketch one out."

I opened my desk drawer and pulled out a notepad and a pencil, then slid them over to Briggs.

While he went about drawing the map, I studied his face. Was he guilty? *Did he do this?*

I'd asked those questions before, in different interrogation settings.

Once, I'd questioned a man who'd been accused of raping a woman in an alley behind a downtown bar in Bozeman. He'd been so cooperative. Seemingly so innocent. So distraught over what had happened because the victim had been an acquaintance from college. Yet he'd done it. He'd looked me in the face and sworn to me that he'd had nothing to do with it.

It was my nature to believe there was good in most people, but I hadn't believed that son of a bitch for a moment. DNA had confirmed my instincts.

*Did he do this?*

In that bastard's case, yes.

With Briggs? *No. Maybe. I don't know.*

If there wasn't a doubt about his mental capacity, it would be a lot easier to decide. But what if he'd done something terrible and couldn't even remember doing it? What if he'd gone out hiking and run into a girl on the wrong path? What if he'd gotten violent with her?

What if he'd gotten violent with his wife and Frank had been right, that he'd driven her away? Or what if Griffin was right about Frank and this was all just gossip spewed in a small town by enemies?

The truth was probably somewhere in the middle, hidden for me to find.

Briggs finished his sketch and handed me the notepad. The map was simple and concise. He'd circled the area where he'd found the purse and wallet. He'd marked where he'd found the boots. From how he'd drawn the map, there really was no reason that the girls would have gone on his trail. If they'd parked on the road and taken the same trail that I'd taken to look over the area, they shouldn't have even gotten close to where Briggs had found the purse and wallet.

Unless he was lying.

He'd had that wallet for days, allegedly. He'd heard about Lily Green's death. Why hadn't he immediately brought it in?

"Did you look through the wallet?" I asked.

"No, I, um...I was going to. Then I sort of forgot about it." He rubbed the back of his neck. "After the fire."

"The purse is in good condition." I pointed to the

handbag. "It doesn't look like it's been outside long."

"Probably hasn't. Leather like that would be ruined in a spring rainstorm."

Either he'd had it longer than he'd claimed. Or someone had put that purse on the mountain along with the wallet. Yes, both could be Lily's. But even then, she'd died early last month. We'd had rain showers since her death. That purse and the wallet should be in worse condition if they'd been outside since June.

There was a chance they'd been sheltered from the worst of the elements, maybe shaded under a tree. Assuming the purse was Lily's. Assuming she had taken the wrong trail. Assuming that she'd tossed the purse and wallet aside before going to the cliff.

Too many assumptions.

"Have you seen anyone hiking in that area lately?"

Briggs shook his head. "It's private property. Only person who regularly goes there is me."

"You're sure?"

He locked his eyes with mine and understanding crept into his gaze.

If there was evidence of anything sinister, he'd be my primary suspect. He had the means. The opportunity. The only solid element missing—the key element—was motive.

Trespassing was weak but a possibility. Maybe he'd seen someone on his ranch and he'd gone into a rage.

It was thin.

I hated thin. It usually meant I was missing something.

The uneasy noise in my head was beginning to scream so loud I wanted to plug my ears.

What the fuck was going on? If Lily really had committed suicide, someone might have been with her that night. She'd had sex with someone.

Briggs?

That would explain why none of her friends had noticed a boyfriend. Maybe she'd been sneaking up to the mountains for an affair with a much older man.

Maybe...

There were too many maybes. But if he'd had her boots up there, it made sense why her feet hadn't been shredded. She'd been wearing them until, what? He'd pushed her? He'd tossed her over the edge?

"Can you tell me where you were the night of June first?" I asked, hating the way his shoulders slumped.

"Home."

"Alone?"

"As far as I remember."

"Were you doing anything? Reading? Texting? Movies?"

He met my eyes and there was so much embarrassment in his face that my heart twisted. "I don't do much these days. I'm, uh...I'm sure I was home. But I don't remember exactly what I was doing."

"Fair enough." I gave him a sad smile. "It's hard to remember specifics that long ago."

He dropped his gaze to his lap.

It was his relationship to Griffin that made me hurt for Briggs. It was the reason we were in my office and not an interrogation room with another officer as a witness.

"That's all the information I need for now." I stopped recording and locked the recorder away, then picked up my keys. "I'll take you home now."

He stood, wordlessly, and followed me out of the office and to the parking lot.

There were no officers in the bullpen, only Officer Smith

stationed at the door. I'd picked this hour specifically, not wanting there to be an audience when I brought Briggs in.

The drive to the cabin was a stark contrast to our trip into town. Briggs kept his hands clasped tightly in his lap, like a pair of invisible handcuffs were clasped around his wrists.

When I stopped in front of his house, he reached for the door, but hesitated, looking at me for the first time since we'd left the station. "I don't think I hurt those girls."

The uncertainty in his words was a knife to the heart.

Lost for words, I had nothing to say as he shoved out of the cruiser and disappeared into his home.

I stared at the cabin's closed door for a long moment.

You never knew what happened inside the walls of a home unless you lived there. But in Briggs's case, I could guess he lived—preferred—a simple life.

He was like his nephew in that way.

The urge to rush to Griffin, to have him wrap his arms around me and chase away this sick feeling, was so strong that when I drove to town, I had to keep both hands on the wheel to ensure I stayed on course.

He was mad. I was angry.

There'd be no comfort in his arms today.

The station was still quiet when I returned. I sat at my desk and replayed the recording from my discussion with Briggs. Then I got to work.

The purse and wallet were taken to be fingerprinted. Even with the recording, I made notes of exactly how my discussion with Briggs had come about and how I'd found the items in his home. Then I left to visit Melina Green at work.

Melina was at the nurses' station when I arrived at the

nursing home, smiling as she chatted with a coworker. Her smile fell when she spotted me. Melina recovered quickly, waving as I approached, but the damage to my feelings was done.

I'd forever be the face of the worst day of her life.

It was my burden to bear.

She was getting back on her feet and I was an unwelcome reminder of her pain. As time went on, there'd be others like Melina. Others who'd wince when they saw me enter a restaurant. Others who'd turn the opposite direction when they spotted me walking down the sidewalk.

"Hi, Melina. Sorry to bother you. Can I have five minutes?"

"Of course."

I didn't bother with small talk as I pulled her aside and showed her the video of the purse. She didn't recognize it and assured me that if Lily had purchased that handbag, she was the type of daughter who would have loved showcasing it to her mother.

There were tears glistening in Melina's eyes when I said goodbye.

It was early in the afternoon when I left the nursing home. There was paperwork to do at the station. Reports waited for me to review. The city's budgeting process was beginning for the next calendar year, and I needed to wrap my head around the fiscal data Janice had prepared.

But I didn't return to my desk.

I drove home, needing a couple of hours alone behind my own walls to let my feelings breathe. Then I'd go see Pops and cook him dinner.

Except time alone was not in my future.

Griffin's truck was parked in front of my house. The

moment I eased into the driveway, he stepped out of the driver's side and marched to my porch. Even with my doors closed, I could hear the stomp of his boots on the sidewalk.

I dragged in a fortifying breath, summoning no energy for this fight. I hadn't slept much last night at the hospital— not only because of the stiff hospital chair but also because I'd agonized over how to tell Griffin I was bringing in Briggs for questioning.

Without a word, I joined him on the porch, fit the key into the lock and walked inside.

He followed me to the living room, waves of fury radiating off his chest.

I let my purse plop to the floor by my shoes, then faced Griff, ready to get this argument over with.

It would likely be our last. This was the end.

Later tonight, when I was alone in my bed, I'd mourn the loss of Griffin. My rugged cowboy who carried so much on his broad shoulders. I'd miss him. I'd cry for what we might have been. Probably more than I'd cried over Skyler.

Even furious, Griff was handsome. His chiseled jaw was clenched. His eyes, hidden beneath that baseball cap I loved so much, were ice cold.

"You talked to Briggs." It was an accusation, not a statement.

"Yes."

"Mom and Dad called their lawyer. He's to be present for any other discussions you have with my uncle."

"That's fine. Briggs could have asked for a lawyer to be there today."

Griff looked at the wall, his jaw pulsing as his nostrils flared. "It's all over town. I stopped by the coffee shop.

Lyla said she's been asked about five times why Briggs was arrested today. So now my family is fielding phone calls, having to tell everyone he wasn't arrested and it was just a routine meeting."

Goddamn Officer Smith. He was the only one who'd seen me escort Briggs into my office. Not even Janice had been around, having taken a lunch break. Smith, that asshole, was going to learn a lesson in confidentiality first thing tomorrow morning.

"I'm sorry. I tried to be discreet."

"Discreet would have been having that conversation anywhere but at the police station. Discreet would have been telling me first."

"I did tell you first," I hissed, stepping forward to poke a finger in his chest. "I came to you this morning. Do you really think I want to make Briggs look like a fool?"

He didn't answer.

"I'll take that as a yes."

"I know how this town works. There's a lot of gossip."

"Something you've explained to me many times. Which was why the only person in the station was Officer Smith. I questioned Briggs in my office with the door closed. No one was present. I recorded the discussion. Me and me alone. But I have a job to do."

"A job."

"Yes, a job." I tossed up my hands. "Do you know how many rules I broke by telling you first? If anyone ever found out, my investigation would be compromised."

"What investigation? What do you think you're going to find? Those girls killed themselves, Winn. It's fucking sad. It's fucking horrible. But it's the fucking truth. It was suicide."

"But what if it wasn't?" My voice bounced off the walls. "What if it wasn't, Griff?"

"You think my uncle killed them?"

"No, I don't," I admitted. To him. To myself. "That doesn't mean I can ignore the questions. What if? What if it was your sister who you'd found on Indigo Ridge? What if it was Lyla or Eloise or Talia? I cannot live with the what-ifs. Not when I might have the power to erase them."

He expelled the air from his lungs in a whoosh. "I'm not faulting you for the questions. Just the manner."

"I can't be a police officer for everyone in Quincy but not for you. And if you actually took a step back, stopped acting like a stubborn mule and remembered that I'm more than just the woman sharing your bed, you'd realize that what you are asking of me is impossible. That's not who I am, Griffin. That's not who you'd want me to be."

"I'm not—"

"You are." I sighed. "You are."

He froze. Heartbeats passed.

Any minute, he'd walk out the door and out of my life. It hurt already, to lose him. God, it hurt.

Except he didn't leave me. His frame sagged and he tore off his baseball cap, sending it sailing across the room. Then he dragged a hand through his dark hair. "You're right."

The relief was so profound I laughed. "I know."

He planted his fists on his hips. "I'm pissed."

"Deal with it."

"I will." Griff's arm wrapped around my shoulders and he hauled me into his chest. "Sorry."

Maybe I should have fought for more than a one-word apology, but two seconds against his warm, strong body and I let it go. After Pops and his heart attack, two sleepless nights and the discussion with Briggs, I didn't have the strength to argue with Griffin. So I wrapped my arms around his narrow waist and pressed my cheek against his heart and just…breathed.

"You have me twisted up, woman. So fucking twisted up."

"Want to unwind? Call it quits?"

He leaned away and his hands moved to my face, his fingers threading through the hair at my temples. "I don't think I could quit you if I tried."

"Even if we fight?"

"Especially when we fight."

It wasn't a declaration of love. It wasn't a lifelong commitment. But that statement moved me so much that tears flooded my eyes.

My parents used to fight. Mom had called it *normal* fighting.

In high school, when all of my friends' parents were getting divorced, I'd fret and convince myself that my parents would too. One night, I'd overheard them arguing about something. The details had faded with time, but when my mom had found me in my room later that night, crying, she'd sat down on my bed and promised that the argument was normal fighting.

She'd told me that one day, she hoped I'd find a man who'd fight with me. Who'd love me even when he wanted to strangle me. Who'd never quit fighting because what we had was worth a few angry words.

"I don't want to quit either," I whispered.

"Hey." His thumbs caught the two tears that escaped. "You can't cry, Winn. It destroys me. Don't cry, baby."

I sniffled away the sting in my nose. "It's just been a long few days."

"Lean on me." He kissed my forehead, then hugged me again, squeezing so tight that if my knees buckled, I wouldn't drop an inch.

I leaned on him.

And for the first time in a long time, I knew the man holding me tight wouldn't let me fall.

# CHAPTER 19

## GRIFFIN

"What's funny?" I asked.

Winn had been holding back giggles since we'd left the grocery store. "Nothing."

The twitch at the corner of her mouth said otherwise. "Baby. Spill it."

"I've just never ridden in your truck."

"Okay," I drawled, pulling to a stop in front of my house. "Why's that funny?"

"Because it's filthy." Her pretty laugh broke free. "You are the neatest, tidiest man I've ever met. If I leave a crumb on the counter, you sweep it up. I've never seen your hampers overflowing with dirty clothes. When you shave, there's not a whisker you don't rinse down the drain. But this truck..."

I shrugged. "It's a ranch truck."

Keeping it clean was practically impossible. Working in

the dirt all day meant I'd inevitably bring it in on my boots. The same was true with straw and hay. And most of the time, I preferred rolling the windows down to using the air conditioner, so dust was a given.

"I like that it's messy." She unbuckled her seat belt and leaned across the console, kissing the underside of my jaw. "It makes you real."

"I'm as real as it gets for you, Winslow." I tucked a lock of hair behind her ear.

Her dark blue eyes softened and she leaned her cheek into my palm.

Neither of us moved. We just sat there, touching, our eyes locked as we soaked in the quiet moment.

Still moments had been scarce these past two weeks.

The topic of Briggs had mostly been avoided in that time. It was a raw subject, for us both.

Winn had done what she'd needed to do. She'd been right to put me in my place. Mom and Dad had both taken her side too. Yes, they'd called a lawyer, but neither had faulted her for asking Briggs some questions.

Since then, she'd spent some time hiking around Indigo Ridge and the trails that led from the cliff to Briggs's cabin. She'd asked me first, giving me the same respect she would have any other land owner. Otherwise, she'd gone about doing what she needed to do while I'd focused on the ranch.

We were in the thick of summer haying. The swathers and balers were running from sunup to sundown. The end of July was always a hectic time. We were constantly moving cattle herds from one pasture to the next to ensure the grass wasn't overgrazed during these hot summer days. Weeds had to be sprayed. Equipment fixed. One of our tractors had broken down earlier this week, so I'd spent the better part of two days with our mechanic, both of us covered in grease, working to get it fixed.

By the time I made it home each night, I was dead on my feet.

Winn had been busy at the station and spending time with Covie. She'd leave each morning, and the daily worry about her would settle in as an underlying current to the day. The distraction of work helped, but I wouldn't really breathe until she was here. Under my roof. In my bed.

I liked that my house was becoming her place. A few nights this week, she'd beat me home. I'd find her inside, shoes discarded by the door and wearing one of my T-shirts, her own uniform top usually on the floor beside the hamper instead of inside it. One night she'd been on the porch, drinking a glass of wine.

Sooner rather than later, I wanted this to be her only sanctuary. Considering that the rest of her furniture had arrived at her house in town but she hadn't unboxed it yet, I was taking it as a good sign.

"We'd better get these groceries inside," she said.

"Yeah."

She leaned in for one more kiss, then climbed out.

I met her at the tailgate, popping it open. As she looped plastic bags over her forearms, I did the same before following her inside. Then we came out for the second load since my fridge and pantry had been nearly bare.

"What's this?" she asked, picking up the old hubcap Mateo had found weeks ago.

"Trash. You know the place I bought by Indigo Ridge, across the road?"

"Yeah." She dragged her finger across the word *Jeep*, indented into the metal.

"That guy had about a million old cars parked all over the place. Mateo found that along the road that leads to the ridge. I think I'll be finding rusted parts here and there for the rest of my life."

"Ah." She tossed it deeper into the truck bed before grabbing the last bag.

We worked together in the kitchen to unload. It was simple. Boring and dull. But something about going to the grocery store together, pushing a cart up and down aisles, about moving in tandem through the kitchen, made me fall for her just a little bit more.

Maybe because it felt like this space had been waiting for her all along.

"We bought all this food." She stood at the open refrigerator. "And I have no idea what I feel like eating for dinner."

I chuckled. "Steak and potatoes? I could grill."

"Perfect. What can I do?"

"Kiss the cook."

She shut the fridge and walked over to where I stood against the counter, fitting herself against my chest. Her hands snaked around my waist, dipping beneath the hem of my shirt. The moment her palms flattened on the bare skin of my back, my mouth was on hers. Our tongues battled that delicious war.

Seconds away from tearing her shirt off, I froze when I heard the front door open.

"Griffin, if your dick is out, this is your five-second warning to put it away before the girls get here." Knox's voice carried down the hallway.

I tore my mouth away from Winn's, wiping it dry. "Go away."

He ignored me, emerging from the entryway. When he strode into the kitchen, it was for Winn. "Hi, I'm Knox."

Winn cleared her throat and stepped away, no longer shielding the bulge behind my zipper. "Hi. I'm Winslow."

"Nice to meet you." He shook her hand, then shot me a look. "Finally."

The dinner date I'd promised her at the restaurant hadn't happened. Partly because we'd been busy. Partly because we both seemed content to lock ourselves away together.

"The girls are bringing dinner." Knox went to the fridge and pulled out one of my beers. "And I'm taking the rare evening not to be in charge of a meal."

"Wait." I held up a finger. "What dinner?"

"Mom said you were home and that she saw Winslow's car here. So we're invading." He turned to Winn. "Making sure you know there's no hard feelings about the Briggs thing and that the only one to get riled up about it was you."

Winn's frame relaxed. "Thank you."

"You're welcome." Knox winked at her.

I sighed, grateful for the show of support even if I wasn't overly excited about a full house. "So everyone's coming here?"

Knox shook his head. "Mom and Dad already had plans."

"What if we had plans?"

"Did you?" Knox asked Winn.

"No." She laughed. "Just dinner."

"See?" He tipped his beer to me, then after a drink, went back to the fridge to get me one. "Drink this and relax. Be grateful we've given you two this long."

I took the bottle, twisted off the top and offered it to Winn. "You might need this."

"The girls are bringing sangria," Knox said.

"Oh, I'll wait for that." Winn waved off my beer.

"But..." Knox raised his eyebrows. "Eloise made the sangria."

I cringed. "Baby, you'd better stick with beer. Or I'll open a bottle of wine for you."

"What's wrong with Eloise's sangria?" she asked.

"Mom likes to joke that she gifted us kids her cooking talent, except because she gave so much to Knox and Lyla, by the time Eloise and Mateo were born, there was nothing left for them."

"There's a chance the sangria might kill you," Knox said.

Winn swiped the beer bottle from my hand.

I went to the fridge for my own. The moment the top was off, the front door opened again and the chatter of voices was like someone had found the house's volume dial and cranked it to the max.

"Christ, they are loud," Knox muttered.

"You don't get to complain." I shot him a glare. "This was your idea."

"Actually, it was mine." Lyla waltzed into the kitchen with three plastic containers, each a varying shade of green. "Hi, Winslow."

"Hi, Lyla." Winn waved, and I was glad she was taking it in stride.

Winn was going to be a part of my life—no ifs, just facts—and my family invaded. It was their nature. Hell, I invaded too. Though usually it was by stopping to see them at work instead of showing up on their front doorstep.

Talia and Eloise came in next, the former carrying a platter of preformed burger patties and the latter with a pitcher of sangria.

"Hey, Winn." Talia set the burgers down, then rounded

the island to pull Winn into a hug. "How are you? How's Covie?"

"I'm good. And he's feeling great. Slightly annoyed at the amount of vegetables I've introduced to his life."

"Good." Talia let Winn go, making space for Eloise, who also gave her a hug.

"Hi, Winn."

"Hi, Eloise. How's your hotel?"

"Amazing." My baby sister beamed. "Technically it's Mom and Dad's hotel but..."

"They'd be lost without you." I moved closer to pull her into a sideways hug. "Hey, kid."

Eloise's blue eyes sparkled as she smiled up at me. "Hey, big brother."

"You doing okay?"

She nodded, relaxing into my side. "Just busy. You know how it is during the summers."

The Eloise Inn was the heart of Quincy.

And Eloise was the heart of the inn.

"Eloise is my favorite sibling," I told Winn.

"Uh..." Winn's eyes widened, looking to my other siblings. "Are you supposed to say that out loud?"

"We all have favorites." Knox chuckled. "Lyla is mine."

"Griff is mine," Lyla said, popping the lid on one container, flooding the kitchen with a savory smell that made my stomach growl.

"You all have favorites. Really?" Winn laughed, then pointed between the twins. "And you two aren't each other's?"

"I *love* Lyla most because we shared a womb," Talia said. "But my favorite is Matty."

"Where is Mateo?" I asked, keeping one arm around

Eloise while the other tipped the beer bottle to my lips.

On cue, the front door burst open. "Party's here!"

"He was in charge of beer." Knox came over and clapped a hand on my shoulder. "Hope the sheets in the guest bedrooms are clean."

"Hell." I tipped my face to the ceiling.

So not only were my siblings invading to have dinner, but they were also going to get drunk and sleep over.

Now it made sense why Mom and Dad had opted to skip.

They probably suspected this dinner would get rowdy.

It did.

Eloise convinced everyone to try her sangria, promising that no one would die. There'd been a lot of grimaces but the pitcher was empty and my sisters were hammered.

"Let's build a fire." Talia shoved out of her seat on the deck that overlooked the backyard. She staggered the first few steps toward the staircase that led to the firepit.

"Yes!" Lyla cheered. "And do s'mores."

"No." I shook my head. "It's too dry for a fire."

"You're no fun," Eloise slurred from her chair beside mine. Her eyelids were barely open to slits. "Winn, your boyfriend is a bummer."

She giggled from her seat on my lap. "He's not so bad."

"No offense, Winn," Mateo said from his seat beside Eloise, "but your opinion doesn't count. You're the only one who will get to see Fun Griff tonight."

"Eww." Talia gagged.

"Too far, Mateo." Lyla cringed.

Winn buried her face in my shoulder and laughed.

"Mateo, remember when Griff was the fun brother?" Eloise asked.

"Griff was never fun."

"Excuse me." I leaned forward to shoot him a glare. "I bought you beer when you were underage."

Mateo scoffed. "When I was twenty. Six days before I turned twenty-one. That's not fun."

Winn sat up straight. "Contributing to the delinquency of minors?"

"Don't listen." I covered her ears with my palms. "You guys are fucking killing me tonight."

Knox walked out from the house with two fresh beers, handing one to me. "Sounds like you need this."

"Thanks," I muttered. "I'm going to start locking the goddamn door."

Winn snuggled deeper, kissing my cheek. "You're having fun."

"Yeah, I am." I grinned, holding her close as she yawned.

The sun had set hours ago. The stars were putting on their nightly show, twinkling down from their throne in the midnight sky.

I was beat, and even though tomorrow—today— was Sunday, my task list was long. But I didn't want to be anywhere else but in this chair with Winn on my lap, listening as my brothers and sisters razzed me ruthlessly.

"What else can we tell Winn?" Lyla asked.

"Nothing," I grumbled. "You've done enough."

Any embarrassing story from my life, they'd told it. *Shitheads.*

"What about that time he got caught freshman year with that girl under the bleachers at the football game?" Mateo asked.

"No, thanks." Winn waved him off. "Let's skip that one, please."

"That wasn't me," I said. "That was Knox."

"And that was a fun night." Knox laughed. "I lost my virginity that night."

"Way too much information." Eloise stood from her chair. "I need to go to bed."

"I'll help." I nudged Winn, both of us standing to help, because Eloise looked like she was five seconds from passing out.

"Where's everyone sleeping?" Mateo asked.

As they started debating who got which bedroom, I led Eloise inside with Winn following.

The entryway split my house in half with the kitchen at the back. In one half was the living room, the office and the master. In the other, three guest bedrooms and two bathrooms.

The architect I'd hired to design this place had made a joke once about the need for abundant bedrooms. We'd met in town to discuss blueprints, and during that lunch meeting, each one of my siblings and my parents had stopped over to offer their opinions.

For years, I'd lived in the loft apartment above the barn at Mom and Dad's. It was where Mateo lived at the moment. But as I'd gotten older, it had been time to build my own house.

Knowing that this was my forever home, I'd spent the money. I'd given myself plenty of space, not just for the family I might have, but for the one I already did.

The first guest room had three twins, two bunked on top and one below beside a dresser. The walls were planked in a distressed barnwood, much like the siding that covered my actual barn. The gray and brown striations gave it enough character that I hadn't needed to buy art.

I pulled back the blankets on a bottom bed, making

space for Eloise to sink down.

"I'll get her a glass of water." Winn slipped out while I helped my sister take off her shoes.

"I love her, Griffin." Eloise gave me a dreamy smile. "But when you marry her and have babies, don't get rid of my bunk beds."

"Okay." I chuckled, tucking her in. Much like I'd tucked her in as a kid when I'd babysat for Mom and Dad to have a date night.

Winn returned with a glass of water. "Good night, Eloise."

"Night, Winn."

I kissed my sister's forehead, then eased out of the room, hitting the light.

"Come on, baby." I took Winn's hand and led her down the hallway, past the living room and kitchen to our side of the house.

The master bedroom's vaulted ceilings were lined with thick, wooden beams like those in the living room. The fireplace in the corner of the bedroom had a floor-to-ceiling stone hearth. Large-paned doors opened to the farthest end of the deck—my other siblings were still talking and laughing outside.

The moment I closed the door behind us, Winn began undoing the buttons of the flannel she'd stolen from the walk-in closet earlier when she'd gotten cold outside.

"I'm beat," she said. "I hope they don't care that we disappeared."

"They won't." I took over for her, undoing the buttons. Then I eased the shirt off her shoulders, letting it pool at her feet.

"I forgot how this is."

"What is?"

"Family gatherings."

"You mean you forgot how loud and obnoxious they can be?"

"And wonderful and entertaining."

I put my hands in her hair, kneading her scalp. "Did you have these sort of nights with your parents?"

"We did." She gave me a sad smile, her head lolling into my touch. "It was with their friends, since they didn't have siblings, but as a kid, they'd host summer barbeques and everyone would laugh for hours and hours. Like tonight. This was fun. I needed it."

"I'm glad."

"Did you have fun?"

"I did. Though some of those stories weren't exactly ones I wanted you to hear."

She laughed. "You really streaked down Main Street with a gorilla mask over your head?"

"Yep," I muttered.

Knox had told her all about how I'd lost a bet my senior year and the price was a naked sprint down Main. Thankfully, there'd been no stipulation that I had to keep my head exposed, so I'd borrowed the mask from a buddy's Halloween costume stash.

"To this day, I don't think Mom knows it was me."

"I want to be there the day she finds out."

My heart swelled. "You will be."

"Your family is incredible. You're lucky to have them."

"I am." I nodded.

It was too soon to declare they'd be hers too. That tonight, each of my siblings had found a quiet moment, like Eloise had before falling asleep, to tell me they loved Winn.

"They've claimed you now."

She locked her eyes with mine. "Have they? And what about you?"

"Oh, I claimed you a long time ago." The night I'd met her at Willie's. I hadn't realized it at the time, but from that night on, she'd been mine.

"What are we doing, Griffin?"

"Thought it was sort of obvious." Falling in love with her had been effortless.

"Yeah," she whispered. "I guess it is."

I opened my mouth to say the words but hesitated. Not tonight. Not with my brothers and sisters outside, their laughter bouncing off the walls. Not when I hadn't taken her on a first date.

The words would come in time.

So I dropped my lips to hers, starting with a slow tangle. The heat built gradually but with intensity, like the sun on a clear July day.

With clothes stripped, with her bare skin against mine, we came together. One slick slide of my body into hers, and there was nothing to keep us apart.

We didn't need the words. Her eyes locked with mine as her toes curled into my calves, as her body trembled beneath mine.

We didn't need the words.

For tonight, living them was enough.

# CHAPTER 20

## WINSLOW

"I'm going to go hang out with Pops for a while today," I told Griffin as we ate breakfast at the kitchen island.

"I've got to head up to the south side of the ranch where we've got some horses grazing and make sure the creek still has enough water for them. If it's too dry, and I suspect it's getting that way given how hot it's been all week, I'll have to move them closer to a spring. Want to come with me?"

"How long will it take?"

"Probably most of the day."

As wonderful as a Saturday spent with Griff on the ranch sounded, I hadn't spent enough time with Pops in the past two weeks. Or at my own home. Since the night of the impromptu sibling dinner here, I hadn't gone to my house for anything but five minutes to grab the mail.

"I'd better skip this one. I need to go to the house and

clean. It's dusty and stale. Maybe build that TV stand that's been sitting in the box."

"Or..." Griffin set his fork down, twisting in his seat to face me. "You don't build the TV stand."

"My television is on the floor."

"But that one isn't." He pointed over my shoulder to the flat screen mounted above the living room's fireplace.

"At some point, I'm going to want to watch TV at home and not have to sit on the floor so it's at eye level."

"How many minutes have you watched TV at your place in the last month?"

"Zero."

"Exactly."

"But I already bought the stand. Why wouldn't I build it?"

"Because you don't need it."

"Yes, I do."

"Winslow." My name, stated in a way that sounded like I was missing the point.

"Griffin."

"You watch TV here. You sleep here. Your stuff's all over the bathroom and your clothes are covering the closet floor."

"I need to do laundry."

"Yeah, and when you do that laundry, it's going to be in the washer and dryer right down that hallway." He nodded toward the laundry room.

"Do you not want me to use the washer and dryer?"

"No." He chuckled, shaking his head. "It's yours. Just like the bathroom's yours. The bedroom. The closet floor. This kitchen. That TV. This house is yours."

I blinked. "Huh?"

He laughed again, fitting his wide palm to the nape of my neck. "Think it over. You want to keep your place in town for a while, that's fine by me. You want to get it listed before summer's over and the market has its seasonal dip, then we'll get ahold of your realtor and bring the horse trailer to town to move everything out here."

My jaw hit the floor as he slid off his stool, kissed my forehead and disappeared toward the bedroom, probably to find some socks so he could go on about his day.

*Did he just ask me to move in? To live here?* Actually, no. He hadn't asked. There hadn't been a single question mixed in with his string of brain-scrambling statements.

Did I want to move in? *Yes.* I loved this house. I loved the comfort that came with turning off the highway and onto his quiet gravel road. I loved sunsets on the porch and waking in Griffin's arms.

But it was too soon, wasn't it? I'd lived with Skyler for years. I'd just separated my life from another man's. And I did love my little house in town.

That cute, charming little house with the red door that I'd neglected for weeks and weeks.

Griffin, his feet in socks, snuck up on me, still frozen on my stool.

I waved him off when he reached for our plates. "I'll clean up."

"Okay." He kissed my hair. "See you later. Dinner?"

I nodded.

"Have a good day, baby."

"You too," I murmured, the words coming on autopilot.

It wasn't until he was out the door and the rumble of his truck vanished that I shook myself out of my own head and loaded the dishwasher. Then I went to the bedroom and grabbed a load of laundry.

I worked around the house for a couple of hours, waiting to transfer my clothes to the dryer. I dusted the living room. I vacuumed the bedrooms. I mopped the floors.

Should I move in? Maybe that question was unnecessary.

Every pair of panties I owned was beneath this roof. Most were in the hamper, or the vicinity of the hamper. But the others were stowed in a drawer in the closet. He'd given me three drawers, half of the dresser. The same was true in the bathroom.

I cleaned. I brought groceries here after work. The Durango was parked out front whenever I was on duty and driving the station's Explorer. All that was missing was my mail in the mailbox.

Except I knew that if this fell apart, I had a place to go.

Deep down, maybe that was the problem. Maybe that was the reason I couldn't find myself immediately saying yes.

Because he still hadn't said those critical three words. Neither had I.

Each time he kissed me, each time he made love to me, I felt them.

So why couldn't I give them a voice?

By the time the dryer dinged and my clean clothes were in a drawer or hanging on a closet rod, I still wasn't sure what to do. So I headed into town to visit the man whose bear hugs always grounded my feet.

Pops opened the front door to his house before I'd even shut off my Durango. When I stepped out, he held up a hand, halting my steps on the sidewalk. "Now I'm going to warn you right now, Winnie. I had bacon for breakfast. The house and my clothes reek of it. I know it's not on the diet plan, but dang it, I'm going to have it once a week. Maybe twice."

"Okay." I laughed and walked into his outstretched arms. As expected, one hug and I was steadier. "How are you feeling today?"

"Productive. Mowed the lawn this morning. Picked up around the house. Now I get to relax with my best girl."

"You'd better be talking about me."

He chuckled, slinging an arm around my shoulders to bring me inside. "You know I am."

We settled on the back deck, watching the river flow. The lazy swirl, the lap of ripples along the banks, was as soothing as a sunset on Griff's porch.

*My porch.* It could be my porch.

"You look nice today," Pops said.

"Really?" I was in a simple white tank top, denim cutoffs and tennis shoes.

"It's not your clothes, sweetheart." His eyes softened. "Are you happy here? In Quincy?"

"I am. Quincy agrees with me."

"Or maybe it's Griffin."

"Maybe." A smile tugged at my mouth. "He asked me to move in with him."

"Yeah? And what did you say?"

"Nothing. Yet. I'm not sure what to do. It's soon."

"Pfft. Soon is relative."

"I lived with Skyler for years. Don't you think I need to be on my own for a while?"

"Winnie, you might have lived with Skyler, but trust me when I say, you were on your own."

I opened my mouth to argue but the words died on my tongue. Pops was right. I'd lived with Skyler, we'd been engaged, and I had most definitely been on my own.

"You two coexisted," Pops said. "That's not the same as companionship."

"I don't think I realized how lonely I was in Bozeman," I admitted. "Since Mom and Dad."

And then I'd come here, and from the very first night, I'd had Griffin. He'd chased away that loneliness with such ferocity, I hadn't even realized how much I'd needed someone to burst into my life and shake it up.

"You went through an awful ordeal," he said.

"So did you."

He reached over and put his hand over mine. "It's not the same."

For the first time in weeks, I thought about the crash. It had been…how long had it been? The last nightmare I could remember had been after the Fourth. Weeks of peaceful sleep and Griffin was the cause.

"I made a decision yesterday." Pops patted my knuckles. "Want you to be the first to know."

"You're retiring."

He nodded. "It's time. This little health blip put things in perspective."

"A little blip?" I rolled my eyes. "You had a heart attack."

"Minor."

"A heart attack, minor or major, is not a blip."

"Call it what you want, but it made me realize I'd rather spend the rest of my time without heartburn. I see these other old-timers sitting at Lyla's shop each morning, talking about the weather and the gossip in town. I think that would suit me just fine."

"You're going to get bored."

"Guaranteed. I'll probably drive you crazy. Stopping by unannounced. Staying over uninvited."

I laughed. "In that case, I fully support your retirement."

"Good."

"I'm proud of you, Pops. All you've done for Quincy."

"You know, Winnie?" He sat a little straighter. "I'm proud of me too. It's been a good run as mayor. A long, good run. But you have to promise me one thing."

"Name it."

He leaned in close. "The day you fire Tom Smith, you'll tell me first."

"Deal. Well, I'll tell Tom Smith first. But you second."

"Before Griff."

"Before Griff." I winked. "I hope whoever becomes my new boss is as great as you."

"You're biased."

"No, I'm not."

In my short time here, Pops had given me the freedom to do my job. He was always there as a resource, but he didn't micromanage the station or demand to know what was happening with certain cases.

I was sure that Frank had given Pops an earful about Briggs Eden, but Pops hadn't waded into the fray. He trusted me to do my job and make the right decision.

"Can I talk to you about something confidential? While you're still my boss?"

"I'm all ears."

"It's about Lily Green. And Harmony Hardt."

I told him about the wallet and the purse. About how I'd found them at Briggs Eden's cabin and everything he'd told me when I'd brought him into the station last month.

It was all information I hadn't wanted to burden him with after his heart attack. That and nothing else had come from my investigation. There were no more leads to follow, no more questions to ask. Gossip about Briggs had mostly faded away too.

"There were no fingerprints besides those belonging to Briggs," I told him. "Not even the girls' prints. Which leads me to believe that someone put them up there for Briggs to find."

"Why?"

"I'm not sure." It had been bothering me for a month, but as I turned it around in my head, over and over, nothing made sense. I'd even called Cole in Bozeman to get my former partner's opinion on the case.

Cole had been as stuck as I was.

And without evidence, I was stuck.

"Maybe someone is trying to set Briggs up," I said. "To tie him to both Lily and Harmony. That purse might just be a replica of Harmony's. Maybe it was Lily's."

Without fingerprints, I wasn't sure. I'd tried to hunt down a recent purchase on Lily's credit card statements but there was nothing that had shown her buying a leather purse. I'd even stopped by some shops downtown to see if they sold it and no one had recognized it.

"If the purse was Lily's, it would explain why it was in such good shape," I said. "Maybe she bought it and never showed it to her mother." And it would explain why it had been with the wallet. "She might have dumped both before..."

"Poor kid." Pops shook his head.

"There's one more option. Briggs might have been there the nights they died, and he took Harmony's purse and Lily's wallet."

"And then left his trophies on a bookshelf for you to see?" Pops blew out a long breath. "It's a stretch."

"Maybe he doesn't remember where he found them. Maybe he wasn't lucid."

"For Lily, it's probable. From everything you've told me, he's slipping. But Harmony Hardt died years ago. I don't think Briggs has been experiencing severe symptoms for long. Let me play devil's advocate. What if he was there? What if he had something to do with it?"

"I have no evidence." Speculation, however, I had in abundance. "Someone could be setting him up. Someone who wanted me to think that he might have had a hand in their deaths."

"Who?"

I shrugged. "The only person I've ever heard talk badly about him is Frank."

"And that's all old drama." Pops waved it off. "Frank's a good friend, but between me and you, he's always had a bone of contention with the Edens. It's jealousy. Plain and simple. So take whatever he's told you with a grain of salt."

"I have." I sighed. "I just…I feel like I've let these girls down."

"You want answers."

"Very much." For their families. "I'm missing a piece. Had Lily left a suicide note or had there been a sign she was struggling, I might not feel like this. But as it stands, I can't let it go."

"You need to." Pops put his hand on my forearm. "I'm saying this as your boss. You've done everything you can to make sense of their deaths. But, Winnie, people go through dark times. You know this."

"I do."

"It doesn't always make sense."

"You're right." My shoulders slumped. "I was ready to

put it away. To let it go. Then the purse and wallet showed up, and I just...gah. I hate dead ends."

"They exist in this world to torture people like you."

"You're not wrong."

"What's Griffin say about all of this?"

Since our fight a month ago, Griff hadn't brought up Briggs other than to give me an update on what the doctors had found.

Harrison had been taking him in regularly to meet with a specialist. There wasn't much they could do, but they'd enlisted him in a drug trial and everyone was hopeful it would slow the dementia's progression. But it was early on and that road was long.

"Griff knows I have a job to do and he's respecting my position," I said.

"Because he's a good man."

"He is."

"A heck of a lot better than Skyler." Pops spewed the name with a lip curl.

"I thought you liked Skyler."

He arched a white eyebrow. "No. He was never good enough for you. Your parents thought the same."

"What?" My mouth fell open. Mom and Dad had always been so nice to Skyler. They'd invited us over for regular dinners. They'd helped us move in together. "Why do you say that?"

"He's an asshole." Pops chuckled, his chest shaking. "We used to talk about him behind your back."

"You did?" I smacked his shoulder. "Why didn't anyone tell me?"

"We all knew you'd figure it out eventually. Though I think your dad was losing patience. When you got engaged, he about lost it. The pissant didn't even bother asking for his permission."

I couldn't believe I was hearing this. I stared unblinking at my grandpa's profile as he watched the river flow like he hadn't just dropped a bomb on my lap.

My parents hadn't liked Skyler. If anyone but Pops had told me, I wouldn't believe it.

But in a way, it made me feel better. That they'd landed on the same conclusion I had, though much earlier.

"Wow." I shook my head. "And Griffin? Is there anything you want to tell me now?"

Pops turned and gave me a sad smile. "They'd love Griffin."

I pressed a hand to my heart as my eyes flooded. Dad would have dropped everything to help me move my stuff into Griffin's house. Mom would have loved sitting on the porch to watch the sun set behind the mountains.

"I wish they could have met him," I whispered.

"They did meet him."

"What? When?"

"Oh, it had to have been years ago. They came to visit. You were busy working, so it was just them for a weekend. We all went down to Willie's for a drink. Harrison and Griffin were both there."

"Griff didn't tell me."

"The bar was packed and he's not exactly unpopular. But I recall your mom made the comment that she wished you'd find a man like that. A sexy cowboy. Your dad teased her mercilessly for that. Said he was going to go home and buy a pair of boots to wear around the house naked."

"Oh my God." I buried my face in my hands, torn between laughing and crying. Because that was so them.

And the fact that they'd met Griff, just knowing they'd seen his face...I didn't know why it was important to me, but it was.

Tears won out over the laughter, and as a few leaked down my face, Pops put his hand on my shoulder.

"I miss them."

"Me too," he said.

"Thanks for telling me."

"We don't talk about them enough, sweetheart."

"That's my fault." It had been too hard for too long.

"I'd like to. If you're all right with it."

I nodded. "I'd like that too, Pops."

He squeezed my shoulder, then stood. "How about a snack? I'm hungry."

"I can get it."

"You stay."

The whoosh of the river was my soundtrack as I replayed my conversation with Pops. For too long, I'd held Mom and Dad close. I'd hoarded their memories. But we needed to bring them into our lives.

Griffin might not have known them like Skyler, but that didn't mean he couldn't. Through my memories, he'd know them. Through my love for them, they'd be part of our future.

Pops returned with a plate overflowing with red grapes, whole-wheat crackers and baby carrots. All things I'd brought him earlier this week.

"Are you in a rush to head home?" he asked after the plate was empty.

"No. Why?"

"How about a game of backgammon?"

"That would be fun." I hadn't played in ages. Not since

before Dad had died. Backgammon had been his favorite game to play with Pops. Then he'd taught me.

Pops and I played for hours, until the heat from the afternoon sun drove us inside to the dining room table, where we played one last game.

"That was fun." He grinned as he put the board away.

"It sure was. But I'd better head home."

"Whose home?"

"Griffin's," I corrected, wrapping my arms around his waist. "Thanks, Pops."

"Love you, sweetheart." He hugged me tighter, then let me go. "Have a good night."

"Love you too. Bye."

We'd played longer than I'd expected, and by the time I got outside, it was close to dinnertime. I pulled my personal phone from my pocket—the station phone was in the other, and though carrying two phones was a huge pain in the ass, since Pops's heart attack, I hadn't gone anywhere without either, fully charged.

I was about to call Griffin and see if he wanted me to stop downtown and pick up something for dinner, but before I could unlock the screen, the clank of metal on metal carried from the house next door.

"Hey, cutie," Frank called from the garage. He was wearing a grease-stained pair of jeans. A red rag was hanging out of a front pocket.

"Hey." I stuffed my phone away and smiled, muffling a sigh when he waved me over.

His attitude toward Griffin at the hospital still grated on me, but this was Frank. This was my grandpa's best friend and the guy who'd been there when I hadn't been to drive Pops to the hospital.

"How are you?" I asked, stepping into the garage. The smell of metal and oil was so strong I scrunched up my nose.

"Oh, fine." He tossed out a hand to the Jeep. "This vehicle might be the death of me. Especially if Rain keeps losing parts."

I laughed. "How'd she lose parts?"

"Lord, if I had the answers to solve the mystery that is my beloved wife." He laughed and kicked a tire with his boot.

"Frank—oh, Winnie!" Rain poked her head out the door that connected the house to the garage, and when she saw me, she rushed out, coming my way to pull me into a hug. She wore an apron tied tight and was holding a meat tenderizer.

"Hey, Rain."

I'd seen her a few times since I'd moved to Quincy, each on my trips coming and going to visit Pops. She was one of those lucky women who didn't seem to age. Her hair was the same light brown as I always remembered, her skin smooth except for a few fine lines around her eyes and mouth. Her hug was as fierce as those I remembered from my childhood.

Mom had always joked that for a slender woman, Rain was as strong as an ox.

"Are you cooking?" I nodded to the tenderizer mallet.

"I am." She shook it and laughed. "Chicken fried steak. Frank's favorite. How are you, little bird?"

"Good." I smiled at the same nickname she'd called me since I was a kid. "Frank was just telling me about a few missing parts for the Jeep. Did you go wild cleaning the garage?"

"Never." She laughed. "This is his mess."

"Then how'd you lose a part?" I asked.

"Driving," Frank answered. "Somehow this summer,

she lost a hubcap."

A hubcap. The tire he'd kicked was missing the cap. My eyes darted to the front wheel. It was capped with the hubcap I'd seen in the back of Griffin's truck weeks ago on a grocery store run. The one he'd told me Mateo had found on the road to Indigo Ridge.

"I saw a hubcap like this..." I locked my gaze with Rain's. "I didn't realize that you drove the Jeep."

Her smile faltered. "Well, sure. It's my only car."

Why would she go on the road to Indigo Ridge? That was private property.

Something prickled at the back of my neck. An uneasy feeling. I didn't need a mirror to see the color drain from my face.

Rain must have noticed it too. "Frank, close the door."

It took me three seconds too many to register that sentence. It took me three seconds too many to look between my lifelong friends and realize what I was seeing. Because in those three seconds, Frank punched the garage door opener clipped to the Jeep's driver-side visor.

And Rain lifted the mallet.

It took me three seconds too many to shed my personal bias and grasp that these people—neighbors, friends—were not as they seemed.

Three seconds too many.

Before the lights went out.

# CHAPTER 21

## GRIFFIN

*Hi, you've reached Winslow Covington. Please leave a message and I'll return your call as soon as possible. If this is an emergency, please hang up and dial 9-1-1.*

I growled at the voicemail greeting, checking the time again.

Seven forty-eight.

The summer nights were long in Montana and the daylight would last for almost another hour, but it was getting late. She'd missed dinner. She had agreed to dinner, right? I'd left her shellshocked this morning but Winn wasn't one to ditch without a phone call first.

For the past hour, I'd assumed that something had happened at the station. Maybe an accident or an officer who'd called in sick. But as the minutes wore on and she still hadn't returned my calls, the churning in my stomach was becoming unbearable.

I pulled up Covie's number and called it for the third time. Four rings and it dropped to his voicemail.

"Shit."

Bad news traveled at the speed of light around Quincy. If there'd been an accident or something else significant, someone in my family might have heard about it. So I started with the most likely source of news. *Dad*.

" 'Lo," he answered.

"Hey, it's me."

"Hi, how'd the creek look today?"

"Dry. Moved the horses down. All good. Listen, have you heard about anything happening in town today?"

"Uh, no. Why? What happened?"

"Nothing." I sighed. "Winn isn't home and she's not answering. I wasn't sure if something came up and I hadn't heard about it yet."

"No news here. Want me to make some calls?"

"No. Not yet." If Dad started calling his buddies, there'd be rumor of an emergency before there was an actual emergency.

"Okay. Keep me posted."

"I will. Thanks."

"Call Eloise," he said. "If there's something going on, she'll know before the rest of us."

"Good idea. Bye, Dad." The moment the line went quiet, I called my sister and asked her the same question.

"I've been at the front desk all evening," she said. "There hasn't been anything going on that I've seen."

And if there'd been a streak of cruisers blazing down Main with their lights flashing, she'd have noticed. "Okay. Thanks."

"You're worried."

"Yeah. I am."

"I'm going to make some calls."

"No, not—"

Before I could finish, she'd hung up on me. "Damn it."

There was no stopping Eloise, and if I knew my father, he was on the horn at the moment too. If Winn was just out and about, she wasn't going to like being hunted down.

"Then she needs to answer her fucking phone," I muttered, hitting the number to her personal phone again. It rang and rang.

Winn had been good about keeping it close and charged since Covie's heart attack. But when it transferred to voicemail for the tenth time since I'd called, I hung up and paced the kitchen.

*She's okay.* This was probably just part of her job. A random, purposeful disappearance when she was too busy to answer my call. Chances were she was dealing with something important and my constant calls had been a distraction.

But damn it, I was coming out of my skin here.

We were going to have to come up with a system or something. A text, anything, for her to signal she was all right.

There was no way she'd give up being a cop.

There was no way I wouldn't worry.

"Fuck it." I swiped my keys and ball cap from the counter and headed for the door.

She was probably at her place, building that goddamn TV stand and freaking out about moving in. Yes, it was soon for this big of a step. But my feelings for her weren't going to change. So why not live under the same roof?

She was practically living here already. She'd cleaned the house today and the scent of furniture polish clung to the air. Bleach lingered in the bathrooms.

Maybe I could have asked. Said it more eloquently. But ignoring my calls wasn't the way. Was a text too much to ask for?

The trip to town took too long—I called each of her numbers two more times. My chest was too tight, my heart beating too fast. The sinking feeling in my stomach plunged to the floorboards when I turned down her street and her driveway was empty. Every window on the house was dark.

"Damn it, Winn."

I didn't bother stopping at the house, but simply hit the accelerator and headed around the block. The station was my next stop, but her Durango wasn't parked in her reserved spot. I didn't bother going inside either. I'd call there next, but first I wanted to check with Covie, so I steered myself toward the river.

Covie's street was as quiet as Winn's and my heart climbed out of my throat when I spotted her car parked outside his place. "Oh, thank fuck."

*Christ.* I'd about lost my shit.

I hopped out of my truck and forced myself not to jog to his door. The doorbell got punched, not pressed, because as my blood pressure returned to normal, anxiety was replaced with anger.

There was no reason she shouldn't have answered. Covie too.

When his footsteps sounded from beyond the threshold, I was practically shaking as he flipped the locks.

Except...

If she was inside, why was the dead bolt on?

"Griffin?" Covie cocked his head. "What are you doing here?"

She wasn't inside. *Fuck.*

"Is it Winnie?" he asked, the color draining from his face.

"She's not home. I tried calling you."

"I fell asleep with the TV on. She left here hours ago to meet you for dinner." He looked past my shoulder to her Durango. "I didn't realize her car was still here."

"Have you heard anything from the station? Was there an accident or something?"

"Not that I've heard. You've called her?"

"About a hundred times." I dragged my hand through my hair.

It was probably nothing, but every cell in my body vibrated that something was wrong.

"Let me call the station." Covie waved me inside, leaving me in the entryway as he rushed to the living room. The lamp beside his recliner was the only light on in the house. The TV was muted on the movie he'd been watching. His free hand trembled as he made the call. "Hi, this is Walter. I'm looking for Winslow. Is she at the station or out on a call?"

*Say yes.*

The panic in his gaze made my knees shake.

"Yeah, okay. Thanks." He ended the call and shook his head. "She's not there. Mitch is going to ask around and call me back."

"I'm going to keep looking." Maybe she'd gone for a walk. Maybe she'd been at the river and slipped. If her phones were wet, that would explain why she hadn't called.

"I'll come with you." Covie followed me to the door,

stepping into a pair of tennis shoes.

The darkness was coming faster than I liked. "Would she have walked somewhere? Maybe bumped into someone who needed help?"

"I don't know," Covie said, following me down the sidewalk.

We were feet away from my truck when a loud crash came from next door.

Our faces whipped to the Nigel house.

"What the—" Covie held up a finger. "Let me check on Frank."

We didn't have time to worry about fucking Frank. "Covie—"

"Two seconds. Maybe he saw her leave."

"Fine," I grumbled, following him across the lawn that separated their homes.

The garage door was open but the lights were off.

Frank sat on the concrete floor, one knee bent, the other leg straight and his foot tipped to the side like he didn't have the strength to keep it upright. His back was against a tool bench, his face hidden in the shadows of the dark space.

"Frank?" Covie hurried toward his friend, bending low. "What's going on? Are you hurt?"

Frank shook his head, his glassy eyes rolling more than blinking as he cast a glare my direction. "Get out, Eden."

"Are you drunk?" Covie stood and frowned. "We're looking for Winnie. Have you seen her?"

"This is his fault."

Was he talking to me? "Excuse me?"

"I hate you."

"The feeling is mutual. Now answer Covie's question. Have you seen Winslow?"

"Winnie." His expression went from cold and furious to sad and apologetic in a blink. He dropped his eyes to his lap. "Oh, God."

"Hey." Covie dropped to a crouch, putting a hand on Frank's arm to give it a shake. "What's going on?"

Frank's shoulders curled in. "It was just for fun, Walter. It was never serious."

"What was fun?" Covie asked him.

"We're wasting time." I wanted out of this goddamn garage. We should be searching for Winn, not listening to this asshole's drunken babble.

"One minute, Griffin." Covie held up a finger. "Frank, what are you talking about? Do you know where Winnie is?"

"You need to understand, Walter." Frank straightened in a flash, grasping Covie's forearms and holding him in place.

I took a step forward, the hairs on the back of my neck standing up.

"Understand what?" Covie asked him.

"It was sex. Only sex. You know I like sex."

Sex. With who? My frame locked. My hands balled into fists. If Frank had so much as touched a hair on Winn's head, they'd never find his fucking body.

"What are you talking about, Frank?" Covie's calm voice was a stark contrast to the fury that raged through my veins.

I clamped my molars together to keep quiet.

Frank wouldn't say a goddamn word to me. Maybe, if we were lucky, he'd forget I was standing here, because all that mattered was Winn.

"The girls," Frank whispered.

My heart lurched. *The girls.* There was no question who

he was referring to. I knew, deep in my soul, exactly which girls he meant.

Lily Green. Harmony Hardt.

Where the fuck was my Winn?

"Frank." Covie pulled his arms free of his neighbor's hands. Then in a swift motion, moving faster than any man that age should be able to move, he was on his feet, hauling Frank up with him.

"Ah!" Frank cried as Covie shoved him into the tool bench.

"What. The. Fuck. Is. Going. On?" Covie barked.

Frank collapsed into Covie's shoulder, trying to hug him.

But Covie pushed him off, shoving him again. The tools on the bench rattled. "Talk. Now."

"It's an addiction. It's not my fault. I like sex and that's all it was. I swear."

I gulped. "What's he talking about, Covie?"

If Frank had raped Winn…

Red coated my vision and it took every ounce of strength to stand here and not move.

"Who?" Covie asked. "Lily Green?"

The guilt in Frank's eyes was answer enough. "We kept it a secret. They were all secrets. We'd meet out of town at a hotel. Have some fun. That was it. Sex. They wanted it as much as I did."

"What did you do to them?" The words were hard to form through my clenched jaw.

"Nothing. I didn't do anything." Frank's eyes searched Covie's. "You need to believe me. I didn't do anything. I wouldn't have hurt them."

"They're dead," Covie spat.

"I know they're fucking dead!" Frank's roar filled the

garage, bouncing off every surface.

"Tell me." Covie shook Frank again. "Tell me. Where is Winn?"

"She shouldn't have asked so many questions."

That statement had me flying across the room, ripping Frank out of Covie's grip. "What did you do to her?"

"Nothing." He gulped and there was real fear in his eyes. Because I would murder this motherfucker, and he knew it. "I wouldn't hurt her."

"Then where the fuck is she?" I bellowed.

The stench of whiskey on his breath was overpowering as he lost it, breaking down into a fit of sobs. When I dropped him, he collapsed to his knees.

"Where's Rain?" Covie asked him.

Frank didn't answer. He buried his face in his hands and cried.

Covie bolted for the door that led to the house, whipping it open. "Rain!"

There was no answer.

He came back and scanned the empty space. "Her Jeep is gone. Maybe she's shopping. Let's call her. See if she knows where he might have taken Winnie."

The sound of the river grew louder as Covie went for his phone.

The river. The mental image of Frank holding Winn's head beneath the water exploded in my head. Her lungs filling with water. Her lifeless body floating downstream. I squeezed my eyes shut, willing the picture away.

When I opened them, they landed on the safe in the corner. Maybe Frank had taken out a pistol. Maybe he'd pressed the barrel to her head. My stomach roiled.

"I told her not to do it this time." Frank's babble tore

through my brain.

"What?"

"I told her not this time. That it was different. But Winnie knew. She's too smart. She's always been too smart."

"Wait." I held up a hand. "You told who not to do what?"

His whisper was barely audible. "Rain."

# CHAPTER 22

## WINSLOW

The blood trail coating half of my face made opening both eyes almost impossible. With my hands bound behind my back, there was no way to wipe my eyelid clean. Every blink was sticky. Every breath strained. Every step excruciating.

"Rain—"

"Shh." She poked her knife at the gash in my head. The metal tip barely made contact with my flesh, but even the graze was enough to send me to the dirt.

The crack of my knees against the rocks rang through my bones like the vibration of a bell, but instead of a beautiful chime, it was agony. Sheer agony.

My head spun in a dizzy circle, like a spinning top the moment before it collapsed. Blackness tickled at the edges of my consciousness but I shoved it away, forcing a breath into my lungs. *Breathe.*

I'd had the wind knocked out of me countless times in physical training or karate. I'd strained muscles and earned thousands of bruises. But this was my first concussion. Each move was sluggish, and all I wanted was to sleep. Just for a minute.

I leaned forward, the ground beckoning, and twisted enough so that when I dropped, I hit my shoulder and not my face. Wrong move. The second I crashed, pain ripped through my arm. Either my shoulder was dislocated or I had a fractured bone.

When I'd been unconscious, Rain had done something to my arm. Maybe, when she and Frank had been loading me in the Jeep, she'd dropped me. Maybe she'd stomped on me or used the meat mallet again. Something was definitely wrong because my muscles didn't want to work right and any strength in my left hand was gone, stolen by the ache.

But before I could close my eyes and succumb to the dark, Rain's knife was back, the tip digging into the smooth skin at my neck.

Pain had a way of cutting through the haze.

"Up." She gripped my elbow and forced me to my feet.

I swallowed the urge to puke as I stood. "Please."

"Shh." She shoved me up the trail. "Walk."

One foot in front of the other, I rushed nothing. For every step, I took two breaths.

*Think, Winn.* My brain didn't want to think. My brain wanted sleep. *Wake up. Fight.* "Why are you doing this?"

"Stop talking."

"Rain, please."

She lifted the knife to my head, to the place where the blood felt thickest. "Quiet."

I clamped my mouth shut and nodded, taking another step.

Up and up Indigo Ridge.

To the end.

Was this how Lily Green had died? Forced to make this miserable climb? Was this the path that Harmony Hardt had walked too? What about the others?

It hadn't been suicide. *I was right.* All this time, my instincts had been pushing me to this conclusion. But those same instincts had failed me too. They'd failed me for not suspecting Frank. For not seeing the monsters who'd lived next door.

Now it was too late.

The sky was the purest of navy blues above my head. The stars appeared to be dancing in a dizzy circle, but it was my fuzzy head playing tricks on me. The one spinning was me.

Rain had slammed that meat tenderizer into my skull and, in a blink, there'd only been black.

I hadn't even raised an arm to block the strike. I'd be disappointed in myself later. If I survived this.

That had to have been hours ago. I'd woken in the back of her Jeep at the base of the ridge. When she'd waved a vial of smelling salts under my nostrils, only the faintest of golden glows had been left on the horizon. The light was nearly gone now. And there was just enough moonlight to see the narrow trail that loomed ahead.

Rain didn't relent for a moment. She pushed me up that trail, step by step. My lungs were on fire and my legs burned. She breathed like she was lounging on a couch, not hiking to the apex of a cliff.

*Rain.* How had it come to this? Who was she? The pain

in my heart made this all so much harder to believe.

"I thought you loved me," I whispered.

"Loved you?" she scoffed. "Liked you. Yes. You go too far with using that word. You're like my cheating husband. Always spouting words of love."

"He loved them?"

"He was obsessed with them. Leaving them notes. Arranging their secret rendezvous. Even when he promised me he'd stop, he didn't. So this is his punishment."

"You could divorce him."

"That's too kind. Did you know this used to be one of his favorite hiking spots? He proposed to me here. Now he can hike this ridge and think about what he's done. About what he's made me do."

"I never touched Frank."

"No, you asked questions." She shoved my elbow, nearly knocking me off-balance. "You should have let it go. They got what they deserved. So did he. And it could have ended there if you had done what everyone else in this goddamn town has done for years and believed what you were supposed to believe."

That these girls, at least some of them, had killed themselves. And yes, everyone had simply believed.

"I told him to stop this." Rain's seething words seemed more for herself than for me. "I told him the last time had to be the last time or I'd bring him up here next."

"If you want to take me to town and collect him instead, I won't argue."

She laughed, the musical, sweet laugh that I'd known since childhood. It sent a chill up my spine. "Keep going, Winnie."

"Rain, please."

"Don't beg. It doesn't suit you."

I gritted my teeth and took another step. Then another before I stopped.

Why was I making this easy on her? Screw this bitch. With a smirk at my lips, I dropped to my knees, the pain unbearable but I grunted through it. Then I shifted and sat on my ass.

"What are you doing?"

"Taking a breather." I lifted one shoulder, stretching my neck in an attempt to wipe some of the blood off my face. It hurt like a mother, but when I straightened, there was a red smear on the strap of my white tank.

"Get up," she barked.

"No, thanks. I'm good here." My head throbbed, but my focus was sharpening. I let it wake me up. I let it push me to fight.

At the dojo where I'd trained in Bozeman, my senseis, Cole included, had always said the best way to learn was to face an opponent better than you. Rain was better positioned. She had the knife. I had a concussion.

But I couldn't lose this fight. I couldn't die on this ridge.

"Get. Up." Rain kicked my ankle, the sole of her hiking boot scraping the skin raw.

I winced, took that pain and added it to the rest, embracing it as fuel. "No."

"I will kill you here."

"And drag me the rest of the way?" I huffed. "Even a rookie cop would be able to tell that my body was dragged. So unless you want everyone in the county to start asking the questions I've been asking for months about these alleged suicides, no, you won't kill me here."

The air was lodged in my lungs as I waited for her to

respond. A bold move, asserting myself, but at this point, what did I have to lose?

*Griffin.*

I would lose Griffin.

*Find me, Griff.* When I didn't show up for dinner, he would go looking, right? He'd find my car. He'd ask Pops. Hopefully they'd go to Frank's place and see through that bastard's bullshit.

Griffin had been right about Frank, and I'd been too clouded by family history to see the lies.

"Did you put Harmony's purse and Lily's wallet on the trail for Briggs to find?"

Rain kicked my hip and it took every ounce of my willpower not to cry out. "Get up."

"Or maybe you put them out there for me to find, hoping that I'd think Briggs had killed them." I shifted as I spoke so my body would shield my hands.

The dirt was like sandpaper against my fingertips as I clawed at the ground, searching for a sharp rock or edge that I might be able to use to break the zip tie at my wrists. Cops preferred cuffs because even behind the back, a person could break the ties. All you had to do was make some space and slam down hard. But I couldn't lift my shoulder, not with enough strength to break the tie.

"It almost worked. I did suspect him."

"But you did nothing."

"You didn't leave me enough evidence," I sneered, at her and the trail. This spot where I'd plopped down was smooth.

"Up. Now." Another kick. Another wince. But otherwise, I didn't move.

"Did you hit them over the head like you hit me? Was that how you got them out here?"

"Shut up."

"I didn't find any blood around Lily's car. No signs of a struggle. What did you do? Trick her into thinking she was meeting Frank?"

Rain's glare narrowed. "Stop. Asking. Questions."

"That's a yes," I muttered. "Let me guess. You wrote a note—you said that's how Frank contacted them." Which was why I hadn't found anything in Lily's text and call history. "Lily came out to the country expecting Frank. Maybe you promised a little late-night stargazing. A romantic picnic and—"

"Shut up!" The knife's blade glinted silver as it whipped out and slashed through my bicep.

My cry was swallowed up in the night. There was no one but her to see the tears, so I let them fall. Angry, desperate tears. But I would not be silenced. Not tonight.

"You hit them, like you hit me. That was why there weren't any traces of drugs in their system." Any injuries caused by her knife or a wound to the head like mine had been covered up by the sheer brutality of their deaths. When all that remained of a person's skull were fragments, piecing them together to see a prior injury was nearly impossible. "Did you make her walk up the trail too? When did she take off her boots?"

"Why do you care?"

"Tell me. Before we end this, the least you can do is give me the truth."

Her lip curled. "She kept slipping in those boots."

"You should have left them on her feet."

She nudged my tennis shoe. "I'll fix that mistake with you."

"Good luck," I deadpanned. "No one will believe I

committed suicide."

"You've had such a hard time, though, haven't you? Struggling to fit in. That awful breakup with your fiancé. The folks at the station have been unwelcome at best. You're alone and rumor is that Griffin Eden is about to dump you too. He's been in love with Emily Nelsen for years."

I scoffed. "I hadn't heard that one yet." But I had no doubt that rumor had been started by Emily herself.

"Oh, I'll concede that Emily is a fool, but she's been after Griffin for a long, long time. There will be some people in town who'll believe she's finally caught his eye for good. Combine that with the tragic death of your parents, and it's no wonder you've been so depressed."

"It's a stretch. Too big of a stretch."

"I've been *stretching* for years."

I looked up and met her cunning gaze. "It didn't work with me."

"Almost. It would have worked on Tom Smith."

"But Tom Smith isn't the chief." I jutted out my chin. "I am. And I will see you rot in a prison cell for this. For those girls."

However many she'd killed.

The knife shook in Rain's hand. "I will kill you here. I will drag you if I must."

"Fine."

Her hand came to my hair, bunching it in her fist. True to her word, she began to drag. The pain was excruciating and I screamed again, the sound so raw and brutal it ripped through my throat just as a clump of hair tore loose.

"Stop." Tears clouded my vision as my limbs shook. "I'll walk."

That only made her pull harder.

"I'll walk!"

It took Rain a moment to let go, and when her fingers peeled free from my hair, the relief drew another flood of tears.

I staggered to my feet, my head spinning worse than it had before. The trail was wider here than it was in most places but it was still narrow. Maybe she wouldn't have to push me over the edge. Maybe the gash in my scalp and these unsteady feet would kill me for her.

God, if I did fall, I hoped Griffin wouldn't find me. I didn't want my broken body, my death, to haunt his nightmares.

"Move," Rain commanded, the knife by her side. Its blade dripped with my blood.

I started the climb, glancing over my shoulder once. I could run. It wouldn't be easy with my hands tied, but I could race her down this ridge. Maybe if I bought myself enough time, someone would come searching.

"You'll never outrun me," Rain said, reading my thoughts. She moved to stand behind me, blocking any attempt to escape. If I tried to bowl her over, I'd probably trip and roll down the trail.

Step by step, Rain urged me forward. Her knife bit into the small of my back when I didn't move fast enough.

She'd have to cut my wrists free at some point, right? If she wanted this to look like a suicide, she couldn't keep my hands bound. She must not have bound Lily's at all because there'd been no tie marks.

The cuts on my wrists from the ties stung and throbbed. I'd pulled hard enough for them to dig in, just not break. It was a small comfort, knowing that I'd fought enough for my corpse to raise more questions.

Maybe she'd climb down after pushing me off the cliff

and cut the ties then.

*Before. Please, let her cut them before.*

That would be my only chance to fight. It wouldn't be much of an opening, but it would likely be the only one.

The trail curved and with it my stomach twisted. The top was near.

Except getting there was going to be a bit more difficult. Griffin had blockaded the trail.

I laughed when I spotted the fence. It was tall and sturdy. The only way past was to climb over the top. When had he done this? If I survived this night, I'd kiss him for it. I'd kiss him for the rest of my life.

"What is this?" Rain spat the words as she took in the freshly dug fence posts and braces between them.

"A gift from Griffin."

She studied it, looking it up and down. "Go."

"Where?"

"Over." The knife jabbed my bicep. "Climb it."

"There's barbed wire at the top."

Rain didn't give a shit if I cut myself to pieces, but she'd have to climb this too. She looked forward, then behind us. "Go. Up."

I opened my mouth to refuse but past her shoulder a flicker of light broke through the night.

She followed my gaze, her own widening.

"Help!" I screamed.

"Winslow!"

*Briggs.* He was coming this way from the trail that led to the cabin. The light must be a flashlight.

"Bri—"

"Shut up." Rain lifted the knife to my throat. "Go. Down."

I didn't argue as she shoved me back the way we'd come. Down was a move in the right direction.

She pushed and pushed, so fast we were practically jogging. When we passed the place where the two trails merged, her knife stayed on my pulse, its blade slicing tiny cuts into my skin.

"Faster," she hissed.

I searched frantically for Briggs's light. It was on the trail, but he was still yards away. Too far to stop us as we passed.

He'd be chasing us down the mountain.

My knees ached as she pushed, and I braced each time my heel landed, worried the last shreds of my strength would unravel and I'd fall forward.

"Stop." Rain's hand wrapped around my elbow.

Her gaze whipped behind us, checking to see if we were alone.

So focused on jogging forward, I hadn't kept track of where we were on the trail. The slope beside us was the steepest along this path except for the cliff itself. The face wasn't a sheer wall of rock like it was at the top, but the vertical drop was enough to make my stomach plummet.

Bushes cluttered the slope, their leaves gray against the growing moonlight. They'd hurt but they probably wouldn't kill me. No, it would be the rocks hiding beneath those shrubs that would break me.

Rain would push me over, then race to the bottom and disappear before Briggs or anyone else could catch her.

Her knife came to my side. She nudged my arm, sending another wave of searing pain through my body as she eased in close, her voice a whisper in my ear. "Think you'll fly, little bird?"

"Fuck you," I whimpered.

"Let's find out." Her knife left my side and her free hand pressed between my shoulder blades, ready to shove. She was fast.

But I was ready.

Summoning every ounce of my strength, I twisted away, my feet sliding on the dirt path. My arms were heavy and my legs tired, but I managed to kick at the back of her knee, forcing her off-balance.

"Goddamn you," she shouted.

But I was already moving, stumbling to my feet and pushing my legs to run.

"I will catch you," she threatened, the sound of her footsteps close behind. Her hand reached out and brushed my hair.

I slipped, skidding more than running, but the momentum was in the right direction as I rounded a slight curve.

A new light flickered in the distance. *Headlights.*

I pushed faster. Harder. If I could just get to the bottom, Briggs would—

Rain's hand clamped on my scalp. One of her fingers slid into the sticky, slick gash above my temple, and the pain was so blinding there wasn't anything to do but slow.

And fight.

I whirled on her, my knee raised. Years of training came to my rescue. My kick snapped fast, right into her stomach.

I wasn't dying today. I had things to live for. I had to move into Griffin's house. I had to learn how to ride Jupiter. I had to spend more sunsets in his rocking chair and nights curled in his bed.

Rain grunted but kept her balance. She swung out with the knife, slicing toward my belly.

I dodged, barely, my footing unsteady. My second attempt at a kick missed her hip by inches.

And when she swept the knife again, her strike was true. Agony erupted through my stomach. Red seeped through my shirt, hot and wet.

"Winn." Griffin's voice sang through my mind.

"No." Rain stabbed again, the blade sinking into my side.

I gasped, the pain blending with the rest.

She took my wrist and pulled, hard, dragging me past her body in an attempt to fling me over the edge.

I dropped to a knee, my skin tearing against a rock.

"Winn!"

Griff's voice rang through my mind again. Or maybe it was Briggs.

Rain's gaze flickered over my head to the base of the trail.

I followed her eyes, twisting as best I could. The headlights. The voice. He was here.

Fight. I gritted my teeth, squaring my shoulders and planting my toes beneath me. Then I shot forward, like a spring, and slammed my shoulder into her ankles.

Rain stumbled.

And then it was her time to fly.

Over the edge. Her screams dying at the first clash with a rock.

Then there was silence. Sweet silence as I collapsed onto the ground, tilting my gaze to those swirling stars.

"Winn." Griffin's voice came louder and louder, then he was there, picking me up.

"You found me," I whispered.

He shifted, digging into his jeans for a pocket knife. One

flick and the tie at my wrists was gone.

I tried to lift an arm to touch his cheek but I didn't have the strength.

"Winn. Baby. Stand up. We need to get you to a hospital."

I sagged against him as his arm wrapped beneath my shoulders.

"Oh, fuck." His hand pressed into the wounds on my stomach. "Okay, I'm going to carry you."

He made the move to stand and the pain that lanced through my body conjured one more scream.

"Fuck. This will hurt. You have to stick it out for me, okay?" He looked up the trail. "Briggs!"

"Coming!"

"Hurry!"

Briggs could hurry. Griffin could run. But I wouldn't make it. He might carry me down this mountain and drive into town, but Rain had won.

There were words to say. Apologies to make. Promises to ask him to make. But in the end, I had no time.

"I love you."

"No, Winn. Don't say it." He shook me as he stood. His boots began pounding down the trail. "Stay awake."

"Say it back. Just once so I can hear it."

"No."

"Griffin." My voice cracked. "Please."

He didn't slow. "I love you. Fuck, but I love you."

"Thank you."

Then I let out one more breath.

And the stars vanished.

# CHAPTER 23

## GRIFFIN

"Wake up, baby." My lips brushed against her knuckles. "Why isn't she waking up?"

"She lost a lot of blood," Talia said.

"I can't lose her." I clutched Winn's hand. "I can't…"

The lump in my throat that had been there for three days felt like a noose around my neck.

"You should get some sleep." Talia put her hand on my shoulder. "Get out of this chair and walk around at least."

I shook my head. "I'm not leaving her."

"Griff—"

"I'm not leaving."

Talia sighed. "Can I bring you anything?"

"Coffee."

"Okay." She squeezed my shoulder, then slipped out of the room.

She wasn't the only person who'd tried convincing me to go home. My parents. My siblings. Covie. The nurses. The doctors. Everyone was trying to get me to disconnect.

To let go of her hand.

Because there was a real chance that she wasn't going to wake up. She hadn't once since I'd carried her off Indigo Ridge.

"Come on, Winn. Wake up," I whispered against her skin. It felt too cold, and she looked too pale in the bed. The gash on her head had been stitched, the blood cleaned from her face and hair. But her lips were this ugly gray shade. Her eyelids blue and her cheeks hollow.

"We have so much ahead of us. But I need you to wake up."

In the days that I'd been here, I'd begged her countless times. Because maybe if she could just hear my voice…

"Find your way back to me. Please. You can't leave me yet."

There was so much I had to tell her. So much good she'd done that she deserved to celebrate.

"Winslow." I closed my eyes. "I love you. We've got a lifetime together. But you have to wake up, baby. You have to wake up. Find your way back to me."

She didn't move.

My sister brought me coffee all morning.

Covie came in and sat quietly by my side through the afternoon.

The nurse brought me a fresh blanket after midnight.

Winn didn't move.

Until the sun began to rise on the horizon.

Those beautiful blue eyes opened. Finally.

And she found her way back.

# CHAPTER 24

## WINSLOW

"Ready?" Griff asked as we stood beside his truck.

I clasped my hand with his. "Ready."

We walked, side by side, to Melina Green's front door. My pace was slow and awkward. Everything over the past two weeks had been slow and awkward. But it gave me time to study her yard as we walked.

Her flower beds were overflowing with purple coneflower blooms. The lawn had been recently mowed and the scent of grass filled my nose. Robins chirped as they landed in the large oak tree that shaded part of her house. A fresh morning.

A new day.

Before Griff could knock, the door opened and Melina stepped outside. Her face was alight with gratitude.

"Hi." I smiled.

"Hi." Her eyes turned glassy and then she was there, hugging me too tight.

It hurt. My shoulder had been dislocated and only yesterday I'd stopped wearing the sling. But I didn't dare flinch. I simply squeezed Griffin's hand because he'd been helping me bear the pain for the past two weeks.

Melina held me for a long moment, until Griffin must have realized I was hurting because he put his hand on her shoulder.

"Should we go inside?"

"Of course." She let me go, wiping the tears away, and waved us inside.

Sunlight streamed through the bay window in her living room. Griffin and I sat on the smooth leather couch, his arm going behind my shoulders the moment I was down so I could lean into his side.

My body was healing but it wasn't happening as fast as I'd like. He'd tried to convince me to put this visit off for another week and spend yet another day resting at home. But it was time to get back to life.

Living was precious. Every moment. If the night at Indigo Ridge had taught me anything, it was to make the most of my time on this earth.

For a first major excursion out of the house, visiting Melina was exactly the way to start.

"How are you feeling?" she asked, taking the chair across from the couch. "Can I get you anything?"

"No, thanks. And I'm okay. This guy has been taking good care of me."

Griffin leaned over and kissed my hair. "When she listens. She's not the best patient."

I elbowed him in the ribs. The fast movement caused a

stitch of pain and I grunted.

"See what I mean?" he teased.

"Thank you for coming over." Melina looked to the fireplace mantel, crowded with framed photos of her daughter. "And for everything you've done for Lily."

"I was just doing my job."

"No." She gave me a sad smile. "You did so much more."

In the past two weeks, numerous suicide cases had been reopened and their files flooded with new information. Frank had been arrested the night Rain had tried to kill me, and his confession had shocked the entire community.

Four of the seven suicides in the past decade hadn't been suicides. He'd been having an affair with each of those young women and each had been murdered by his wife.

Frank had mastered secrets and deception, somehow convincing the women to keep their trysts a secret. He was a charismatic man. Good-looking. I didn't fault those girls for falling for his act. I only wished one of them had left a bread crumb. Or that the former chief had pushed harder to find one.

Now that we knew where to look, evidence was pouring in.

Frank would meet each of the women at hotels in neighboring towns. Credit card receipts showed that he'd paid for their nights together. They'd communicated by paper notes, never signed, but his handwriting had been easily matched. Lily Green had kept a few of the notes. Melina had found them when she'd finally worked up the courage to clean her daughter's room. The notes had been hidden beneath Lily's mattress.

Maybe if I'd pushed her to look sooner, I would have recognized Frank's handwriting.

He'd drop those notes to Lily at his trips to the bank. Harmony Hardt had worked at a restaurant in town and he'd admitted to leaving her messages on the backs of his receipts.

There was more to uncover, but the gist of it was all over town. Frank would sneak his affairs, fooling everyone but Rain. And when she'd finally snap, there would be a death.

Rain's first victim had died of an overdose. She'd lived alone and it was believed that Rain had broken in and forced her to take the pills—Frank hadn't known the specifics and Rain wasn't alive to ask. Apparently the overdose hadn't been enough of a punishment for Frank, so Rain had switched her tactics.

"I still can't believe it." Melina shook her head. "Rain used to volunteer at the nursing home. She'd come in and do painting classes with the residents. She always seemed like such a sweet woman."

"You weren't the only one who was fooled." She'd fooled me my entire life. Pops too.

He'd taken this hard. Pops had loved Frank and Rain. Truly. He'd believed they were family and this betrayal had hit him so hard that he'd decided to move.

After decades of living in the house that had been my grandmother's, that had been my father's, Pops was moving. He couldn't bear to live next door to the Nigel house.

So he was taking mine.

Griffin had gone over yesterday to collect the rest of my things. Most of the furniture I'd bought was going to charity. There were a few families in the area who'd fallen on hard times, and if my furniture could give them a pick-me-up, then I was happy to give it away. It wasn't like I needed it at Griff's house—our house.

Melina's jaw clenched. "What will happen to Frank?"

"He's being charged as an accessory to murder. His lawyer might encourage him to plead not guilty, but he will go to prison."

His confession was going to work against him. He'd likely say that it had been coerced or was given under duress. There was nothing to do but wait and let it play out in court. But I had confidence in my officers.

Mitch had been the one to respond to the call that horrible night. Pops had stayed with Frank to ensure the bastard hadn't tried to skip town. Meanwhile, Griffin had taken a gamble and raced to Indigo Ridge, calling Briggs along the way.

If not for them both, I would have suffered Rain's fate.

"I think I hate him more than I hate her," Melina said. "Maybe that's a strange way to see it. But he knew. He knew she'd killed and he kept having his affairs."

"It's not strange." Because I felt the same way.

"I'm glad she's dead." Melina's eyes widened when she realized what she'd said. "Sorry."

"Don't be," Griffin said. "You're not the only one."

He hadn't said much about Rain since that night. He'd told me that her body had been found on the side of the mountain, her neck broken from the fall. Otherwise, he'd stayed quiet.

Too quiet.

There was fury in his gaze. A flame so hot it burned the same shade as those stunning blue irises. The rage had surfaced a few times in the past two weeks, mostly when I'd been in pain.

He'd clench his jaw. He'd ball his fists. He'd keep it in check until I was feeling better. Then he'd call his mom or one of his sisters to come and hang out with me while he went for a hard ride on Jupiter.

Thank God for that horse. He'd helped get Griff through the past two weeks. But sooner or later we'd have to talk about what had happened.

"Have you spoken to the other parents?" Melina asked.

"Not yet. You're my first visit." The others I'd go see once I was back to work at the station, but I had another two weeks of rest at home. The surgery to repair the stab wounds had gone well, but combined with the concussion, my body had been through a major ordeal.

The doctors had needed to restart my heart on the operating table.

"I can't imagine how they're feeling." Melina dropped her gaze to her lap. "To think for so many years that their girls...I'm just glad to have the truth."

"I'm sorry you lost her."

"Me too." Her eyes were brimming with unshed tears.

Even with time, there were wounds that would never heal.

A tear dripped down Melina's cheek. Then another. She cast her gaze once more to the photographs of her beautiful daughter.

"We'll get out of your hair." Griffin stood first, holding out a hand to help me to my feet.

We said goodbye to Melina, leaving her to find whatever peace possible, and climbed into Griffin's truck.

The moment the door was closed, I let out the breath I'd been holding.

"You okay?" he asked, sliding behind the wheel.

"Just tired."

"That's enough for one day."

"I wanted to visit Pops. See how the packing is going."

"It's going fine. He knows where to find us. You're taking a nap."

I frowned but had learned in the past two weeks that arguing was pointless. So I relaxed into the seat as Griffin drove us home.

"I'm proud of you." He reached over and lifted a hand off my lap, bringing it to his lips. "You never gave up. Even when we all told you to drop it. Maybe if I hadn't..."

"This isn't your fault."

He looked over and the pain in those eyes shot straight to my heart. "I thought I'd lost you."

"You didn't."

"But—" He swallowed hard, his Adam's apple bobbing. Then he drove in silence, taking us home. Three cars crowded the space next to my Durango. One belonged to Harrison. The other, Pops. The third, Briggs.

"So much for that nap."

"They get ten minutes," Griff said. "Then I'm kicking them out."

"No, let them stay." It filled my heart that so many people had come to check on me. On us.

Griff stared at the back of Briggs's truck, making no move to go inside.

"What?" I asked.

"For a while, I worried it was him. That he'd done something and blacked it out."

Briggs had come every day since I'd been released from the hospital, each time with a bouquet of flowers. I'd be forever grateful that he'd found his way to the hiking trail in the dark. "He saved my life."

"He did."

"If his dementia gets worse, if he needs help, we're moving him in."

"Yes. Into Mom and Dad's house." Griffin nodded. "They talked about it. They're going to start having him down more. Checking on him more. When it's time, they'll move him to their place."

"We have room."

"So do they. And I get you to myself for a while."

"Okay," I whispered.

His shoulders slumped. His eyes stayed glued to the windshield as the air conditioner blew through the cab.

I rested my head against the seat, reaching over to slide my hand down his arm. "Hey. I'm okay, Griff."

"Yeah." He cleared his throat, then jumped into action, shutting off the truck and hopping out, rounding the hood to get my door.

Whatever he was feeling was locked away because we had company and it wasn't the time.

The guys were all inside when we walked through the door. Pops wrapped me in a gentle hug before guiding me to the living room to sit. Briggs had brought another bouquet of flowers, daisies today. Harrison had brought one of Anne's cherry pies. Between Anne, Knox and Lyla, we had enough food in the fridge to feed the entire Eden family for a week.

Our family stayed for an hour, mostly talking to Griffin about the goings-on at the ranch and what was happening in town. After lunch, when my eyelids began to droop, Griffin kicked them out, but not before they helped make a dent in the food and the pie.

I yawned twice before Griff lifted me from the couch and carried me to bed. "I can walk."

"I can carry you."

"Fine." I leaned against his shoulder, breathing in his spicy scent before he set me down beside the bed, pulling away the covers to tuck me in.

My head was on the pillow when he crouched down to kiss my hair. "I'm going to head out for a quick ride."

"No, you're not." I caught his wrist before he could run away. "You're going to come to bed too."

"You'll rest better if I'm not here."

"Not true and you know it. Lie with me. Please."

He blew out a frustrated breath but he didn't deny me. Griff stood and kicked off his boots, then unbuckled his belt so it wouldn't dig into my back. Then he eased onto the mattress, carefully sliding one arm beneath my pillow, inching close until his chest was flush with my spine.

But he didn't hold me. He hadn't held me since I'd come home from the hospital.

"Put your arm around me."

"I don't want to hurt you."

"I'm okay, Griff."

"I don't—"

"I'm okay. Please don't pull away from me. I'll drag you back if I have to, but it'll hurt."

He sighed and buried his face in my hair. Then slowly, his arm wound around my waist, resting against the spot where the bandages were gone but the stitches remained.

"See?" I twisted, the move causing a bit of a sting but I shoved it down. "Don't carry this on your own. Don't shut me out."

His frame slumped against mine. "It rocked me."

"Me too."

"The idea of you going back to work, I just…I worry. I've never felt this kind of fear before. It's making me unsteady."

"Then we lean on each other. We worry about each other. But we can't let it run our lives. I'm okay."

"You're okay," he breathed, pulling me closer.

"Good." I burrowed into his arms. "Now kiss me."

He barely grazed the corner of my mouth.

"A real kiss."

"Winn—"

"Kiss me, Griffin."

He frowned, but obeyed, his lips lingering against mine.

"Stubborn," I mumbled before dragging my tongue against his lower lip until finally, he kissed me like I wanted to be kissed, breaking away when we were both breathless. "I love you."

He touched the freckles on my nose. "I love you."

"After our nap, can we do something?"

"Depends. What do you want to do?"

I smiled. "You owe me a first date."

# EPILOGUE

## WINSLOW

*ONE YEAR LATER...*

"Hey, baby," Griffin answered. "Having fun?"

"Don't even start," I muttered. "You know I hate traffic duty."

He laughed. "You volunteered."

"Because I'm trying to be a good boss."

"The chief of police doesn't need to man the speed traps."

"We don't have speed traps, Griffin."

"Sure," he deadpanned. "So you're not parked behind the bush off the highway at the John Deere dealership."

*Not anymore.* I glanced in my rearview at the bush and the dealership. "What are you guys doing?"

"We're getting ready to go for a ride around the ranch."

"By ride, you'd better mean in a truck and not on Jupiter."

Griff had made a comment this morning that Hudson was old enough to start riding with him on the horse. I'd thought he was joking. He'd better have been joking. My baby was not getting on a horse. Not yet.

"He's got to learn sometime."

"Griffin," I warned. "He's two months old."

My husband chuckled. "Yes, we're riding around in the truck."

"Good. Have fun."

"I'm going to swing by Mom and Dad's. Say hi. See how Briggs is settling into the loft at the barn."

"Give them all a hug for me. Maybe two for Briggs."

Briggs had moved in last week. It had been Mateo's idea to have Briggs closer to Harrison and Anne, but since Briggs didn't want his cabin to sit empty, they'd traded homes. Mateo was now in the mountains while Briggs was closer to family.

In the past year, he'd started on some medication that seemed to help but every now and again he'd have an episode where his mind would falter and he'd lose time and place. The worst incident had happened a month ago, prompting this move. Briggs had gone hiking and gotten lost. When Griffin and Harrison had gone out to find him, he'd gotten combative with them both, not having a clue who either of them was.

When Harrison had told Briggs later what had happened, Briggs had made us all promise that if he acted like that again, they'd put him in a home. Mateo had suggested the barn loft as an alternative. We hoped that maybe if Briggs was living closer to the place where he'd grown up as a child, it would give him more of a foundation.

None of us knew what would happen, but it was worth a try.

"Will you take your mom's pie plate when you go?" I asked.

"It's already loaded."

In the background, my son whimpered.

"How's Hudson doing?"

"He's ready for a nap. We'll drive around. Let him conk out in his seat. Then head to Mom's."

"I've got"—I checked the clock on the cruiser's dash—"four hours to go. Then I'll be home."

"We'll be waiting. Love you."

"Love you too." I ended the call and continued driving toward Main.

Technically, I was still on maternity leave. I had three weeks left. But we'd been a bit short on staff for the past few months, ever since I'd fired Tom Smith—pregnancy had zapped my patience. So even though I was supposed to be at home, I'd been covering a few shifts to lighten the load at the station until we could get another officer hired.

The tourist traffic had lessened considerably this past week now that the school year had begun. It was nice to see a few empty spaces downtown, though soon there'd be hunters and then the Christmas crowd.

Quincy during the holidays was magical.

Though I was biased. Memories of childhood Christmases here with Pops and my parents were some of my fondest. And this past year had been unforgettable.

Griffin and I had gotten married three days before Christmas. The ceremony had been a small, intimate affair at The Eloise Inn. He'd dazzled in a black suit. I'd worn my mother's wedding dress. After Pops had walked me down the aisle and Griffin and I had exchanged vows, we'd opened the hotel's doors for a reception that had strained the building's seams.

Most of the guest rooms had been reserved for family, and for the first time ever, I'd stayed at The Eloise. Griffin and I had locked ourselves in the best suite for three days.

Ours was the last wedding hosted at The Eloise before the renovations had started. Harrison and Anne had bought the building next door and annexed it to the hotel for events. And the restaurant no longer resembled an open dining room, but a trendy, upscale steakhouse.

When I'd been pregnant with Hudson, Griff and I had gone down three times a week because my cravings had been out of control. Knox had been like a magician, always making exactly what I hadn't even known I'd wanted.

We hadn't planned to get pregnant so soon, but after the incident on Indigo Ridge, my birth control had been interrupted and we'd decided not to bother.

Life was short. Griffin and I were going to live it to the fullest, and this family we were making together was the light of my life.

My hand drifted to my belly. Maybe we'd visit the restaurant as often this time around too. My children would be less than a year apart. Hopefully, that meant they'd be close friends, if not when they were little, then when they were older.

I reached the end of Main and headed down the highway. Traffic was light and most cars I passed would do a little dip, their fenders dropping as they tapped their brakes. Ten miles later, I was about to turn around and head back to town when I spotted a gray sedan with New York plates pulled over on the side of the road.

Slowing, I eased onto the shoulder and flipped on the cruiser's light bar so other cars would give us some space.

Then I made sure I had my sidearm on my hip before I got out and approached the car.

Griffin had insisted I wear a vest when I was on patrol duty. It was hot on top of my black blouse, but my husband worried. So I wore the vest.

The driver's side window of the sedan was down, and the sound of a baby crying hit me first. That unmistakable sound twisted my heart. So did the sound of a woman sobbing as hard as the infant.

"Hello?"

The woman behind the wheel didn't hear me.

"Miss?" I called.

She gasped and practically jumped out of her seat belt.

"Sorry." I held up my hands.

"Oh my God." She slapped one hand to her heart while the other tucked a lock of blond hair out of her face. "I'm sorry, Officer. I can move my car."

"It's all right." I leaned to peek inside. "Is everything okay?"

She nodded and wiped furiously at her face, trying to dry the tears. "Just a bad day. Actually, a really bad day. Maybe the fifth worst day of my life. Sixth. No, fifth. We've been in the car for days and my son won't stop crying. He's hungry. I'm hungry. We need a nap and a shower, but I'm lost. I've been driving around for thirty minutes trying to find this place where we're supposed to be staying."

"Where are you going?" I asked, casting my eyes to the backseat.

Her baby continued to wail, his face red and his tiny fists clenched.

She reached for a sticky note, holding it up. "Juniper Hill."

"Juniper Hill?" Only one person lived on that gravel road.

"Yes. Do you know where it is?" She tossed her hand toward the windshield. "My directions led me right here. But there isn't a road marked Juniper Hill. Or any road marked, period."

"Montana country roads rarely are marked. But I can show you."

"Really?" The hope in her sad eyes broke my heart. It was like this woman hadn't had a helping hand in a long, long time.

"Of course." I held out my hand. "I'm Winslow."

"Memphis."

The name didn't surprise me. Eloise had been uttering it for weeks. Knox had been grumbling it for just as long.

"Welcome to Quincy, Memphis."

"Thank you." She breathed and a new wash of tears cascaded down her cheeks.

I hurried to my cruiser, then led the way to Juniper Hill.

Four hours later, after I'd traded out the cruiser for my Durango, I was home.

Griffin was rocking Hudson on the porch, a bottle held to my son's mouth. "Hey. How'd it go?"

"Good." I took the chair next to him and waved for him to hand me my boy. When he was nestled in the crook of my arm, I breathed.

Hudson had my dark blue eyes, but otherwise I hoped he'd resemble Griffin. He already had his father's thick, brown hair. And even at only two months old, he had Griffin's steady nature. He'd rarely screamed, unlike Memphis's son, Drake.

"Remember that girl Eloise hired to work at the hotel?

Memphis Ward? The one who was moving here from New York?"

"Yeah."

"I met her today. She got lost trying to find Knox's house. Her son is about the same age as Hudson. But not as cute."

"No child is as cute as Hudson."

"Exactly." I pulled the empty bottle from my son's mouth and lifted him to my shoulder, kissing his cheek as I patted his back. "She seems sweet. A little frazzled but I guess we all are on our bad days."

Griffin shook his head and chuckled. "I still can't believe that Eloise convinced Knox to let a stranger live above his garage. He's gonna go nuts. The whole point of him building that house on a nowhere road was to avoid people."

Eloise had been struggling to find dependable employees at the inn lately, and when Memphis had applied, she'd been so far overqualified that Eloise had assumed it was a joke. Though she'd done a virtual interview, and when Memphis had accepted the job, Eloise had been thrilled.

Only a week later, after trying to find an apartment and coming up dry, Memphis had called Eloise to back out of the job. Except my sister-in-law wasn't one to be deterred by road blocks. She'd convinced Knox to let Memphis stay at his place for a few months until a new rental opened up in town.

Memphis was going to be renting the studio apartment Knox had built above his garage. The apartment intended for company because he didn't want to have people crash in his guest rooms like they did when they came to visit us.

"Your sister should be the next mayor."

Griffin chuckled. "Speaking of mayors."

A familiar blue Bronco came rolling down the road with Pops behind the wheel. Since he'd retired earlier in the year, he made it a point to visit a few times a week and spoil his great-grandson.

"He's going to steal you from me," I told Hudson. "And I just got home."

"He's not alone." Griffin nodded to the road again, and sure enough, a line of cars came our way. "I guess we're hosting dinner."

Hours later, after Anne and Lyla had cooked for us all, the house was full of laughter. Pops and Harrison were watching a football game. Talia, Mateo and Eloise were on the deck. Knox hadn't made it over, probably because he was at home stewing about his temporary neighbor.

Griffin and I were on the couch, cuddled together as our son slept in his father's arms.

"Should we tell them?" he asked.

I looked into those bright blue eyes and nodded. "Yeah."

"Gather around," he called, and when the living room was packed with family, he grinned. "Family announcement."

Family. His. Mine.

*Ours.*

And eight months later, our daughter, Emma Eden, joined the fray.

# EXCLUSIVE BONUS CONTENT

# GRIFFIN

"Ready, buddy?"

Hudson gripped the rope to the sled. "Ready, Daddy."

I lifted my boots from the snow and planted a hand, shoving us down the hill.

My three-year-old son's laugh was music to my ears as we flew down the slope, the glittering flakes blowing into our faces.

Winn held Emma propped on a hip at the bottom while she tracked us with her phone, the camera capturing every moment until we skidded to a stop.

"Again!" Hudson struggled to climb out of the sled in all his winter gear. Like his sister, he was bundled in bibs and a puffy coat. The stocking hat on his head had drifted too far down his forehead and he had to tip his chin back to see.

"Let's fix this hat." I pulled off my gloves, folding back the hem of his hat, then giving my boy a high five.

"Me me me." Emma squirmed for Winn to set her down. Once her boots hit the ground, she toddled my way and crashed into my legs.

I hoisted her up, then bent to grab the sled. "One more?"

Winn nodded. "Yeah, and then we'd better go. Pops is coming over in an hour and I need to get dinner in the oven."

"Okay, baby." I brushed a kiss to my wife's lips, then carted my daughter up the hill.

One more run turned into two. Hudson's pout won me over, and despite the setting sun, I hauled him and his sister up the hill for our final sled ride before loading them into the truck to drive home.

"That was fun." Winn spun and smiled at the kids in the back. "We should go again tomorrow."

"You got it." If sledding made my wife and kids smile, then I'd take them every day. We'd find the time.

Our two kids kept us running from sunrise to sunset and often the hours in between. The ranch was thriving. Winn was the community's beloved chief of police. Life was a blast. This was a happy I hadn't even realized possible.

All because of the woman I'd met at Willie's. The woman who'd seduced me in the backseat of this truck. It was overdue for a trade-in, but I couldn't bring myself to part with it.

Turns out, I was a bit sentimental when it came to my wife.

"Let's do baths before dinner," she said as we unloaded the kids and started stripping off the winter layers. "Then if Pops stays late, we can just put the kids to bed."

"I've got 'em."

"Thanks, baby." She gave me a kiss, then retreated to the kitchen, her beautiful face flushed from the cold.

I'd put in some work later tonight to give her cheeks that same color. I'd be using my tongue.

The kids were both wrapped in hooded towels when I heard Covie's voice carry from the hallway. The kids heard him too.

"Pops!" Hudson led the charge, the towel flying like a cape over his shoulders as he raced for the door.

Emma was right on her brother's heels, racing into Covie's open arms.

Neither of them noticed Janice standing by, watching on.

"Hey, Covie." I held out a hand for a shake, then nodded to Janice. "Hi, Janice."

"Hi, Griff."

"Welcome." I waved them both into the house, wondering why Winn's assistant was here.

And why Covie had his fingers laced through hers as they came into the living room.

Winn emerged from the hallway that led to our bedroom, having changed into a long-sleeved tee. One look at Covie and Janice's hands clasped and her feet stuttered to a stop. "H-hi."

"Hi, sweetheart." Covie pulled Janice to the couch, the pair of them sitting without a centimeter in between.

"You said you told them I was coming." Janice shot Covie a glare from behind those red-framed glasses.

"Decided a little surprise might be the best way to tackle this."

"Tackle what, exactly?" Winn came into the living room, Emma walking over, still wrapped in her unicorn towel.

"How about we put some clothes on these kids, then we

can talk?" I suggested.

Winn picked up Emma while I chased Hudson down the hall to their respective rooms. When they were both dressed in pajamas, we returned to the living room to find Janice and Covie still on the couch.

I flipped on a cartoon for the kids, then sat in the chair across from the new couple, waiting as Winn perched on its edge. "So you two are...dating?"

"Engaged," Covie corrected, holding up Janice's left hand. Sure enough, a diamond ring glittered beside her knuckle.

Winn's jaw dropped. "You're engaged?"

Janice winced and jammed her elbow into Covie's ribs. "In my defense, I never liked keeping this a secret. But *someone* was worried that it might cause problems at the station."

"What? How? When?" With each question, Winn's voice grew louder.

I put my hand on her knee. "Let's start with congratulations."

Her mouth opened and closed, then opened again. Nothing came out.

"I'm sorry for keeping this a secret, Winnie," Covie said with a grin. "But it was actually sort of fun to sneak around like we're kids. Me and the younger woman."

"Oh my God," Janice groaned. "You're making it worse."

I laughed. "How long have you two been together?"

"Five months," Covie answered. "I just proposed this morning."

"Five months?" Winn shot off the chair.

"I'm sorry." Janice stood too. "It just started as a little fling and then it became more. You know how that goes. But

I love the old fart and we have so much fun together. Now that I'm retiring next month and we're engaged, I hoped that maybe you'd give us your blessing."

"Of course she will." Covie stood and walked to Winn, putting both hands on her shoulders. "She makes me happy. She keeps me feeling young. I love the hell out of her."

Winn stared at him for a long moment, then the shock disappeared. Because I knew my wife. And she loved so deeply that she'd never deny her grandfather a sliver of happiness. A soft smile pulled at her beautiful mouth.

She stood on her toes and pressed a kiss to Covie's cheek, then she stepped past him and pulled Janice into a hug. "Congratulations. And welcome to the family."

*That's my girl.* I grinned.

The rest of the night was a flurry of questions. I loved that about my wife. Her curious mind. Her thirst to understand.

Emma and Hudson had that too. Most two- and three-year-olds were curious but I saw the same spark in their eyes that I loved in their mother's.

By the time Covie and Janice left for the night, the kids were tucked into their beds. The stars were shining in the winter sky and the full moon cast its silver rays over the snow-covered trees and meadows.

Winn and I stood at the window, watching the Bronco's headlights disappear.

"I sort of love them together," she said.

"I sort of love them together too."

She dropped her head to my shoulder. "I love you."

"I love you." I turned her, framing her face in my hands. "The flush is gone from your face."

"What flush?"

"From sledding."

"Oh." She laughed. "Because I'm not freezing my ass off."

I dropped my mouth to hers. "I like the flush."

"Yeah?"

I swept her up in a fast move, tossing her over my shoulder. Then I smacked her ass as she giggled on the walk to the bedroom.

Where I earned back the flush.

Bonus Scene – Indigo Ridge

Griffin

"You're going to be late for pictures."

I checked the time on my phone. *Fuck*. I was going to be late. "I've got time."

Mom's nostrils flared as she shot a pointed look at Dad. "I'm blaming this on you."

"Me?" His jaw dropped. "I just wanted to go for a ride before the wedding. It was your son's decision to check the fence."

"Good thing I did. Otherwise we wouldn't have noticed that fallen tree."

Dad and I had managed to get it off the fence and restring the barbed wire. It wasn't tight, and I'd need to go back and splice it correctly. But it should keep the cattle in until I could get back to it after Christmas.

After the wedding.

"Shower." Mom clapped her hands twice. "Hustle up."

Just like she used to round us all up as kids. Two sharp claps and an order.

And just like I had as a kid, I obeyed.

She was not in a mood to be argued with. I'd save my compliments about her hair and dress for when she'd cooled off.

Dad hurried for his bathroom while I headed for the one down the hall, where I'd stashed my black suit. Then I rushed through a lukewarm shower, scrubbing away the scent of snow and horses before hopping out to shave.

I quickly dressed in my white shirt and black slacks. The burgundy tie Winn had picked out was to match the red roses she'd be carrying in her bouquet. As I knotted it at the base of my throat, I checked the time.

Hell. I was supposed to have left ten minutes ago.

With a tug, I pulled my jacket off its hanger, slung it on and bolted from the bathroom.

Dad's hair was wet and he was fumbling with his tie as Mom cinched a coat around her waist, covering her green velvet dress.

"I'll drive," I said, swiping my keys from the counter.

I made up five minutes on the drive by breaking every speed limit from the ranch to Quincy. Every time the engine revved in my truck, the waves of irritation and fury rolling off Mom seemed to double.

The moment I parked at The Eloise, she flew out of the passenger seat, not waiting for either Dad or me as she stormed inside the hotel.

"Shit," Dad muttered as we rushed to follow. "She's pissed."

"Yep."

But we weren't more than five minutes late, and no one but Mom seemed to care.

We strode into the room my sisters had decorated for the ceremony, finding the pastor from our church waiting. Knox and Mateo, my groomsmen, stood at the ready.

I gave each of my brothers a hug, then took up my spot at the altar, making sure my tie was on straight. And when

Winn walked down the aisle, escorted by her grandfather, I pressed a hand to my heart to keep it from escaping.

She was beautiful. So beautiful it hurt.

The fence issue earlier was something I should have skipped. But it hadn't really been about the fence. I'd been keyed up and anxious for this moment. This, right here, when the best woman I'd ever met agreed to tie her life to mine.

The fence had been a distraction. A way to keep my nerves at bay.

God, she was gorgeous. Her blue eyes sparkled. She floated more than walked, the train of her white lace dress skimming the floor. It had been her mother's wedding dress. Winn had wanted to wear it today.

When she reached the altar, she hugged Covie, then took my outstretched hand.

"You're stunning." I bent and kissed her temple. "Feel like marrying me?"

Her smile stopped my heart. "I do."

● ● ●

"How much longer do we have to stick around?" Winn asked from her seat on my lap.

I chuckled. "In a hurry to go upstairs?"

"I'm ready for you to strip me out of this dress. The zipper keeps scratching." She squirmed, her luscious ass rocking against my cock.

I'd been fighting a hard-on for hours. Enough was enough. She wanted out of that dress? Then we'd ditch the crowd and head upstairs to our room.

Our ceremony had been small, just family. But after it was over, we'd invited friends from around town to come down to the hotel and party. Most of Quincy had shown up.

The dance floor was packed. The bar had already run out of whiskey. And we'd be lucky if the fire marshal didn't fine us for being overcapacity in the building. Though considering he was the band's drummer, we were probably fine.

The party was taking on a life of its own, and all I wanted to do was celebrate alone.

With my wife.

"Let's go." I helped her to her feet, reaching for my suit jacket, which I'd draped on the back of my chair. As I pulled it free, a white envelope fell out of the pocket.

"What's that?" Winn asked.

"I don't know." I bent to pick it up. My name in Mom's handwriting was scrawled across the face.

I tugged open the flap and pulled out a letter. When had she written me a letter? It had to have been earlier. She must have slipped it into my jacket pocket while Dad and I had been out on our ride.

A woman came up to Winn, stealing her for a hug, so I unfolded the page and read Mom's note.

*Dear Griffin,*

*I had an idea this morning to write you something special on your wedding day. Something inspirational. Maybe some advice. Apparently all of my sage wisdom is escaping me today. I've been staring at this piece of paper for two hours and nothing useful is coming out of my brain. I can't ask your dad for help because you two went out riding this morning. So I guess you'll be reading this entirely pointless note while you're getting ready.*

*You're going to be a wonderful husband. There's not a doubt in my mind. And the only advice I have for you today is don't be late. Now stop reading this nonsense and finish getting ready.*

*You're getting married today.*

*I love you. I'm proud of you. And I'm happy for you.*

*xoxo*
*Mom*

I laughed and read the note a second time. *Don't be late.* Damn, I loved my mom.

Scanning the crowd, I spotted her on the dance floor with Dad. A smile lit her face as he twirled her in a spin, then dipped her for a kiss. Her irritation from earlier had vanished before Winn had ever set foot down the aisle.

Winn's hands snaked around my waist just as I refolded the letter and tucked it back into the envelope. "This zipper is really bothering me."

I pulled her into my side, dropping my mouth to hers. "Then let's take off that dress."

# ACKNOWLEDGMENTS

Thank you for reading *Indigo Ridge*! Special thanks to my editing and proofreading team: Elizabeth Nover, Julie Deaton, Karen Lawson and Judy Zweifel. Thank you to Sarah Hansen for the stunning cover. Thank you to all the members of Perry & Nash for being the best superfans I could ask for. A huge thanks to the incredible bloggers who read and spread the word about my books. And thank you to my friends and my wonderful family for your unconditional love and support.

# Don't miss the rest of the Edens!

*Don't miss the exciting new books
Entangled has to offer.*

*Follow us!*

@EntangledPublishing

@Entangled_Publishing

@EntangledPub

AMARA
an imprint of Entangled Publishing LLC